COLD PRESSED

A SEACROFT NOVEL

ALLISON TEMPLE

COLD PRESSED

No strings attached is all Oliver can offer. He's hiding a broken heart that holds him back from diving into a new relationship, but he'll go on a blind date to make his family happy. Just one date, though; he doesn't have time for love to derail his plans.

Divorced and demoted to the night shift, Nick has his own problems. He's got an ex-wife who needs him and a kid with one foot in juvie. The last thing Nick needs is to butt heads—or other body parts—with a tempting hipster who wears a sad smile on their blind date.

Their chemistry can't be denied, though, in an argument or in bed. No strings sex is uncomplicated, and that's what Nick and Oliver need. But getting into bed together is one thing. Staying out of each other's hearts soon becomes so much more complicated than either one imagined.

Cover Design: Cate Ashwood Designs
Developmental Editing: Christa Soulé Désir
Copy Editing and Proofreading: LesCourt Author Services

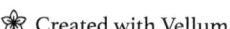 Created with Vellum

For all the parents.
It is inevitable you will screw up your kids.
And if you don't, they will do it for you.

ACKNOWLEDGMENTS

Thanks to Adriana at The Fix + Co. in Etobicoke who welcomed me into her shop and let me ask a hundred annoying questions about juice and entrepreneurship. Also to Courtney, who helped me understand what a flax egg is . . . sort of.

For news on future releases, join the A-List, my monthly newsletter at allisontemplebooks.com/newsletter.

1

---

*I*f it had been anyone but Brian, Nick would have laughed the suggestion off as ridiculous in an instant. If it hadn't come at the end of a double shift, Nick would have recognized the terrible idea before Brian even finished talking.

Instead, because he liked Brian, and because he was hours past when he should have gone home, Nick didn't see it coming until too late.

"When's the last time you had fun?" Brian asked.

"That depends on your definition of fun." Nick's eyes felt like sandpaper, and his stomach was curdling after he'd downed one too many coffees to push through the darkest hours of his night shift. Fun sounded like a ham sandwich and a warm bed. Nick was a man of few needs.

"Well . . . just . . . fun. Go out. With someone. Have a few drinks. Maybe a meal. You know. Fun."

Nick stretched his arms overhead and glanced at the clock. He had seven minutes to go, and then he was out of here. The day shift would arrive any minute now, and it didn't matter if someone had the plague. They were going to drag their asses to this desk, and Nick was out.

"We go out all the time," Nick said. Their guys' nights had

been happening less since Brian had gotten back together with his wife, but Nick could only be happy for him about that.

"No, not with me."

Nick's eyes were bleary, but as he blinked, he realized Brian was blushing.

"I don't understand."

"Jess wants to set you up on a date." Brian's whole face was strained. The lines around his eyes creased into deep furrows. His lips pressed tight, and his throat bobbed up and down like he was trying to swallow a goldfish.

"Jess wants to—"

"Please say no."

"Then why would you—"

"Because I told her I'd ask you, and I can't say no to anything she says these days. But you can. Please say no, and then we can forget this whole thing."

Now Nick was blushing too. Hopefully this was not the moment a call came in for a five-alarm fire or an MVA. He wouldn't be able to function, and the way Brian's face was trying to pucker in on itself was hilarious.

Brian swallowed his goldfish and exhaled loudly. "I told her we shouldn't bother you. That you hardly ever talked about dating anyone, but she said that was all the more reason to ask. Forget about it. I'll tell her it was a bad idea."

Nick was happy that Brian and Jess were back together. But if the joyful reunion was turning to matchmaking, that might not be such a good thing after all.

"Is it someone I know?"

"No. I don't really know him either."

Him. That put a different color on it. Not many people knew about Nick's bisexuality, but Brian was an exception. After fifteen years working together for the Seacroft Fire Department, he and Brian didn't have many secrets left. Brian had stuck with him after the accident that cut Nick's firefighting career short, and Nick had been there to help Brian mourn the end of his marriage and then celebrate its sudden recovery last fall. No point in keeping things from someone who had your back for almost half your life. Brian was always discreet, no matter what Nick told him.

That discretion didn't apparently extend to the wife Brian was obviously still trying to win over, however.

"It was her idea," Brian said, as if he had read Nick's mind. "I don't know how she knew about . . . " He waved vaguely toward Nick. "Look, forget about it. It's a stupid idea, but I told her I'd ask. You know Jess. She gets excited about things."

Brian deserved to be happy. But Nick's warm and fuzzy feelings about Brian's domestic bliss had limits. He kept his private life private for a reason.

"I'll think about it." He pulled himself to his feet. Two minutes to go.

"No, forget I said anything." Brian stood from the chair he'd pulled up so he could sit by Nick's desk. He appreciated Brian's willingness to hang out at dispatch, while most of the other firefighters stuck to the dorm room and lounge on overnight shifts. "I'll tell Jess you weren't up for it. It wouldn't be a bad idea, though, you know. For you to meet someone. You spend a lot of time by yourself."

"It's complicated." Nick gave him a tired smile.

Brian squeezed Nick's shoulder. "Yeah, I know."

Sharon approached the desk, her hair slicked back into a tight braid, coffee mug in her hand.

"Good morning, fellas," she said.

"Morning," Brian said. "Dave on his way?"

"He called five minutes ago." Sharon scowled. "Sick."

Damn. Dave was one of the good ones. Working dispatch for the Seacroft Fire Department wasn't a glamorous job. Mediocre pay, long shifts, and no chance of ever moving up into another position—because they didn't exist—meant SFD's dispatch roster was small and absenteeism was rampant, but Dave was pretty dedicated to the job.

"Could be legit," Nick said. "I heard there's something going around the school, and Dave has kids."

Sharon didn't appear convinced. "His social media feed had a lot of rowdy-looking pictures this weekend. Do you think hangovers are considered a communicable illness?"

"It does seem to hit groups of people at once," Nick said.

Sharon grinned and gave them both a mock salute. "Have a good day. Sleep well."

———

Fifteen minutes later, Nick was changed and heading across the street to the municipal lot where he'd parked the night before. When the new fire station was built, some genius on the planning committee decided to merge the staff lot with the town hall lot. It seemed like a reasonable idea in theory—the department was small, and the town hall only needed parking during business hours—but in reality, Nick spent a lot of time fighting for spots with people trying to pay their property tax bill.

This morning, despite the early hour, the lot was already busy with colorful tents and canopies lining the front row. Was it that time of year already? The farmer's market in Seacroft was always popular with local residents and the summer tourists, shrinking the parking lot even further. Most of the vendors were still setting up, but Nick would have to hurry if he wanted to get out of there before shoppers started circling.

As he walked down the row of stalls toward his car, he mulled over Brian's offer. His love life had been nonexistent for more than a little while. Sometimes he missed having someone to come home to, talk to, and—yes—have sex with on at least a semi-regular basis. But dating was a lot of work. He hated the small talk, the pressure to come off as interesting and appealing when he was divorced, a failed firefighter with not much to offer but a tiny paycheck, an erratic work schedule, and a mid-century—but not in a trendy way—bungalow in an older part of town. He'd tried a hookup app once, but he'd deleted it the first time someone sent a dick pic without so much as a *hi, how are you?* If he wanted to see a complete stranger's penis, he'd watch porn like everyone else.

Still, something about Brian's offer niggled at the back of Nick's mind. Was there any harm in one date?

As he came to the end of the row of market vendors, Nick spotted a tall guy who was turned away from him. The man's broad shoulders pulled his blue T-shirt tight across his back. His hair was dark blond, piled into a messy bun. Nick ran a hand over his own buzz cut. He liked a man with long hair. It gave a guy something to hold onto.

Maybe it was Brian's mention of a date. Maybe it was time. Either way, Nick let himself have a minute to imagine the feeling of Bun-Guy's hair coming loose in Nick's fingers. He tugged it back, tilting the man's head to one side so Nick could kiss him the way he liked. The man groaned as he settled onto his knees, and—

The man glanced over his shoulder, almost as if he could hear the direction Nick's thoughts had taken. Sweet Jesus, his face was more distracting than his back. Even from this distance, his eyes were bright blue, and the V-neck of his T-shirt framed his throat and showed off the definition of his chest.

The man waved at someone.

Specifically, he waved at the tow truck driver who was about to pull Nick's car away.

"Hey!" As tired as he was, getting the word out took a minute, and by then he was already running. "Hey! Stop! That's my car!"

"That's your car?" Bun-Guy stepped in front of him.

"Yes! Stop!" Nick tried to move past him, but the other man

followed, preventing him from chasing after the truck. It pulled onto the street and drove away, taking Nick's rusting sedan with it. The vanity plate, PRTYGRL, taunted him as the truck and his car rolled away.

"That was your car?" Bun-Guy said.

"Yes. Fuck!" Nick ground his teeth. He did not have time to deal with this. "They never tow. I parked here all winter, and they never towed it."

"But you can't park here on market mornings."

"What?" Nick's gaze swung back to the other man. Jesus, up close he was even better looking. His eyes were the same color as his shirt, and his beard had about nineteen shades of brown and blond in it.

That Nick was able to count them was one of the perks of living with a hairdresser—again—he supposed.

"You can't park here on market mornings." The guy pointed to a post over his shoulder where a municipal parking sign hung.

Seacroft Historic Farmers Market
Vendor parking only, first three rows
Saturday midnight to noon
May 15 to October 31

Well, shit.

"I'm really sorry," Bun-Guy said. "If I'd known you were going to come back, I wouldn't have called them."

Nick went cold. "You called the tow truck?"

The guy straightened his spine and crossed his arms over his chest. "You parked in my spot."

"Excuse me?" Was his name engraved on it? Nick paid his taxes, and this was a public lot. What gave this guy any bigger claim on this 140-square-foot patch of asphalt than anyone else?

And yet. "This—" the asshole with the hair spoke slowly as he gestured around them at the now-empty parking space, "—is my spot. It's where I'm supposed to put my stall, and you were in it."

"I'm sorry to be so inconvenient."

"More like inconsiderate. People have businesses to run."

"I was at work." He forced himself to keep his voice low and even.

Bun-Jerk's forehead wrinkled. "And I'm trying to get to work, but you were in my way."

Nick's fists clenched as he stepped into the guy's space. He was an inch or so taller, but Nick was bigger. "Your way? What is it you do, exactly? I work in a place that saves lives, and you couldn't wait another twenty minutes to, what, sell your turnips?" Nick took another step forward. They were virtually nose to nose. He didn't like to use his size to intimidate people, but this guy was pissing him off, and he looked like he could take it.

His intuition was proven right when the asshole stepped in too, so they were nearly chest to chest. "You're not twenty minutes late. The sign says midnight. You're seven hours late. They should have towed that junker ages ago."

Nick flinched. The car wasn't fancy, but it did its job, and that was still no excuse for this moron taking it upon himself to ruin Nick's morning. He clenched his teeth as he and the other guy stared each other down.

Someone coughed. A small group of nervous-looking farmers and market vendors had gathered, watching Nick and Bun-Jerk nervously.

Nick was tired. The stupid car wasn't worth it.

"Fine." He took a step back. "Thanks for the grace period. I hope you enjoy your turnips." He gave the asshole one more glance. The early sun was turning his hair and skin golden like a statue, or a god.

Too bad his face and his personality didn't match.

2

$\mathcal{T}$he cab hit every possible red light between the fire department and Nick's house. The driver had a lead foot, and each time a traffic light turned green, they were nearly catapulted into space. Nick had never been prone to motion sickness, but he practically tumbled through the cab door when the car lurched to a stop in front of his house.

His morning did not improve. The old bungalow's front windows were open, and yelling filtered out from inside.

"Don't give me that!" Anya's voice was edging into shrill, which meant the argument had already been going for a while.

Hayden's reply was, of course, inaudible, and Nick stood on the lawn, half inclined to wait until whatever was going on was over. His whole body sagged with fatigue. If the morning had already descended into yelling matches, he wasn't going to bed yet. Sighing, he made his way up the walk and pushed open the front door.

"It's not negotiable." Anya had her hands on her hips as he entered. "In fact, it's a legal requirement. You have to go."

Hayden didn't say anything. He was slumped in a kitchen chair, somehow managing to look supremely annoyed and disinterested at the same time.

"What's going on?" Nick asked.

"It's Saturday."

Market day, the hot blond guy in Nick's head said.

Shut up.

"And?" Nick went to the fridge and opened it, scanning for something he could eat quickly before he collapsed in bed. If he played this cool, maybe the tension in the room would relax as well.

"Saturday is community service. He has to go." Each word made Anya's voice pitch up higher. Her heavily-mascaraed eyes were wide, and little spots of color bloomed on her cheeks. Nick had known that look for years. She was on the verge of crying. So much for playing it cool. At least Nick wasn't the cause of it, unlike so often when they'd been married. Either way, time for him to step in.

"Your mom's right." Nick pulled a Tupperware out, dumped its contents—cold pasta and sauce—onto a plate, and popped it into the microwave.

"But I'm sick." Compared to Anya's voice, Hayden's was monotone, like every word was an effort.

"Bullshit you're sick," Anya hissed. Nick glanced at her, raising one eyebrow in a silent signal that he could handle this.

Hayden didn't give him a chance, though. "I am sick! I can't go!" With a deep sigh, he pushed himself up from the table and shuffled out of the kitchen without another word. The heavy black tracking bracelet around his ankle was clearly visible against his white sock. Despite his don't-care attitude, the kid was pretty self-conscious about letting the bracelet show, even at home, and kept it covered in long pants. That he was still in a T-shirt and his red basketball shorts might be a sign that he really was ill.

Or he's getting more devious.

Nick hated how suspicious he'd become of everything Hayden said.

9

"I'm not calling the probation officer!" Anya shouted after him, even though Hayden didn't turn around to acknowledge her. "You call him and explain yourself, or he'll be on this house so fast it'll make your head spin!"

Hayden's bedroom door slammed shut.

The microwave beeped, but Nick didn't bother to pull the plate out, his appetite gone.

"I'll call," he said.

Anya whirled on him like he might be a new target. She wore sparkling silver earrings that jingled like a warning bell. "No, you won't. It's his responsibility. We agreed on that."

"I'm not doing it for him." Hayden wouldn't call, and if Nick didn't do it, there would be an angry PO pounding on their front door before lunchtime. That visit wouldn't be pleasant or short, and Nick needed to sleep.

"Can you talk to him? Get him to go? It's not even that bad today. They're helping direct traffic around the farmer's market."

Of course they were.

"He's only a little late. He could still make it. Please?" Anya grabbed her keys from the table. The market wasn't the only thing open early on Saturdays. The salon she worked at would be open at nine, and she liked to stop for a coffee at the diner on her way in, mostly so she could share her latest tale of woe to whoever was there.

"I'll try." A pointless effort—nothing helped when Hayden got that sullen look in his eyes—but seeing Anya so upset hurt, so he'd give it a shot. "Go to work. We'll be okay."

She shrugged her purse onto one shoulder. "You're the best. Are you working tonight?" Nick shook his head. "Maybe we could do something, then. The three of us. Watch a movie. Like a family."

Like a family. She smiled sadly at him. The girl he'd known, the one he'd loved and married and then lost, was still in there. Her hair was darker than it had been in high school, dyed black that glowed red in sunlight. It hid the grays Nick wasn't supposed to know were there, but no amount of makeup or hair dye could hide the tension she carried on her petite frame all the time now. She didn't like the yelling matches with Hayden any more than he did. Normally, she would talk tough about loss of privileges and consequences, but holding fast was hard when all she really wanted was her son back.

"Yeah. Yeah, that sounds nice." It sounded like a pipe dream.

Anya turned to the front door and froze. "Where's my car?"

Nick winced. "Oh. About that."

"Babe. Where is my car?"

Normally, he'd have scowled at the pet name, even though she'd been using it for twenty years. This morning, though, as the acid dripped from her words, Nick dipped his head. He had ten inches of height on her and would never make himself appear small enough to escape her wrath, but he could damn well try.

"There was a problem this morning, after my shift."

"What kind of problem?" She wore her favorite lipstick, a peachy-pink she'd told him once was called Shrimply Devine, and her mouth pursed into a thin line, prepared to pass judgment on whatever he said next.

"It got towed."

"What?" The shriek didn't reach quite the same level it had before, but close.

"It was an honest mistake!" Nick held his hands out, palms up. "I parked in the municipal lot. I parked there all winter. But today was the first morning of the farmer's market and—"

"You got my car towed! Do you know how expensive that's going to be?"

"It's fine. I'll pay for the tow."

"Damn right you are! What am I supposed to do now? I have to go to work!"

Her anger wasn't really directed at him. She was reacting to

Hayden and leftover adrenaline, but Nick knew when to back away slowly. He fished his wallet out of his jeans and put a twenty on the table.

"That will cover a cab and anything else you need today."

Anya glared at him, but she took the twenty. "I can't believe you got towed."

"I had some help." A lot of help, in fact. In the form of a six-foot-two hipster with a superiority complex and too much hair.

When she was gone, Nick called the probation officer. He didn't sound very happy, but that was par for Nick's course. Every minute he spent on the phone was a minute he wasn't asleep, and stringing sentences together was a miracle. He used his patient work voice, the one he used with panicked families. Eventually, the officer relented, although he promised to make a note of this absence in Hayden's file.

Exhaustion weighed on Nick's shoulders. Far too much drama for one day, and it wasn't even eight o'clock yet. He shuffled up the hall and knocked on Hayden's closed door.

"Yeah?"

Nick pushed the door open to find Hayden lying on his bed. He'd hit a growth spurt and seemed to be too long for the mattress in every direction. The foot with the tracking bracelet hung off the side. As a kid, he'd slept like that too, arms and legs splayed all over the place, but then he'd been small, and the position sweet. Now, the tracker was like an ugly scar.

"Are you really sick?" Nick asked from the doorway.

"Yes."

The room was a disaster, and the smell of teenage boy wafted over him and out into the hall—beautiful normalcy amid the storm they lived in.

"There isn't another reason you don't want to go to community service?" Getting a straight answer out of Hayden about anything was a distant memory, but Nick had to try.

"Would you leave me alone? I don't feel good, okay?" When

Hayden was a baby, people said his eyes were just like Nick's. He hoped he'd never looked at anyone with the impatient loathing filling his son's gaze right now.

"Hey, don't look at me like that. I'm the one who called your PO. How do you think it's going to look, missing community service, at your next court date?"

"I don't care."

"You should care. If you want that thing off your leg, you *need* to care." Now he was starting to sound like Anya. Despite giving this speech almost daily, they might as well be shouting at a brick wall, but they had to keep trying.

Hayden shifted, shoving the foot with the bracelet under a pillow. "It's all stupid. It doesn't matter. The judges hate me."

Time to go. When Hayden turned to the *me against the world* argument, continuing was fruitless.

"Pick up your room before your mom gets home, okay?"

Nick went down the hall to his room. He slid out of his jeans and shirt and into bed. His curtains didn't do much to block out the daylight, but he'd gotten used to it ages ago, like he'd learned to sleep alone again after his divorce.

And then his ex-wife and son had come back to his house. While there certainly had never been any question of Anya sharing his bed again, having her and Hayden in the building meant Nick had needed to adjust all over again. He didn't want to resent their presence—they needed his support—but mornings like this were hard, especially when their situation had no end in sight.

Nick rubbed a hand over his eyes and down his chest. With the motion, the fantasy with the guy from the market returned. He skipped over the memory of the angry words shouted after Nick's car had disappeared down the street, but the rest . . . Nick's hand roamed over his body. Before it had all gone wrong, the guy had been amazing. The hair, the face. A man could dream about things like that.

Nick wanted that. Just not with some asshole turnip farmer who liked having Nick's wreck of a car towed.

On a whim, he reached for his phone. He sent a short text to Brian.

I'm interested. Set me up.

The little bubble indicating Brian was replying popped up on the screen. The message appeared shortly.

I'll tell Jess. His name is Oliver. That's pretty much all I know.

Nick lay back on his bed, ignoring the nervous pang in his chest as he set the phone down.

Just a date.

What was the worst that could happen?

———

"Now put the longer peg in the small hole."

Small hole? Oliver stared at the board in front of him.

"They're both the same size."

Seb held up the instruction booklet and pointed to an illustration. "It's this one."

Oliver checked the board again. As the only thing board-like in the entire package of parts and bits they'd opened, it had to be right, yet it looked nothing like the black-and-white drawing.

"Let me see that." He took the page and squinted at it, then held it at arm's length until the image came into focus again.

"Want to put your glasses on?"

Oliver didn't need to look at his brother to see the shit-eating grin on his face.

"Shut up." He set the page down, rotated the board, and popped the peg into place. He smiled up at Seb. "See? No problem."

Seb snorted and sorted through the remaining selection of screws and brackets on the counter until he found the match and handed it to Oliver. "Same thing, other side."

Oliver fought his impatience. The chairs were a good idea. People would have a chance to linger in the shop if they felt more comfortable. Foot traffic was harder to come by than he'd expected, and getting them to stay was even harder. But a lack of customers meant money wasn't exactly plentiful either, so buying the flat-pack, DIY kind had seemed like a reasonable solution at the time. Except he and Seb had been at this for over an hour, and they'd only managed to assemble one and a half out of the five chairs.

"I bet I could get a couple of kids from the high school to come put the rest of these together for you. They'd be cheap. You could practically pay them in pizza and chips, or—" Seb glanced around the shop. "Kale chips and beet juice, anyway."

"Would you shut up and help me turn this over?" He couldn't afford to pay students, or anyone else. Oliver was used to putting in extra hours to get things done, but spending his only day off listening to his little brother's wisecracks was not in his plan. He thought he'd escaped these jokes when he and Seb graduated from high school, finished college (Oliver more than Seb) and moved on to adult milestones like jobs and boyfriends (lately, Seb more than Oliver).

But they were so close to being done with the second chair, even if it wobbled, and Seb's help was free. Oliver bent, clutching the four rubber feet that would keep the chair from sliding on his white tile floor. As he knelt, someone knocked on the shop's front door. The sound made him flinch, and one of the feet tumbled out from between his fingers, bounced a few times on the floor, and skittered under the butcher-block counter.

"Shit!" he shouted, as the bell over the door tinkled. Since he'd opened his shop, Pulpability, three months ago, he'd lost dozens of screws, nuts, washers, and now rubber feet into the void under that counter. No hardware ever returned from that portal.

"How's it going?" Seb's partner, Martin, stood in the doorway, looking nervous. Honestly, he always looked a little nervous with his thin shoulders and brown hair that never quite got out of his eyes.

"Fine, except now I'm going to have to drive four hours back and forth to IKEA to pick up one stupid rubber foot."

Seacroft was unexpectedly far from almost everything convenient, including IKEA. But the cost to ship the chairs was exorbitant, so he'd made the drive even though it had taken most of a day. Doing the trip again for a single foot, though, was insult to injury.

"Better wait until we finish the other ones." Seb nodded at the other boxes lying on the floor. "You never know what else we might lose."

"Thanks for the vote of confidence." Oliver put the rest of the feet on the chair. Let it wobble. The chairs were important, but he had other things that needed to get done.

"I bet we could get Cassidy and her friends to assemble the rest," Martin said. Cassidy was one of the students he had been tutoring. "I know she's looking for ways to earn money before she goes to college in the fall."

"That's what I said. Smart idea, Dr. Lindsey!" Seb grinned, and Martin returned the smile shyly.

Witnessing Seb's descent into domestic bliss was so weird for Oliver. With his white-blond hair and collection of tattered T-shirts and torn jeans, Seb seemed a bit ethereal, like he couldn't be bothered dealing with the real world. But then Martin showed up and tethered him firmly to the ground. It didn't help that Martin was so obviously devoted to Seb as well. They were disgusting, really.

"Are you ready to go?" Martin asked, gray eyes on Oliver.

"Go where?" Oliver pulled the next flat-pack off the pile and lugged it toward the counter. Now they had started, he was anxious to finish, like people were already lined up down the street to sit in his chairs.

"Brunch?"

"Oliver doesn't do brunch anymore." Seb rolled his eyes. "Too many trans carbs and refined fats."

"It's trans fats and refined carbs. And I do brunch."

Seb scowled. "Not in any way that makes it fun for the rest of us. You want the fruit platter, but can they skip the yogurt? And can you have the kale salad, but could they serve it to you in smoothie form?"

Oliver made a face. "That's revolting." And he'd kill for a plate of greasy eggs and bacon right now, not to mention about six cups of coffee, but he was trying so hard to set an example for any potential customers who might stop by. Walk the walk and all that.

But Seb's shoulders squared in the way they had done his whole life whenever he was spoiling for a fight. He pulled one of the bottles from the fridge nearby and read from it in an exaggerated Southern accent. "One hundred percent cold-pressed celery stems, with organic lemon juice and parsley oil." He grinned and let the accent drop as he said, "*That* is what's revolting."

"It's not supposed to be fun. It's a cleanse, not brunch."

"And to make it worse, you're calling it *Cleanse-liness is Next to Godliness*. First off, the pun is terrible. Second, how do you even fit that on a label?" Seb grabbed his leather jacket from a hook by the door. "We'll be back in a bit."

"You're really leaving? I thought you were going to help me with these!" He gestured at the remaining boxes. He didn't point out that the product had originally been called *Cleanse Getaway* but that, like everything in the store, Oliver had changed the name to avoid thinking about Cooper's face every time he took a bottle from the fridge.

Turned out, he thought about him anyway.

"I'll be back. A man's gotta eat." Seb shrugged into his jacket.

"You're sure you don't want to come?" Martin asked as he held the door open for Seb.

Oliver bristled under Martin's kind expression, but he forced himself to breathe slowly and not let his frustrations show. Martin had a tendency to retreat at the first hint of conflict—and conflict was basically stuck in the "on" position when it came to Oliver, Seb, and the rest of their family. Oliver actually liked his brother's new partner quite a bit—better than he liked Seb most days—but being the third wheel to their epic sweetness, trailing after them through Seacroft's sleepy, picturesque streets, was not a comfortable role.

If you'd asked him a year ago where he saw his life going, Oliver would not have pictured this at all.

"Oh." Seb turned from where he stood in the doorway. "One more thing."

Oliver rolled his eyes. "Yes, Columbo?"

"Martin's brother and Jess want to set you up on a date. You're cool with that, right?"

A date?

"You didn't ask him yet?" Martin's eyes were wide under his shaggy hair.

"I'm asking him now." Seb shrugged. He grabbed an apple from a bowl by the door and bit into it.

Oliver scowled. Those were his display apples. "You need an answer immediately?"

Seb wiped apple juice from his chin. "Not if it's the sort of thing you have to think over."

"I'm pretty busy." He glanced at the unassembled chairs. Not to mention the workshop he'd scheduled for next week. He had to find a way to reach new coaching clients. And it hadn't even been a year since—"I have a lot going on here with the shop. I don't know about adding anything else to it."

"That's what I figured." Seb turned to go.

"But Brian says he's a good guy," Martin put in. "And what's the harm in a date?"

"We never dated." Seb slung an arm over Martin's shoulder and kissed his temple. "We went straight from awkward friends to living together."

"Well, yes, but that's because your apartment burned down and my brother got back together with his wife, and now there's the gallery, so we just ... "

Oliver smiled as Martin listed the chaos that had thrown him and Seb together. Not the most auspicious of starts, but more than six months later, they were going strong.

And Oliver was still waking up alone on sleepy Sunday mornings in a house he'd been supposed to share, and relying on his brother's help putting his folding chairs together.

"Details." Seb waved off Martin's list. "Besides, who's going to love my brother when he starts pushing his foul celery water on them?"

No, this was not at all how he thought this year was going to go. It had all been planned. Organized down to the dollar and the minute, and instead, here he was.

Alone.

Seb and Martin turned to leave.

Would throwing a blind date into all the turmoil really be all that bad?

"Wait," he said.

"You're coming to brunch?" Seb asked over his shoulder.

"That too." He grabbed his coat. "But I meant I'll go on that date."

After everything else, what was the worst that could happen?

3

*N*ick's track record when it came to dating could pretty much be described as poor. After his marriage ended, he'd waited years before even trying to meet anyone new. It hadn't gone well. He'd seen interest fade too many times as he'd explained he worked at the fire department, but that he wasn't a firefighter. Throw in an ex-wife and a kid, and he was a bad bet. He might be good for a night of fun—although one-night stands always felt awkward to him—but he didn't have a lot to offer in the long term.

And he had never actually been on a date with someone he hadn't already known at least a little. Seacroft was small. Finding a stranger to meet for dinner was nearly impossible. So his expectations for dating someone he didn't know were outdated. When Nick thought of a blind date, he imagined being at a restaurant, wearing a specifically-colored hat, or maybe with a flower on his table, eyes fixed on the door for a face he'd never seen before. Instead, once he'd confirmed he was interested with Brian, an email followed a few days later from Jess, sent to Nick and oliver.j.stevenson@webmail.com.

Hi Nick and Oliver,

I'm so glad you guys have decided to meet! Brian and I think you'll be really great together.

In case you'd prefer to chat, I'm including your phone numbers too.

Good luck!

Jess

A few hours later, a second email arrived from the new address.

Hi. Nice to meet you. When should we get together?

O

Oliver J. Stevenson was a man of few words. And he wanted Nick to do the heavy lifting when it came to planning, even though Nick barely wanted to go on this damn date in the first place.

Got any restaurants you like?

Nick

The reply took another few days.

Not really. I'm new in town. I've been to the diner downtown a few times, so maybe something else?

O

Not helpful. Everyone had been to the diner. Oliver might as well have said he'd tried the McDonald's by the highway.

While Nick tried to come up with somewhere interesting to go, his home life continued to rattle around his ears. Hayden had recovered from his mysterious illness in time for school on Monday, but then Wednesday he hadn't come home from class on time. A cop car pulled into the driveway a little before five o'clock, and a grim-faced police officer had opened the back door to let Hayden out of the cruiser.

"He was at the school," the officer said.

"I had to stay late to help my teacher after class."

"Which class?" Nick asked.

Hayden shrugged.

"Did you call anyone to let them know you had to stay late?"

Another shrug. Nick bit back frustration at Hayden's inability to understand how serious this was. And underneath the frustration was Nick's discomfort that he didn't know how to reach his son, powered by years of regret that he'd squandered his chance to be a full-time parent. Now he wasn't close enough to Hayden to help him—whether he wanted help or not.

"His probation officer will be calling you later." The officer nodded and returned to his car. Hayden slunk into the house.

The PO called as Nick was getting out of the shower before his shift. Anya got to deal with it. Her face was grim, her words clipped. Hayden, commanded to the kitchen table for the conversation, stared blankly ahead the whole time.

"You are on house arrest," Anya said, once she was off the phone. "That means you're either here or you're at school. That's it. There is no leeway on that."

"I *was* at school!"

"When you weren't supposed to be! The probation officer called the school, and none of your teachers said they'd asked you to stay behind."

Hayden slumped in his chair.

"It's not fair," he mumbled down into his hands.

"Fair? You want to talk about fair?" Anya's hands were on her hips, and she stretched to the very edge of her limited height.

They couldn't keep going like this. Nick needed to find a way to fix things. Give them space, but also repair their fractured relationships.

Or, at least, he needed a break.

As he changed into his uniform at work, he punched out a text on his phone.

Tomorrow night? Angelo's. Dinner at 6?

The reply came back pretty quickly.

Who is this?

Nick grimaced.

Sorry. It's Nick.

He almost wrote *Nick from Jess's email*, but that sounded weak. The point was, he was ready to make a decision, if only not to be home on his night off. Even if they had nothing in common and the date was a disaster, Nick needed a few hours to breathe.

Sure. See you then.

That was it. A date. Not a lot of enthusiasm, and Nick still didn't know anything about Oliver, not even what he looked like, but he didn't have time to dwell on it. His shift was busy. A car accident, two false alarms from one of the apartment towers on the north side of the highway, and a request for assistance from the department in the next county kept Nick's attention off his mystery man.

Social media only occurred to him the following day. Nick wasn't really much for it. He didn't have a cat needing its day documented, and you could only take so many pictures of your microwaved leftovers in the fire department kitchen before your life truly started looking sad.

Apparently, Oliver J. Stevenson had a similar theory about social media. Finding him took some work. In fact, Nick wasn't even sure he'd found the right guy since it said he lived in Charlotte, but he was the only one in North Carolina, so Nick figured it must be him.

Nick was impressed, though. And intimidated. Oliver J. Stevenson looked like a movie star with short blond hair and a bright smile on a tanned, clean-shaven jaw. And he was living a movie star's life, or close to it. The few photos posted on Oliver's profile were full of sunshine and beautiful people. The most recent ones were tagged with locations that looked like resorts charging more a night than Nick made in a shift.

Yeah, Nick was intimidated.

What exactly was it Jess thought they had in common?

Hayden came home from school on time on Thursday, but Anya came back from the salon in a mood. One of her best clients announced they were leaving, and another, a walk-in from the day before, returned to announce she hated the color Anya gave her and demanded a complete redo at no charge.

"I told her it would be too light. She said she understood. She looked like a haystack yesterday, but she swore she was happy with it, and who am I to judge? I mean, I don't even know her. This is why I hate doing color on walk-ins."

"I'm going out tonight," he said.

"Out? Where?" Anya's eyes flashed, and Nick swallowed hard as old memories from unpleasant fights swam up. He blamed himself most days for their failed marriage, but Anya hadn't been able to back down from an argument toward the end either. In the years after, she'd had a few boyfriends, although none that lasted long. It didn't seem worth it to make a big deal about Nick's date with Oliver.

"I'm going to have a bite to eat."

Coward.

"With Brian?"

Sure. Let her assume that. Who knew what would happen? Oliver the movie star might take one look at poor Nick in his rusty car and decide he wasn't worth the time. If it turned out to be more than that, Nick would tell her then.

Angelo's was an old-school Italian place with the usual flair. Checkered tablecloths. Candles in bottles covered in wax from all the candles that came before. The smell of garlic clung to everything, and, on weekends, they had a guy who played the mandolin.

Nick scanned the restaurant as he arrived. No sign of anyone who remotely looked like a movie star, or even anyone close to Nick's age for that matter. He'd always thought of Angelo's as a popular spot, but he hadn't been in a while, and the Thursday night crowd was more of the fifty-plus set than anything.

He let the hostess seat him at a table toward the back. Nick took the chair facing the door and stared at it with all the intensity and nervous energy of a man waiting for a firing squad.

What was he doing? He was too old for this shit, on the dark side of his thirties. Now he was sitting in the only shirt he'd been able to find with buttons down the front, waiting for a guy who liked to pose on sunny beaches while he showed off his six-pack and his designer sunglasses.

Nick's phone rang. Startled, he fumbled it out of his khakis.

"We have a problem. Where are you?" Anya said, skipping greetings completely.

"I told you, I went to get a bite to eat."

"When will you be back?"

A few seconds ago, Nick would have said he was on his way. He'd have gotten up, sent a short apology to Oliver, and grabbed a burger on the way home. But the tension in Anya's voice said things were not any better at the house than when Nick had left. He closed his eyes, emotions warring between guilt and obligation. He should go home. She needed him, and he'd promised to be there for her, but the idea of it made his stomach knot with anxiety. He didn't want to go home. He needed a break.

"I don't know, an hour maybe? Everything okay?"

"He won't plug in the charger."

Nick growled softly. Hayden's tracking bracelet needed to be charged daily. If the battery died, a signal went to the police station, and then there would be a phone call or, worse, a visit to see what the issue was.

"Let me talk to him."

The only indication Hayden had picked up the phone was the change from household static to sullen silence.

"Hey, buddy. Your mom says you won't plug in your bracelet."

"No! I totally will. I've just got some stuff to do first."

"What kind of stuff?" A teenager on house arrest could only have so many obligations on a Thursday night.

"Just . . . stuff."

"Stuff you can't do while you're sitting on the couch where your mom might see you?"

"No! It's . . . it's so boring. I can't do anything but watch TV."

For any other teenager, mandatory TV would have sounded like a dream, but doing it on a schedule wasn't fun for any of them. Hayden had to sit in the living room every night for two hours while the damn bracelet charged. Binge-watching was the only thing making it bearable for any of them. Nick wouldn't be surprised if the TV options were getting thin, but that didn't make any difference.

"Buddy. You already screwed up by not coming home on time."

"I told you, my teacher asked me to stay late!"

"Go charge up. Do a crossword or something."

"A what?"

A shadow fell over his table, and Nick's heart squeezed. "I gotta go. Listen to your mom."

"Excuse me." The new voice was low as Nick hung up his phone, and it made the hair on his arms prickle. He stuffed the phone back in his pocket as he glanced up.

The long-haired asshole from the market rested one hand on the empty chair.

"Can I help you?" This conversation would be short because that was as polite as Nick was going to be.

The guy squinted at him, and then he smiled, and—dammit, Nick was back in that moment at the market, where this man had been an attractive stranger whose face and body would make the last few minutes of Nick's morning bearable. The smile was a good one, a quirk to one side saying something was funny and this guy was going to tell Nick the joke.

"I hope I didn't interrupt your call," Bun-Guy said.

"I'm waiting for someone." Let him think Nick was moments away from a very important dinner.

"Yeah, about that." The smile grew, bringing a sick feeling to life in the pit of Nick's stomach. "Your name's not Nick, is it?"

He pressed his lips tight.

No.

No, no.

The guy pointed at himself. "Because my name is Oliver and . . ." More of that smile. That goddamn smile. "I think I might be your date."

―――――

Horror spread over Nick's face. It would have been hilarious to watch if not for Oliver's own lingering dismay.

When he'd walked into the restaurant, he'd seen the man whose car Oliver had called the tow truck on. That little confrontation had not been his finest moment. As he'd given his name to the hostess, she'd told him his date was already waiting, but Oliver ignored her, choosing to scan the space in the increasingly futile hope his date might be someone, anyone, other than the dark-haired stranger.

It wasn't.

His mother taught him to be a gentleman. Otherwise, he would have run. But he couldn't be the jerk who stood someone up, even a blind date so obviously doomed from the start.

Fortunately, Oliver had lots of experience dealing with people who didn't want him in the room. One of the perks of being a lawyer—or a former lawyer, at least. He'd have to play this by ear, but he'd do his best to smooth things over.

Nick was on the phone as Oliver approached.

"Excuse me."

Oliver had noticed Nick's eyes at the market, the irises so dark they were nearly black. Last Saturday, they'd burned with enough anger to obliterate a weaker man on the spot.

Just like then, Oliver could barely tear his gaze away from them.

Nick's features, already stern from his phone call, hardened as he gazed up at Oliver.

"Can I help you?" His voice held no understanding of their situation, only cold irritation.

Oliver plowed on, trying to go for blandly polite. "I hope I didn't interrupt your call."

"I'm waiting for someone."

Oliver nearly showed off his best jazz hands. *Surprise.*

"Yeah, about that." He bit at the inside of his lip. "Your name's not Nick, is it?" It had to be. No other guy in the whole restaurant was within a decade of Oliver's age, and the little information he'd been able to glean from Seb and Martin indicated Nick couldn't be more than forty.

Realization dawned on Nick's face. The frown softened, the features going slack. His lips parted. Then the tip of Nick's tongue peeked out as he licked at his bottom lip and swallowed heavily.

Letting the poor guy hang for another second would have been fun, but Oliver was already starting at a deficit. Allowing Nick the upper hand by rediscovering some of the anger that sparked in his eyes as he'd pressed into Oliver's space at the market was not the best game plan. So he pasted on his best *isn't this a funny coincidence* smile and poked a finger at his chest.

"Because my name's Oliver, and I think I might be your date."

Before his height could become intimidating, he sank into the open chair. He kept his hands on the table where Nick could see them and cocked an eyebrow in a silent prompt to say something.

Nick gaped at him for a moment longer, dark eyes blinking rapidly and throat working to catch up. "Excuse me. I think there's been a mistake."

Oliver was so busy cataloguing Nick's features he didn't see the momentary tensing that would have alerted him before Nick stood. He was halfway around the table and headed toward the door before Oliver could react, and then the only thing left to do was to reach out and snag Nick's wrist. The momentum pulled him half out of his chair again.

"Hey, wait."

Nick spun, and the glare was back, speaking of the many horrible deaths Oliver could die, none of which Nick would mourn and many of which he would facilitate.

"Let go of me." His voice was low, mean. His skin was warm, his pulse beating hard under Oliver's hand.

Oliver released his wrist immediately. "Look, I'm sorry. I didn't mean to startle you. I'm as surprised as you are."

Nick huffed out a dark laugh, and his breath brushed over Oliver's cheek. "That's what you're sorry for?"

They were inches apart, just like at the market, and while Oliver's heart thundered and his head struggled to keep up and plan his next move, he kept getting distracted by Nick's closeness. Nick was a little shorter, but broad and built under his wrinkled button-down. In a fight, Oliver stood no chance.

Or in bed.

Fuck.

Thoughts like that were not going to help.

"Let me buy you dinner. As an apology."

Nick tilted his head to one side, exposing the thick cord of muscle running up his neck. Another twinge of attraction and regret twitched in Oliver's chest. Under normal circumstances, with any other guy that looked like Nick, Oliver would have been so pleased to find out this was his date. He'd not only be planning the best way to get to know him, but also probably the fastest way to get him into bed tonight. Too bad he'd blown his chance before he'd even known he had one.

"Please?" he said hopefully.

Nick sighed and settled back in his chair. "Sorry. I'm overreacting. The car—I was in the wrong spot. That was my fault. But you surprised me just now by being—well—you. Sorry."

Oliver arched an eyebrow. "So I'm forgiven? For the towing thing?"

"We'll see." Nick gave him a crooked smile, and Oliver perked up. Somewhere under the grumpy exterior, this guy had a sense of humor. Oliver just had to find it.

He glanced quickly around the restaurant, but their standoff had gone largely unnoticed. The place was busy, but not packed, and the few unoccupied tables around them were a buffer while they got themselves sorted.

A server came and asked if they'd like drinks. Oliver half expected Nick to be a Bud Light kind of guy, but he ordered a glass of red wine. Oliver knew the label he asked for and liked it.

"Make it a bottle," he told the server. He hadn't had a drink since Christmas, but his adrenaline was up, and they could probably both use a glass to calm their nerves.

"That's not necessary," Nick said.

"I told you." Oliver gave him his best confident smile. "I'm buying."

Nick's frown deepened. "It's not about that."

The server hovered nervously.

Oliver turned his smile up to her. "A bottle, please."

The server bobbed an acknowledgment and fled before Nick could protest.

"I'm not much of a drinker," Nick said when she was gone.

"It's only a bottle of wine." Oliver shook his napkin onto his lap. "Might help us avoid bloodshed."

A muscle twitched in Nick's cheek, like he'd been about to smile and caught himself. Oliver took it as the only encouragement he'd get to continue his peace campaign. "So why don't you tell me about yourself?"

Nick coughed and plucked at the buttons of his chambray

shirt. He'd rolled the sleeves up, exposing solid forearms with dark hair.

"What do you want to know?" Nick asked.

"You work at the fire station with Brian?"

Nick cleared his throat. "I'm the dispatcher."

"Not a firefighter?"

The dark eyes turned flat, as if Oliver had said the wrong thing. Other people would have been frustrated, but a tiny shiver of excitement slithered down Oliver's spine. He'd had opposing witnesses who were easier to crack. This might be fun after all.

"No. I was a firefighter, but I hurt my leg, and they put me on dispatch."

"How did you hurt your leg?"

"I fell three stories when a floor collapsed in a burning building."

Oliver whistled low. Hollywood-level heroism right there. "How long ago was that?"

"Three years."

"You must have done a number on your leg, then."

"You want to see the X-rays? I have them at the house somewhere."

Oliver grinned as Nick glowered at him. He should trademark that grumpy-but-sexy persona. Undeterred, Oliver continued. "How long have you lived in Seacroft?"

"My whole life."

"All of it?" He liked this little town, was pleased with his decision to move here. To live here his entire life, though?

Nick unrolled one of his sleeves and rolled it back up again. "You make it sound like forever. I can't be that much older than you are."

"I'm thirty-five," Oliver said.

"I'm thirty-nine." Nick's hard stare dared Oliver to make a joke about turning forty.

"And you've never wanted to live anywhere else?"

Nick shrugged. "I don't see what's so special about anywhere else."

The server came with their wine. She poured Oliver a small glass, which he tasted before thanking her. She poured the rest of his serving and then Nick's too.

"Are you ready to order?" she asked. Oliver hadn't had a chance to go over the menu, but Nick nodded.

"Go ahead," Oliver said, buying time. Nick ordered the cannelloni and a Caesar salad.

"And for you?" the server asked.

"I'll have the branzino," he said. "But it comes with pasta. Do you have potatoes you could serve with it instead?"

She frowned. "We could do mashed potatoes?"

Oliver wrinkled his nose. They'd be swimming in butter for sure, and probably cream too. Or else they'd be out of a box, and those were barely better than pasta.

"On second thought, don't worry about it. I'll have the vegetables it comes with, thanks."

She nodded and left.

"You came to an Italian restaurant, and you don't eat pasta?" Nick said. The tiny twitch at the side of his mouth was back, and he was doing a poorer job of hiding it.

Nick picked the restaurant, but that was beside the point. Oliver generally wouldn't eat the potatoes either, but after Seb had given him a hard time about brunch the previous weekend, he was trying not to come off as too fussy. He was already breaking rules with the wine. Next he'd be jonesing for a cigarette, and it would be all downhill from there.

"Watching my girlish figure." He grinned. Nick grunted but gave him that once-over again—slower this time—lingering on a spot above Oliver's eyes for a moment too long. Oliver ran a hand over his tied-back hair and watched Nick's attention follow it.

Interesting.

"Your hair is long." Nick's expression was confused.

"Is that a problem?" Growing it out hadn't quite been intentional, not at first. He'd been so busy after he'd moved to town, a haircut was barely on his priority list. And then, when Seb started teasing him about getting shaggy, Oliver let it keep growing to annoy his brother. By the time he'd finally thought about actually cutting it, the sides started to cover his ears, and he figured he'd see how long it could go before it bugged him.

So far, it hadn't.

"No, I mean . . . " Nick cleared his throat and shifted in his chair. He might even be blushing, though the restaurant's lighting made it hard to tell. Nick hissed through his front teeth. "Shit. I looked you up. This afternoon. Online. Your hair was shorter in the pictures I saw."

Now Oliver had to smile. With some of Nick's anger gone, he looked awkward, nervous almost. Like a big man sitting on a child's chair and trying to be cool about it.

He wasn't without resources, though, if he'd found Oliver online. Since opening his shop, he'd hardly bothered to check into most of his accounts. He'd posted a few "fuck you" photos from his vacation on Thanksgiving last year, in case Cooper was watching, and then hadn't thought about it much since. Despite all the promises to keep in touch since he'd left the firm, he hadn't heard from most of his former colleagues. He received emails from time to time, and the usual barrage of happy birthday messages when everyone got their automated social media reminders, but aside from that, things had been quiet.

But he'd left that world behind, so losing those connections was expected. They didn't understand what he was doing now, and he didn't know how to talk to them, especially when the answer to "How's everything going?" was a half-hearted "Yeah, not bad."

He stuffed that thought away. He was here, with this surly

not-a-firefighter, who had a temper hiding an awkward core of vulnerability. Time to focus on that.

Oliver ran a hand over his beard, surprised when Nick's gaze followed the movement again. Did he even know he was doing it? Oliver let the tip of his tongue run along the edge of his lip for a moment, and Nick's eyes widened.

Sometimes the littlest gestures were the most important.

Oliver leaned forward, bracing his forearms against the table, and grinned when Nick's posture mirrored his.

"So," he said, "what do you do for fun around here?"

4

*N*ick's throat went dry at Oliver's question.

That smile. Oliver's smile would kill him. It made Nick want all kinds of things. All kinds of fun. And more than a ham sandwich too.

Brian would be proud.

"I don't know. What do you like to do?"

Oliver pursed his lips, then tugged at an earlobe. All that succeeded in doing was dragging Nick's attention back up to Oliver's hair. Nick was glad Oliver had let his hair grow. He'd have something to run his hands through when—

He coughed. He was supposed to be mad at the jerk, not fantasizing about him from across the table. When Oliver had grabbed his wrist, he'd nearly decked him, but he really did seem sorry about the whole incident with the car.

"It's been a while since I had fun." Oliver was grinning again. Nick reached for his wine. "I've been so busy starting my business, I don't have a lot of free time."

It still sounded like he wasn't talking about joining a bowling league. Nick had another drink. "What's your business?"

The smile spread. Nick heated under his collar. "Turnip farming."

"Turnip—oh." Nick wouldn't apologize for that. Not yet. "But what is it really?"

"I opened a wellness and healthy eating lab on Front Street."

"Does your lab say you can't eat pasta?"

Oliver ran his broad hands down his chest and stomach. "I try to limit my carbs. There are some pretty good whole grain pastas, but they wouldn't serve them in a place like this."

A place like this. Oliver probably thought Angelo's was beneath him. Nick helped himself to more wine and motioned to Oliver, who smiled and held his glass out. Well, at least he'd gotten that part right. Nick wasn't much of a wine drinker. He generally preferred beer, but ordering a Bud to go with his pasta felt unsophisticated. The wine wasn't even that bad. Bitter but sweet, and cool on his tongue.

"So you . . . what?" he asked. "Analyze what people eat and tell them to cut back on the butter?"

"No. We—I—it's called a lab because we want our clients to know that what we're offering is based in science. It's not some fad business where we tell you to eat more kale and it will clear up all your ailments from back pain to insomnia."

"Do you have a business partner?"

"Hmm?" Oliver glanced up from his wine.

"You keep saying we."

For the first time, Oliver's confident expression faltered, and the shift made Nick sit up straight. Whatever had made him hesitate, though, Oliver collected himself almost immediately. The smile returned, tighter around the edges, but his posture was relaxed. "No, it's just me. The meal plans are designed by a nutritionist, but she works on contract. She's got five basic plans, and then I can modify them based on what the client needs and how fast they want to see results."

"So it's a weight loss thing?" Nick was still pretty fit, but he'd been riding his metabolism for a long time. As he rounded the corner on forty, he'd need reinforcements soon enough.

"It's a lifestyle thing. If a client comes to me with weight loss goals, I can help with that to a certain extent. But it's more about thinking about the ingredients you're putting in your body and whether you've got the right balance." Oliver eyed him, leaning back in his chair. "You don't look like those are the kind of goals you'd come to me with, though."

Nick arched an eyebrow, but he tried not to preen. "I'm holding my own."

"I think you definitely are."

Nick was too hot under his shirt. He watched Oliver from behind another drink of wine. The movie star was in there. Behind the beard, the hair, and the confident grin was the face of a man who was used to getting what he wanted.

Did Nick want to be wanted?

He definitely wanted Oliver. Had from the first time he'd seen him—up until the car thing got in the way. But since it looked like they were going to get past that, he let his mind wander back to those first moments in the parking lot, where he'd been so taken with Oliver's hair and the way his body stretched his T-shirt. Nick had seen that body in those sunny beach photos on social media, and now he knew the acres of taut skin and muscle he'd seen belonged to the guy in front of him, he really wanted to see it again.

"What were you doing at the market?" Nick asked.

Oliver's jaw tightened, and he took a long drink of wine. "That's an experiment."

The server arrived with their food. Nick's cannelloni was warm and inviting on its plate, with little ripples of steam rising lazily to drag his senses downward.

Oliver's branzino was . . .

A fish. *Huh.* Nick hadn't wanted to ask when Oliver had ordered. He'd seen it on the menu for years and had never bothered to order it, because he didn't know what a branzino was and didn't want to look stupid. Now he was glad he hadn't, because it really was a whole frigging fish, with the head still on and everything. Its shrunken white eye stared at him from Oliver's plate, like it blamed Nick for its situation.

Actually, they could both blame Brian, and he and Nick were going to have a talk at work about boundaries very soon.

Oliver must have known what he was getting, though, because he turned his plate and calmly opened the fish up with his knife. Steam rose, and he inhaled, looking pleased with his choice.

"My mom makes amazing branzino," he said.

"Are you Italian?" The blond hair and blue eyes made it seem unlikely.

Oliver smiled around a mouthful of fish, and Nick had to marvel at whatever genetics allowed a man to still be attractive like that. "We're the most Anglo of the Anglo-Saxons. I think my father can trace his heritage all the way back to before the Norman conquest."

Nick didn't know what half of that meant, other than it didn't sound like they were Italian.

"How's your dinner?" Oliver asked, making Nick blink. He glanced down at his untouched cannelloni, then back up at Oliver, who watched him with a knowing grin.

Nick growled softly and picked up his fork. "So tell me about your experiment and why it was so important to get my car out of the way."

Considering the evening started with Nick trying to storm out or possibly punch his date, he was having a nice time. They finished the bottle of wine, and Oliver ordered a second one. Their conversation was mostly small talk. Oliver told him more about his business, and Nick shared a couple stories from his late nights at the station.

Oliver talked briefly about working as a lawyer and mentioned a few more things in passing about his family. With the casual way he talked about the food his mother would cook, or about a fancy party he'd been to for work, Oliver—whether he meant to or not—made it obvious he came from a very different world and was used to having money available.

Nick did not come from that world. He hadn't meant to talk about his injury right at the start, but Oliver had asked, and Nick needed to make it clear that his career direction had been beyond his control. Most days, his leg hardly bothered him anymore, but his femur never could take the weight of all his gear again, no matter how much physio and weight training he'd done. And yet, despite everything, Nick wanted Oliver to be impressed with him, and telling old war stories was as good as anything else he had to offer.

By the time they were finishing their desserts, he had relaxed significantly.

"When was your last steady relationship?" Nick wouldn't normally bring something like that up so quickly, but they were nearly done with their second bottle of wine now. He wasn't drunk, but he was definitely into that fuzzy place where he could ask those kinds of questions.

Oliver paused as he scraped chocolate off his plate with one of the crumbly cookies that came with his coffee. His cheeks were flushed, but Nick's question made the brightness in his eyes dim. "I was with someone for a long time. It ended last year." He popped the cookie into his mouth, then licked crumbs from his fingers. Nick's pulse fluttered as Oliver's lips smacked together. "What about you?"

Nick balked, then flushed when Oliver smiled, like he'd caught Nick staring. He cleared his throat. "I was married once, right after school. It didn't last. You shouldn't get married when you're that young." He should mention Hayden too and get it over with. Short-circuited career, ex-wife, kid on house arrest. The trifecta of bad dates. Oliver would run screaming.

"So you're bi then?"

Nick took a slow breath before replying. "Is that a problem?"

"Is it a problem that I'm not?" Oliver raised a glass, and Nick clinked his against it.

They both watched each other as they drank. Nick's hand shook as he set the glass down, but he couldn't make himself look away. His heartbeat was unsteady, and a warm glow spread through his belly. Oliver's fingers played over the edge of his wine glass until he sat back in his chair, a broad palm smoothing over the front of his shirt.

Nick didn't know much about clothes. He owned three pairs of the same jeans, and lately he'd taken to buying his T-shirts in five-packs online, while everything Oliver wore was expensive. The shirt fit him too well to be bought at a chain store. The buttons weren't plastic like Nick's. And where Nick had strapped on the ancient watch that usually lived at the back of his dresser, only taken out for special occasions, Oliver sported a black smart watch with a display that flashed on and off as he talked and gestured with his hands.

Oliver seemed like a really good guy, but they were very different. The odds those differences would make for a solid long-term relationship weren't good. And that bothered Nick more than it had any right to.

As if on cue, his phone pinged in his pocket. Oliver blinked, breaking the moment between them.

Nick checked the time. Nearly eight-thirty. How had they been there for more than two hours?

Anya's text flashed on the screen.

Where are you?

He glanced up at Oliver, who was watching him.

"Sorry," he said. "I shouldn't have done that. Don't want to be that guy checking his phone in the middle of dinner."

"We're hardly in the middle of it." Oliver's smiles had softened over the course of the meal, and they held less teasing now.

Nick returned the smile. "I had a good time."

"So I'm forgiven for towing your car?"

Nick snorted. "Almost."

"How can I make it up to you?"

The warmth that had taken up residence in Nick's chest and his full belly started to spread, moving south at Oliver's question and the way his eyes danced as he said it.

The phone pinged in Nick's pocket again, feeling like cold water in his lap. "Probably time to call it a night."

Oliver's smile dropped, but he didn't protest.

The server took away their plates and brought a bill. Nick tried to pay for half, but Oliver held true to his word and covered the whole thing.

They walked side by side out of the restaurant.

"That was fun," Oliver said as they stood in the parking lot.

"Yeah."

"I'll see you around?"

Nick scratched his chin to hide his frown. He'd had a nice time, but he still didn't know why he was here. They had almost nothing in common, and sooner or later, Nick would have to tell him about what was going on at home. No way Oliver would stick around after that.

"I'll be careful not to park my car in the municipal lot on market days from now on." He held out his hand to shake, and Oliver took it. His skin was warm, the grip firm. Nick watched their hands twine together, following the line up Oliver's arm to his shoulder and then to his face.

Being the guy out with someone like Oliver, even the once, had been nice. The movie-star fantasy was fun for a while.

Nick was leaning in before the idea was fully formed in his head. If Oliver gave any indication of backing away or disinterest, Nick would have stopped. Instead, Oliver blinked, and his gaze shifted, moving away from Nick's eyes, toward his mouth. The space between them got smaller and smaller.

The kiss started gently. Just a goodnight peck. Nick would

have been happy with that. Oliver tasted faintly of chocolate and wine. A nice way to end the night.

But Oliver let go of Nick's hand, and his arm wrapped around Nick's body, pulling him in closer.

The feeling came over Nick fast, like a wave crashing down on them. One second, he was trying to be a gentleman, thanking his date for a pleasant night, and the next minute, he was stumbling, taking three uneven steps until Oliver's back met the brick of the rear of the restaurant with a soft thud. They skipped right over apologies, because Oliver opened his mouth, and his tongue slid out to lick Nick's lips while his hands cupped Nick's head and tilted it gently to one side.

Nick groaned, his own hands wrapping around Oliver, pulling them together even as he pressed them against the building. The noise he made was dark, needy. Oliver exhaled as his tongue slipped inside Nick's mouth. When Nick palmed Oliver's ass through his pants, he grunted, but he didn't move away. Instead, he turned them so Nick's back was against the building. Oliver's hardening cock was evident against Nick's hip. Sparks flared under his eyelids and over his skin. Nick's own erection wasn't very far behind.

He could blame the wine. Or his lack of practice. One second, they had been saying their goodnights, and now Nick was grinding against a near-stranger in a parking lot. In another second, he'd be begging Oliver to touch him.

He squeezed his eyes tight and then pulled away.

"Wait," he panted.

Oliver cocked his head back, but kept their hips pressed together. They were both hard, and a little friction would make Nick forget his protest and get back on board with whatever Oliver had in mind.

"I'm sorry," Oliver said. "I thought you—"

"No. I did. Or I guess . . ." Nick put a finger to Oliver's mouth, then trailed it down his throat to his chest. The fabric of his shirt was soft, almost delicate, under Nick's touch. He let his hand drop. "It's better if we don't. This wasn't supposed to be about—"

"It's a date. It can be anything we want it to be." Oliver reached for him, but Nick pressed as far back as the hard surface of the wall would let him, even while his body screamed at him to stop being an idiot.

"Yeah, but—" Nick shook his head. "I had a nice dinner. Let's leave it at that." One night had to be enough. The rest of his life was too much of a mess to drag Oliver into it.

Oliver looked like he was going to argue. He opened his mouth to say something, but then he shut it again before he nodded and stepped away. Nick shivered, even though the evening was warm.

"Fair enough. Are you okay to drive home?" Oliver asked.

Was he? He was dizzy and disoriented, with no idea if the wine or his sexual frustration was causing it.

"I'll be okay. I can walk from here."

It would be the better part of an hour, and Anya would probably kill him for coming home without the car again, but it would give him time to clear his head.

He was half afraid Oliver would offer to walk with him, which would have been a terrible idea, because then they would have wound up naked in the bushes somewhere for sure. Instead, though, Oliver gave him one last smile. "Take care, then. I'll see you around."

Nick hoped that wasn't true.

5

*S*aturday morning came and Oliver was back at the market. He spotted Nick's car parked in the far corner of the lot, as far from the stalls as it could get. He'd forgotten to ask Nick about the license plate at their dinner. It must have been an inside joke, because Nick was clearly not a party kind of person.

Oliver's pride was still nursing its wounds over the abrupt end to their night. He couldn't get the feeling of Nick pressing against him out of his head, or the soft groan he made when Oliver pushed him up against the wall.

Oliver hadn't tried to take someone new home after a first date in a decade and was disappointed to find his charm had not survived intact. The way Nick managed to call it off, at the very moment Oliver would have gotten down on his knees and hoped for a few minutes of privacy, meant clearly, he had slipped.

Regardless, now was not the time for public indecency. Now was the time to woo the citizens of Seacroft with his wares. He set up his stall at the end of the row. When the market board approved his application for the season, he'd hoped the end spot would mean high traffic as shoppers came and went. Unfortunately, he had been placed at the wrong end. Parking was tightly controlled, and only vendor vehicles—and tow trucks—were allowed to enter from the road at the side closest to the town hall. The shoppers had to enter from the other side and make their way past all the other vendors to get to him, but it would be worth it when they did.

The market was an experiment, an unexpected phase in his revamped plan to launch Pulpability. He and Cooper had mapped it all out from the moment they left their jobs until the end of their second year of business, detailed down to the week and the dollar. Unfortunately, the whole plan was on Cooper's hard drive, and he was . . . not someone Oliver could reach out to. He'd done his best to recreate it but, in the six months since he'd opened his doors, couldn't shake the feeling that he'd missed something important.

The first phase was getting the storefront ready, which took most of the winter and more cash than he'd expected. That was thanks, in part, to some reprinting on a lot of his branded materials, but more due to the fact that, in his business's short life, he'd already had to buy not one but two industrial juice presses, after the first one—purchased used from an online marketplace—had given up the ghost after only a month. In addition, he was operating on half the start-up funds, so the budget for things like advertising had been drastically cut back.

All this to say the market had been a necessary contingency to help supplement foot traffic. Deviating from the plan he and Cooper had put together—the details he remembered anyway—felt risky, but he needed to do something to get this kick-started. Oliver had bills to pay. He'd done his best to drum up interest, but every time he saw enthusiasm die on someone's face, his pitches felt more and more hollow.

He hoisted the aluminum bucket onto his table and filled it with ice. He'd only sold six bottles of juice the weekend before, but he'd handed out half his stack of flyers advertising his upcoming workshop—his other new addition to the business plan—and a few walk-ins to the store had followed. Not much, but it was a start.

"Whatcha got there?" A woman stood in front of his stall. She was probably in her sixties and wore a faded purple T-shirt. Curly gray hair sprouted out from underneath an old denim baseball cap that had *Farmers Feed Cities* stitched onto it.

"Good morning." Oliver smiled. He'd learned in law school to start every conversation with a smile. It made most people relax and made nervous people wonder what he knew. "How are you today?"

"Oh, fine." The woman looked over his setup. He'd hung the Pulpability banner over the front of the tent. She had to step a long way back to see it, which was not ideal. He didn't want people stepping away. Oliver made a mental note to hang it lower next Saturday.

"Are you interested in trying something?" He settled the sampler bottles in the ice. The woman eyed them suspiciously.

"What's in them?" She lifted a bottle. Her expression said she was expecting him to say "arsenic."

"Well, the one you're holding there is *Mango Tornado*. It's mango, carrot, ginger, and lime, with a little bit of apple."

She wrinkled her nose. "Seems like a waste of perfectly good apples to me."

Oliver kept his expression patient. "The apples are a base. The real nutritional value comes from the other ingredients."

That got another skeptical look. "Apples are good for you. I eat an apple a day, and I haven't been sick in years."

"Well yes, of course. They've got fiber and vitamin C. Most people should eat more plant-based material. But in a juice like this, you have to remove the peel, which eliminates a lot of the nutritional value in apples."

The woman pursed her lips. "Are you going to be here all season?"

"That's the plan. I'm Oliver, by the way." He reached over the table to shake her hand. She took it, but she still watched him suspiciously.

"I'm Marsha. My husband Glen and I have a booth over there."

"Great to meet you. What do you sell?"

"Glen's family runs an apple orchard. Right now we're selling the end of last year's apple butter and cider. But you wouldn't be very interested in that." Her lips pinched together in a bitter smile. Oliver's cheeks flushed as he pulled his hand back.

Oops.

He was given a merciful reprieve when the sound of a car with little or no viable muffler choked to life in the parking lot. Nick's car pulled out of its parking spot. Something squealed as he came to a stop and took the car out of reverse, but the squealing sound died as he made his slow chugging way toward the exit. He didn't even glance at Oliver as he pulled onto the street.

Oliver had clearly failed to make a positive impression. Or maybe he hadn't managed to claw his way back from being the jerk who had Nick's car towed.

It would all be fine, except even the shadowed sight of Nick's profile in the car brought back all the memories. The rasp of Nick's stubble on Oliver's neck, the wet heat inside his mouth. The firm insistence as Nick grabbed Oliver's ass and showed him exactly how much Nick wanted him.

Oliver's dick twitched in his jeans, and he shifted, tearing his gaze away from the old sedan that rumbled up the street. He turned back to the front of his stall to find, much to his relief, that Marsha had moved on. No need to dig himself in deeper with her by not only insulting her produce but also sporting a hard-on like he had a fetish for classic junkers.

The morning crowd rolled in, and Oliver didn't have more time to fixate on his memories of Nick. He did his best to catch people's attention—those who made it all the way down to his end of the aisle, anyway. Most listened politely as he introduced himself and his business model. Some accepted his offer of a free sample, although their reactions were mixed. The *Mango Tornado* was the most popular. People treated the kale and spinach blend that Oliver called the *Green Monster* like a magic potion that needed to be choked down but would give them superpowers if they survived. No one seemed to like *Beet the Rap*. More to the point, hardly anyone bought anything. Despite all his planning, nothing could have prepared him for the quiet desperation that flared up in his chest whenever someone walked away.

He handed out a bunch of flyers, though, and at least a few people seemed excited about his workshop. One guy, who had the reddest hair Oliver had ever seen, nearly fist-pumped the air when Oliver explained it to him.

"This is exactly the kind of thing I've been looking for!" He smiled broadly, flashing white teeth against his freckled skin.

"Well, I look forward to seeing you there."

The red-headed kid—he couldn't be more than twenty— grinned at him, bought three bottles of *Beet the Rap*, and went on his way. Oliver couldn't help his smile as he watched him go, although it faded when he spotted the death stares coming from Marsha and Glen across the way. The orchard stall was busier than his. Whatever they thought of his opinions on apples, they weren't hurting.

As he packed up for the afternoon, nervous energy twitched under his skin. He'd spoken to more people that morning than the week before, but the crowd had still been small. He'd see how many people actually followed through on their promises to come to the workshop. The market felt like a smart way to introduce himself, but he still had a long haul before he could call Pulpability a success.

He would succeed, though. He'd left too much behind, would have to answer too many questions if he failed.

He drove to the shop, letting himself in through the back so he could put his remaining stock in the fridge and stash his tables and banners.

The shop had a storage room behind the kitchen. He shuffled a few boxes around, trying to create more space. The bottles rattled as he stacked their crates. As he stood from setting down the last one, he banged his head on a shelf hard enough to see stars.

"Ow!" He clamped a hand down on the throbbing spot on his skull, then growled as a stack of paper tumbled to the floor in a rush.

He hissed and swore, rubbing at his head. He wasn't bleeding, so only his pride was banged up. Oliver bent to pick up one of the pages, designed with lots of space for him to write meal plans and other directions. Someday he'd use it to print corporate invoices too, but that was phase four, which wouldn't kick off until the fall at the earliest.

He froze, as he saw the letterhead. Habeus Juice Us. That was wrong. He sifted through the pages on the floor. They all said Habeus Juice Us. They all had Cooper's name next to his. Cold fear fought against a flash of bright anger in his chest.

He'd thrown these out. Getting everything rebranded and reprinted was an unplanned but necessary start-up expense, to prove the business was his and his alone; that although he was on his own now, he could still make it a success.

Except apparently he hadn't thrown all the old papers out. Or they had come back from the dead to haunt him.

Oliver growled and checked the next stack of paper on the shelf. The letterhead said *Pulpability*, like it should

He gathered up the old papers and tossed them in the recycling bin behind the store. He wasn't superstitious, but the purge felt good. Maybe this last remnant, lurking in the back of his shop, had been holding him back. He'd worked too hard to believe in luck, but maybe this was what he needed to turn things around.

He ignored the prickling feeling, like someone was watching him, for the rest of the afternoon.

———

Nick had been a walking, talking hard-on since Thursday. When Brian came by the dispatch office and not-so-innocently asked how Nick's date had gone, he'd barely been able to hold it together. Answering that question in more than a few words would have brought back too many sights and sensations. Oliver and his celebrity smile. Oliver licking chocolate off his fingers. Oliver pushing Nick against the restaurant wall and turning his better judgment to putty in the space of ten seconds.

He'd grunted a few responses when Brian pressed for more information. Mercifully, a call came in, and Nick made a big show of answering it. Brian took the hint, but not before he gave Nick a knowing look saying he didn't believe the story was as simple as all that.

Saturday wasn't much better. When his shift ended, Nick practically ran to his car before his legs could divert him back toward Oliver's place at the market. He'd gone home and locked himself in his small workshop in the basement. During rehab, his physiotherapist told him to find hobbies so he didn't dwell too much on not being at work. His father made furniture, and Nick figured he could do the same, if his career fell apart completely. He'd taken some courses and had his dad's old lathe refurbished. It never panned out, but he still had all the stuff. He spent the day turning spindles and planing arms for chairs, even though he had no idea what he'd ever do with them all once they were assembled.

On Sunday, Anya had the day off, and Hayden was in a reasonably good mood. Nick had to work overnight and spent most of the day napping and lying low, so Anya dragged Hayden outside to help her work in the yard. Nick wasn't much for landscaping. He mowed the lawn and that was about it, so any work Anya managed to get Hayden to do would be an improvement.

Funny. When he'd first been arrested, Hayden would have treated gardening like a fate only slightly better than torture. Any time Anya suggested any kind of chores, there had always been a big show of eye rolling and heavy sighs. Standard reactions in the arsenal of any fifteen-year-old, but Hayden turned it into an art form. Sometimes it escalated into an argument. Other times, Hayden agreed to help and then mostly made excuses to go back to his room while his mother worked.

Now though, two seasons and nearly six months later, and with the warm weather back, the garden was about the only reason he was allowed outside on the weekend. It still required a small amount of mostly symbolic eye rolling—and a phone call to the probation officer to be clear Hayden wasn't making a break for it—but after that, he was essentially a free man as long as he didn't leave the property.

Watching them together was still hard, though. With less tension, and their heads tilted toward each other, the scene they made was almost domestic and happy. In another life, Nick might have had this, his wife and his son working alongside each other in the backyard. But Nick squandered that chance a decade ago.

"Today was a pretty good day," Anya said when they were done. Her skin shone from the sunshine and fresh air.

"Seemed to be," Nick agreed.

Hayden was in the shower. For all his selective adolescent hearing about anything said in the house, he might as well have police radar any time they talked about him. No matter where they were, and what room Hayden was in, he would appear and demand to know what they were saying. The shower bought them a few minutes to say things that would only bring on an argument if he could hear them.

Anya's eyes went nervous. Without her usual mascara and eyeliner, she looked younger than her nearly forty years. "I need a favor for his court date next week."

"Mm-hmm." The court dates happened monthly, with the judge reviewing reports from Hayden's probation officer and from the school. The bracelet was originally supposed to have been on for three months after his sentencing, but in the first month, Hayden had skipped a few classes, and in the next month, he'd tried to leave the house in the middle of a Sunday for no reason he would discuss. Both infractions added another month, so here they were, nearly six months in. Every month, they hoped for good news from the judge, and every month, they were disappointed.

"I don't think it's going to be a good one," Anya said. "The hearing. Not with him missing community service and being late coming home from school. He's had better months, and they still left it on."

"Probably." The ritual frustrated them all. He and Anya gave the lectures and the speeches, and revoked what few remaining privileges Hayden had left. Then Hayden promised to fall in line but followed that up with enough screw-ups to make a weak case when they stood in front of the judge.

"Could you . . ." Anya paused when the water in the shower turned off. She dropped her voice to a whisper. "Could you take him? I know it's not for a little bit, but I already know I can't face it this month." Her eyes were sad when she turned her gaze up to him.

"Yeah." Nick squeezed her shoulder. "No problem."

Except Hayden's court dates were on Mondays. By taking him, Nick would miss out on a huge amount of sleep between his Sunday and Monday night shifts. But Anya wouldn't ask if she didn't need the relief. When they'd been married, she'd asked him for smaller things, and he hadn't been able to get over himself enough to help. He would always regret that, but regret wasn't worth much, so the least he could do was take Hayden to court. It wouldn't be the first time he'd gotten through a shift on a coffee IV and willpower. Nick had promised to be this for her. Time to follow through.

Later, as he drove to work, Nick rolled his head on his shoulders. He was always tired now. They were making the best of a very bad situation, but most days weren't like today. Even when Hayden followed all the rules, showed up where he was supposed to be on time, and didn't kick up a stink about charging his bracelet or cleaning his room or any of the other things that might set him off, the tension at their house was thick. Every day, Nick hoped that today would be the day things turned around, and every day that hope withered into tired disappointment. The cycle was exhausting for all of them.

Oliver's hands on his face popped into his mind again. He'd been caught up in a tornado of lust and arousal, but underneath it all was the tingling sensation of being touched. In particular, of being touched with affection. Nick wasn't an especially touchy kind of guy by nature, but he liked the warmth of Oliver's hands, the rough places that brushed over Nick's skin. No one had given him more than a reassuring squeeze or a pat on the back in a long time, and now that he'd felt it, he couldn't get it out of his head.

He wasn't the right guy for Oliver, and his life was too much of a mess to make pursuing something with him worthwhile, but Nick had to force down a shudder of want as he parked the car. He couldn't be distracted. Anya and Hayden needed him. Oliver would meet someone else who didn't come with all Nick's baggage. Once again, hope shredded itself into disappointment as Nick headed into the station.

Oliver put the whole letterhead thing out of his head. Seb and Martin invited him out for brunch again, and, while he should have stayed home and prepped for the workshop, he'd agreed to go for the distraction, if nothing else. His brother's endless teasing was the rancid icing on the cake.

"It's not that I don't eat bread," he said after the server had taken their order. Everyone else had ordered bacon and eggs, while Oliver asked for an egg white omelet and sliced fruit. He'd do his best not to eye Seb's bacon too longingly when it arrived. God, he missed bacon. "The average American eats fifty-three pounds of bread a year."

"My youngest son doesn't even weigh fifty-three pounds!" Penny said. She owned the diner, and she and Martin formed a fast friendship as they'd rallied the town when the bookstore burned down the previous year.

"Exactly." Oliver nodded. "And the nutritional value of your typical slice of mass-produced white bread is—"

"Oh my God." Seb wrapped his arms around his head and collapsed to the table. "Penny, please don't encourage my brother. Oliver, don't you have an 'off' switch? This is the only day you're not at work. Can't you loosen up and eat like a normal human being?"

Oliver could have pointed out that his whole business model was based on not taking days off. Instead, he smiled indulgently at his brother and patted the back of his head.

"How are things going?" Penny asked as she sipped her coffee.

"Pretty good!" Oliver forced his smile until his cheeks hurt. "I think the market stall is going to be a great addition and more than make up for keeping the shop closed on Saturday mornings."

"You know one of us could work at the store on Saturdays." This was from Martin, who sat next to Seb. Oliver turned his perma-smile toward him. Martin could be painfully shy, so offering to help out in any kind of customer service capacity said a lot. But Seb and Martin were still getting their own art gallery off the ground, so he couldn't ask for more of their time. And anyway, he needed to be able to say he'd made the business a success on his own. Cooper said it couldn't be done, that it would be too much work for one person. But Oliver wasn't afraid of hard work. He could do this.

"It's fine," he said, responding to Martin's offer. "The market will be the boost I need. It gets Pulpability introduced to a different segment of the community and to the tourists, when they start coming, and regular customers will know that's where they can find me through the spring and summer."

"I still think that name is terrible," Seb said as he sat up again.

"No one asked you." Martin wrapped an arm around Seb's shoulders.

"Well, they should have."

Better than Habeus Juice Us.

No. Not thinking about that.

"I'm running a workshop this week, if any of you would like to come." He couldn't ask for more of their help, but a little moral support couldn't hurt.

"What kind of workshop?" Seb asked with narrowed eyes, at the same time that Martin said, "We'd love to!"

"It's about home juicing. It doesn't always have the same benefits as what I've got at the store, but done right, it can be a pretty good alternative."

"I don't believe it. He's still working," Seb hissed to no one in particular.

"We'll be there." Martin elbowed him gently, and Seb grumbled agreement.

Seeing someone wrangle Oliver's spitfire brother into—if not exactly submission—at least a measure of civility was still disconcerting. Seb had always done his own thing. Watching him acquiesce to the quiet man sitting beside him was some kind of magic or miracle.

"So how did your date go?" Martin asked.

Oliver bit his tongue to fight back a blush. "Fine. He seemed like a nice guy."

"That's what Brian says. He told me he and Nick started working at the station about the same time, but Nick had an accident a few years ago. I think Brian still feels like he's letting Nick down somehow."

"He said he works dispatch."

Seb snorted. "Can't imagine that's a very demanding job. Nothing here is. Did you see the headline in the paper yesterday? Controversy over the new possum-proof garbage cans."

"Well, actually—" Penny started.

"What do you think?" Seb turned back to Oliver. "Is Nick the guy you want in your corner when the possum army comes for your family?"

Nick seemed to have the build and the disposition for a crisis. Tough and strong, quiet but purposeful.

Like the way he'd purposefully manhandled Oliver into near public indecency. If he was nursing an old injury, it hadn't been evident as he'd pushed Oliver up against a brick wall.

Their food arrived. Before Oliver could even take a bite, a piece of buttered white toast dropped out of the air and landed on his egg whites. Oliver glared up at his brother; he stared blandly back.

"In case you change your mind."

Oliver tossed the toast back at him. "I'll pass."

"No need for a food fight. I was just making a point. Did Cooper encourage this kind of childish behaviour?" Seb laughed.

Oliver's fork paused, halfway up to his mouth. The omelet tumbled back to his plate.

"Cooper?" Penny asked.

"Oliver's ex-boyfriend," Martin said with a shrug. "I don't know much else."

"He's a spoiled asshole. That's really everything there is to know. I have no idea what my distinguished big brother saw in him."

"I'm right here." Oliver glared at Seb with real annoyance now. Bringing Cooper into this was unnecessary, but Seb lived to push other people's buttons.

"Come on." Seb put his own fork down. "It's been, what? Eight months?"

Nine months and twenty-seven days.

"Something like that."

"I think it's time to dish. You've been very tight-lipped about what happened. You live with a guy for ten years and then suddenly you quit everything. Your job. Your boyfriend. Your life. So shit must have gone down, and either you did the heart-breaking, in which case you finally smartened up and realized what I've known for a decade or more, or he left you, in which case you owe him nothing, and we deserve a good brunch-time story."

The longer Seb spoke, the more all of Oliver's internal organs felt like they were turning to lava. His stomach went acidic, and his heart pounded loudly in his ears. He didn't want to talk about this, because Cooper already took up too much of Oliver's mental energy, and he wasn't even here, but of course Seb didn't care about things like personal boundaries.

"When do your kids finish school for the year?" Martin asked Penny quietly.

"Not for another month," Penny said. Oliver glanced at them. Their faces were sympathetic, and the longer Oliver's silence stretched on, the more Seb's mocking smirk turned to guilt, like he'd realized he was pushing too hard.

"You know." Oliver glared at him. "You can be just as much of an asshole when you want to be."

Seb wordlessly shoved a fork into his eggs, but he wouldn't meet Oliver's eyes.

The conversation moved on, with Martin and Penny doing their best to keep the topics neutral and nonconfrontational. Oliver replied when he was asked a direct question and didn't look at his brother again.

They had always been like this, the two of them.

And now Oliver had made the stupid move of trying to build his social circle off his brother.

On his drive home, he sent a text to Nick.

I have a proposition for you.

6

*N*ick had been on edge since receiving Oliver's text. Reading intention in a text was hard, but Oliver's first message, and the ones that followed, were persistent in a way his emails setting up their first date hadn't been. Oliver wanted to see Nick again, and he wasn't taking no for an answer.

Which was how Nick found himself pulling into the driveway at the address Oliver gave him. He took a few deep breaths as he sat in his car. Nick suggested meeting for a drink somewhere, but Oliver was insistent they meet at his house. Going to Oliver's place felt so personal, but he'd promised he wasn't planning anything weird.

Low-level anxiety rippled beneath Nick's skin. He'd been edgy at work, though the nights were quiet, and short with Anya at home, though she hadn't deserved it.

"What is wrong with you?" she'd finally asked that morning, but he shrugged her off and said he was tired. The words an eerie echo of the many excuses he'd given when they'd still been married, and he hadn't wanted to deal with whatever had her worried that day. The way her expression clouded over was familiar too, and it twisted his stomach.

He wasn't sure why he didn't tell her about Oliver. Possibly because he didn't want her to make a big deal out of something that still might be nothing. Possibly because he didn't want her to worry Oliver would be a distraction from what was going on at home. He was committed, no matter what Oliver wanted.

The house looked new, although the beachfront neighborhood around it was not. Probably a flip. Nick walked to the front door and rang the bell, then nervously stuffed his hands into his jeans pockets. His pulse beat a fast rhythm in his throat, picking up even faster at the sound of footsteps approaching from inside.

Then the door opened, and Nick's nerves and agitation condensed into a tight ball in his gut, weighing him to the spot where he stood. In the late day sun, Oliver's face was devastating. His eyes were dark blue and crinkled at the corners when he smiled. His hair was down, coming to below his chin.

"Hey." His voice made the ball in Nick's stomach squeeze and then spread, a warm rush pouring over his insides and into his groin.

"Hi." His own voice sounded rough.

"Come on in." Oliver stepped aside, and Nick practically tripped as he entered the house.

They stood in the hall for a second, staring. Nick's brain ran a million miles an hour and still came up blank for something to say.

Oliver leaned in and kissed Nick once on the cheek. On reflex, Nick turned his head and caught Oliver's mouth. The kiss was brief, with Oliver stepping back before it could burn into anything brighter.

There still didn't seem to be anything to say.

Oliver ran his tongue over his bottom lip, then pulled an elastic off his wrist, which he used to tie his hair back into a messy bun.

"Let me show you around."

A tour. Nick could do a tour. He ignored the relief that flooded through him.

The inside of the house had definitely been renovated recently. It didn't quite have that new paint smell, but the walls were perfect, without a single scuff or smudge. Oliver showed him an office obviously in frequent use. A glass-topped desk and leather chair were set up with stacks of papers organized in neat racks and a heavily marked-up calendar tacked to a corkboard to one side.

Nick followed wordlessly as Oliver led him to the open-concept living room/dining room/kitchen space. The appliances were all brand new, brushed stainless steel and gleaming. The stove was a six-burner gas range. Such a far cry from Nick's kitchen, with its curling laminate flooring, peeling cupboard fronts, and the ancient range with its chipped enamel.

Oliver touched Nick's shoulder, drawing his attention away from the kitchen. Oliver's hands were strong and broad, the fingers long, the nails cut short. He was wearing another of those V-neck T-shirts like that first morning in the market, serving to show off his muscled arms. Nick watched Oliver's shoulder blades glide over his back as he made his way up the hall. The motion was hypnotic.

An empty room toward the back of the house was followed by a large bathroom. It had a basin sink with brushed fixtures, and a shower big enough that Nick could probably lie down on the tiled bottom and not bump his head.

"And the bedroom," Oliver said as they left the bathroom. The door was open, and, while Nick wasn't brave enough to go in, a heavy wooden dresser and the corner of a bed with dark sheets were visible from the hall. If he got closer, Nick would be unable to keep himself from picturing Oliver in that bed, and then he'd insert himself into that image, and from there he'd embarrass himself in front of this beautiful person he hardly knew.

"It's a nice house," he managed to say.

Oliver took mercy on him and led him back toward the kitchen.

"It's pretty good. The basement is finished too, but I didn't really have anything to put down there."

All this space for one person. It probably had the same square footage as Nick's house, and Oliver wasn't even using half of it.

"Did you get a good price on it?" Real estate in Seacroft was temperamental, but a house this size, especially a renovated one near the beach, would always be in demand.

"I'm renting. I heard the guy who flipped it was trying to get too much money in the sale, and it wasn't moving. It's month to month. I get a place to live. He gets some revenue to cover his mortgage."

"But he could sell it out from under you?"

Oliver smiled. "Trust me. With the year I've had, renting this place month to month is one of the most predictable things I've done. Can I get you something to drink?"

"Just a soda. Or water is fine. I have to work tonight."

Oliver poured them each a glass, and then led the way out to the living room. Nick sat on the couch, surprised and pleased, when Oliver sat next to him.

"Cheers!" He held his glass up, and Nick knocked his own against it.

The house fell into silence again as they drank. Nick fidgeted as his discomfort from the night of their date returned. He didn't know much about Oliver's past, but the house only confirmed what Nick had already guessed. Someone starting a new business didn't pay for a house like this, even if it was a rental, without having some solid money in the bank to start with.

"I had a good time the other night," Oliver said.

"So did I."

"Did you? You left in a hurry."

"I didn't want you to get the wrong idea."

"That you're the kind of guy who kisses on the first date?"

Nick scratched at his scalp. He'd buzzed his hair before coming over, and the short stubble tickled at his fingertips. "That I was more into the date than I actually was."

Oliver's confident expression flickered. "Oh."

"I mean—" Nick struggled to explain it. "I had a nice time. And you—You're—If nothing else, you're a really good kisser. But I have a lot going on in my personal life. It might not be the best time for me to get involved with someone. It's all a bit complicated, and it didn't seem fair to get too caught up in what we were doing."

"Complicated?" Oliver set his glass down on the coffee table.

"Yeah." Nick didn't want to talk about it. Despite it all, he still wanted Oliver to like him.

"What if we made it uncomplicated?"

"What do you mean?"

Oliver smiled and ran a hand over his hair. He undid the bun, then tied it back up again.

"I mean, what if this wasn't about a relationship? You're busy, I get that. I'm busy too. I'm trying to get a business off the ground, and the next few months over the summer are going to be critical. So, what if this wasn't about dates and getting to know each other? What if this wasn't about me meeting your friends and you meeting mine and all the things that go with it?"

Nick's heart stuttered. "You're talking about sex."

Oliver cocked his head to one side and looked Nick up and down. "I am." He leaned in and hesitated like he was waiting for Nick to say something else. When he didn't, he pressed his lips to Nick's. His mouth was soft.

Like that night after dinner, it could have been a simple kiss ending almost as quickly as it began. Except, the second Oliver's skin brushed against his, something caught fire. One second Nick was a sane, rational person, and the next he had Oliver's T-shirt caught in his fist, pulling the other man toward him while his tongue slid along the seam of Oliver's lips.

Oliver growled, coming to his knees and opening his mouth to let Nick inside. The air warmed between them as blood rushed in Nick's ears and started to collect lower. His reaction was as instinctual as breathing.

They were half on top of each other, with Nick's hands in Oliver's hair and one of Oliver's knees planted between Nick's thighs, when Oliver finally broke away.

"What? Why did you stop?" Nick asked.

Oliver grinned. His hair had come loose at the sides, and his lips were swollen, and when he smiled again, Nick had to grab the glass on the table and swallow the rest of his water to keep from leaping across the couch and pouncing on top of him.

"I have a proposal," Oliver said.

Nick chuckled as he set his glass down. "I'm all ears."

———

Oliver had to restrain himself. The attraction present between them the other night was still there, louder and even more demanding now that they had four walls and a door separating them from the rest of the world.

If only Nick understood the kind of effect he had on Oliver. That superpower would bring nations to their knees.

"What I'm proposing is uncomplicated. Neither of us has time to make a big deal out of this. I'm suggesting we take our personal lives out of the equation. Let's scratch this itch between us. That's it. No personal drama. No commitment. It lasts as long as it's convenient and it feels good. That's all."

Nick brought his hands behind his head and leaned back against the couch with a heavy sigh. It might have been an innocent thing, but it only succeeded in showing off the width and length of his body. Oliver wanted to skip the rest of his prepared speech and touch every inch of it.

"Just sex," Nick said, dark eyes focused like lasers on Oliver's face.

"That's all. We agree to that upfront and stick to it, no matter what."

Nick rolled his head along the back of the couch. His eyes—Oliver didn't think he'd ever get enough of Nick's eyes—were still so dark they were black, and the color was high on his face. Even if he said no to the larger proposal, Oliver hoped he'd agree to screw around a bit more today. Letting him go without getting to feel his body on Oliver's one more time seemed impossible.

"Okay."

Oliver blinked, caught off guard. It couldn't be that simple? "Okay?"

"Sure. What's the worst that could happen? We mess around for a few weeks and one of us gets our heart broken."

Well, that was grim. And it defeated the point. Oliver couldn't stand to have his heart broken more than once a year.

"It won't come to that."

Nick rolled toward him, like he meant to kiss him again, but Oliver stopped him with a hand on his chest.

"What?" Nick frowned.

"I have a few more things. Rules, if you will, before we go ahead."

"Rules?"

"I used to be a lawyer. We like to have our bases covered."

Nick sighed and rolled back. "All right. Let's hear it."

Oliver ducked his head to smother a laugh and winced when his hair pulled at its elastic. He went to undo it and tie it back for the third time since Nick had arrived, then thought better of it and let it hang loose instead.

"First," he said, "we both get tested before we do anything

too involved. This arrangement doesn't have to be long-term, but I'm not extending the experience with an STI."

Nick shrugged. "The fire department makes us get tested every year. Even me, despite the fact I never leave the station. We did it a few months ago. I can get a copy of the report if you want."

"Fine. I'll make an appointment this week."

"Next?"

"This arrangement isn't serious, but if either of us is thinking about seeing anyone else, and especially about sleeping with anyone else, we tell the other one. It's not about exclusivity, it's about honesty, and I hope you'll respect that."

Another shrug. "You're the first person I've been with in years. The odds of me finding someone else so quickly, when I've lived in this town my whole life, are slim."

Well, that had been easy. If Nick were going to balk at anything, Oliver expected that condition to do it. Asking to keep this casual but exclusive was big.

"Last thing." Oliver slid a hand over the hard expanse of Nick's chest. "We don't do anything sexual without both parties agreeing."

Nick arched an eyebrow. "That's kind of obvious, isn't it?"

"I wanted to get it out there. I think it's pretty clear I want you." Oliver circled his thumb across one of Nick's nipples, making him inhale sharply. "But wanting doesn't mean we're compatible. I don't role-play. I'm me and you're you, just as we are. I don't like to be tied down. I don't mind toys, but I don't like pain. If your mouth, your hands, or your dick go anywhere near my ass, you get to clean up before they go anywhere near my mouth again."

Nick grinned, maybe the first real smile Oliver had seen from him. The white teeth against his tanned skin were bright.

"Don't call me babe," Nick said

"I didn't."

Nick put his hand over Oliver's where he still teased Nick's nipple. "That's my condition. Don't call me babe. Or sugar or honey or sweetie. My ex-wife liked pet names. I am not your darling, your baby doll, or anything else you can think of."

"What about party girl?"

"Party girl?" Nick's mouth pinched like the word tasted rancid.

"Yeah." Oliver took a chance and ran his free hand over Nick's close-cropped hair, gratified when Nick closed his eyes and leaned into it. "Your license plate says Party Girl. Can I call you that?"

Nick opened one eye to glare at him. "It's Pretty Girl, and no, you can't."

"Pretty Girl?" Oh, this was going to be fun. "Of all the things you could put on a license plate, you chose Pretty Girl?"

His laughter was cut off when Nick gripped his shirt again and hauled Oliver onto his lap. No more time for jokes before Oliver straddled Nick and Nick's strong arms were wrapped around him, pulling them close as Nick tried to devour Oliver in one bite.

"I'm in," Nick said.

Laughter turned to need, low in Oliver's gut. He had his arrangement—and a pretty girl to boot.

7

*H*ayden's court date went as well as could be expected, which was to say the judge took about thirty seconds to review the reports, glanced over the top of his wire-frame glasses, and announced that Hayden could do four more weeks of house arrest for missing community service and not being where he was supposed to be after school. Hayden, in the suit they bought specifically for court appearances, hung his head and said he understood.

The ride home was a different story. Getting to the courthouse took over an hour each way, and while the drive up was always full of moody silence, Hayden chose to blow off steam on the drive home after being on his best behavior during the invariably long wait to be called and the brief appearance before the judge.

"It's not fair!" he said as Nick pulled the car out onto the highway. "I was sick! It's not like I didn't go to community service because I didn't feel like it."

"You heard the judge," Nick said. "Next time, you have to get a sick note for something like that."

Hayden rolled his eyes. "That's stupid, though. The doctor's office isn't even open on Saturdays. What was I supposed to do?

Make sure I stayed sick until Monday so I could go get a note? Then the stupid judge would have given me another four weeks for missing school instead!"

"Do you want to talk about what happened the day you were late? You're normally really good about coming home on time. And we both know your teacher didn't ask you to stay. So do you want to explain what really happened?"

"No."

"Are you sure? Because it's not like we don't know you're hiding something. You know your mom and I want to help you. But we can't if you don't—"

"Would you get off my back, okay? I was late, what's the big deal?" Hayden kicked angrily at the dash, making the glove compartment pop open.

"Hey!" Nick reached over to slam the compartment shut again. "There's no need for that."

"Well then, stop bugging me. I was late. I couldn't find my backpack, and I was late, so what?"

"You couldn't find your backpack?" That was a new one. "Don't you have a locker to keep your stuff in at school?"

Hayden stared out the passenger side window.

"Well?"

"Yeah."

"So you couldn't find the backpack that was in your locker?"

More glum silence.

"Hayden?"

"Forget about it. I couldn't find it, and then I did. I was late. I'm sorry I'm not perfect!"

"But don't you understand that's exactly what you have to be if you ever want that thing off your ankle? You have to follow every letter of the law and more."

"But it's so stupid!"

"Well, you should have thought of that before you started picking on your friend online, shouldn't you?"

"He's not my friend."

The kid knew how to argue semantics like nobody's business. Maybe, when this was all over, they'd talk about a future career on the other side of the courtroom.

Maybe Nick could get Oliver to talk to him. He'd said he'd been a lawyer. Maybe if Hayden talked to someone whose day was more than video games and not doing homework, he'd be inspired to do something with his life, or at least toe the line long enough to get off house arrest.

But he and Oliver agreed to stay out of each other's personal lives, and, in a way, that was a relief. Nick was doing his best, but he struggled when it didn't seem like things were ever going to get better for them.

Oliver was an escape, and Nick should have felt guilty about using him, but hadn't they agreed to it? Oliver's mouth on Nick's was enough to make him forget everything for a few minutes, and so far, they'd only managed some pretty serious kissing and a little groping. Who knew what would happen if they ever got naked? He needed to find out, even if it meant playing by Oliver's rules.

The other night, Nick had been so turned on he thought he'd burst, but Oliver had been insistent on his condition about STI tests before anyone got to have an orgasm. Nick had left for work even more agitated, with a side of deep sexual frustration for good measure. He'd never wanted to jerk off in a bathroom stall so much, but he was an adult with a measure of self-control, so he suffered through his shift silently. He could wait. Nick needed to know what Oliver felt like—under him, in him, it didn't matter. He needed to know, and he needed the moments of escape it could offer him.

Because, despite the reprieve Oliver offered, an angry teenager still sulked silently next to Nick as the miles on the highway rolled by. He would always love his son, but liking

Hayden was difficult these days, and the shame of that ate at Nick more every day.

He'd emailed Oliver his STI test results as soon as he'd found them. If it made him look overeager, so be it.

"Dad?" Hayden's voice dragged him back to the present. It was bittersweet that, despite everything, Hayden still called him "Dad." Nick didn't feel very qualified for the job most of the time.

"Yeah, buddy?"

"Can we get something to eat? I'm starving."

Nick sighed. Anya would say he shouldn't reward bad behavior with things like junk food. And strictly speaking, Hayden's house arrest conditions meant they were supposed to drive straight home from the courthouse with no deviations. But they'd waited almost three hours for their case to be called, and Nick was hungry too.

Billboards advertised fast-food joints and a gas station a few miles up. If the probation officer kicked up a stink about them stopping, Nick could say they had needed gas.

"Sure, buddy," he said. "Do you want burgers or pizza?"

———

Oliver was chopping mangoes when the bell above the door at the front of the shop chimed. Technically, he'd already closed for the day, but he'd take even latecomers if they were interested in buying something. He poked his head out into the front of the store and was disappointed to see Seb and Martin. Martin smiled, but Seb's grin was a little more uncomfortable.

"Hey!" Oliver did his best to sound upbeat. "What are you guys doing here?"

"We're here for the workshop," Martin said.

"Martin thinks you need help setting up." Seb scanned the shop without ever meeting Oliver's gaze.

"We *want* to help set up." Martin ignored Seb's pout and shrugged out of his jacket.

"Not much left to do." Oliver glanced around. The tall chairs faced the bar, and he'd brought six of his own chairs from home for people to sit closer. If a dozen people showed up, he'd call it a success, although he had forgotten to count his brother and Martin in that number.

Seb sighed heavily and sank into one of the tall chairs. It wobbled under him, and he glared at Oliver.

"What is your problem?" Oliver asked.

"Don't mind him." Martin put a hand on his shoulder. "He's having a supply problem, and it's making him grumpy."

"I'm not grumpy!" Seb crossed his arms over his chest. "I'm used to having the next book at my fingertips. Do you know how hard it is to find a pictorial history of mid-century manufacturing on the right grade of paper?"

Seb was an artist who worked with reclaimed books. His carvings had a decent following, but the last six months since the bookstore that used to be Seb's source for new material—and also where Seb had lived in an upstairs apartment—burned down had been difficult. He was coping, and Martin's moderating influence was all to the good, but losing easy access to new books clearly did nothing for Seb's artistic temperament.

"Here." Oliver went to the fridge and pulled out a bottle of *Neural Neutrality*. He passed it to his drama queen brother.

"What is it?"

"Swiss chard, apricot, and carrot. It's supposed to provide mental clarity and a calming effect."

Seb rolled his eyes, but he took the drink.

"I've got a few more ingredients to prep, but you guys are welcome to hang out. It's a bit tight in the back." Oliver turned toward the kitchen.

"That's what he said," Seb muttered.

Oliver's hands shook as he gripped the knife. Seb was an ass.

But that tiger showed its stripes years ago, and Oliver still chose to move here.

Except he hadn't meant to be in Seacroft alone. Cooper should have been here too. But Cooper made his choices, and now Oliver was making his.

As he finished the mangoes and started in on the carrots, a hushed but intense conversation took place in the front of the shop. Oliver couldn't pick out the words, but Martin was clearly trying to make a point, and Seb was definitely opposed to it.

The conversation died, and Seb knocked on the doorframe over Oliver's shoulder. His self-confident smirk wasn't quite as bright as usual.

"Did you need something?" Oliver asked.

"I'm sorry." Seb's jaw was tight.

"For anything in particular? Or should I take that as a blanket statement?"

Seb sighed and glanced over his shoulder. He flinched at the hiss of rushed words, like Martin was giving restrained stage-mom directions from just out of sight.

"I'm sorry about brunch the other day. About giving you a hard time about Cooper. You know I never liked him, but he was obviously important to you for a long time. Whatever happened, it's your business." Another glance over his shoulder and more deep sighs followed. "But if you ever want to talk about it, you know I can take off my jackass hat for a few minutes."

Oliver grinned. "Just a few, though, right? Any more than that and your life force starts to fade?"

"I'm trying to apologize here."

Having Martin hovering in the wings was probably killing Seb. That knowledge would have to do.

"Thanks. I'm okay. It's not something I need to talk about." Oliver had moved on. Never mind his hands had shook as he'd read the STI test results, or the wave of relief that washed over him when it had all come back negative. He hadn't realized he was holding onto fear that Cooper left him with more than hurt feelings, but having the results on paper gave him peace of mind.

Before Oliver and Seb's little brotherly bonding moment could become too serious, the bell over the door sounded again. Oliver skirted around Seb, putting his bright business-owner smile back on.

The newcomer was the guy from the market, the enthusiastic red-haired one. His eyes widened as he took in Oliver, Seb, and Martin.

"Am I late?" He hovered at the door, like he might need to make a run for it.

"Hi!" Oliver said as he came toward him. "Welcome. You're the first to arrive!"

"I am?"

"Don't mind them. Family doesn't count."

"Get out while you still can!" Seb's words, soft and high, were followed by a grunt. Oliver would have to remember to thank Martin for kicking Seb later.

For now, though, his priority was this new customer. Oliver nearly went to throw an arm around him, if only to shield him from Seb's snark, but he managed to stop himself. Instead, he went for a friendly smile and a handshake.

"I'm Oliver. I own Pulpability."

"Avery." The guy smiled too, and his freckles disappeared under a blush that almost matched the color of his hair.

"You were at the market, weren't you?" Oliver led him toward one of the chairs at the front.

"Yeah! I saw your booth, and I knew I needed to find out more about what you do. I'm really into being healthier, you know, and this sounds really cool!"

Oliver glanced over Avery's shoulder to Seb. *See. It's really cool.*

"That's great," he said. "Have a seat. I'm going to give it a few more minutes to see who else arrives, but for showing up early, you get the best seat in the house."

In the end, the turnout was . . . meager? Was that the best word? Underwhelming. Seb, Martin, and Avery were joined by three other women Oliver might have recognized from the market. The extra chairs he'd brought from home sat empty as he passed out handouts and tried to stay positive.

"Hi, everyone. My name is Oliver Stevenson. Thank you so much for coming to Pulpability." His perma-smile stretched his cheeks until they ached.

It started out pretty well. Oliver introduced his products and demonstrated a few easy recipes people could make at home. The small crowd was engaged. Avery, in particular, asked a question almost every time Oliver paused for a breath.

"I'm not a nutritionist," Oliver said, when Avery asked if specific kinds of apples had better nutritional benefits than others. What was with the apple obsession in this town? "But I don't think so. If you want more information, though, the Pulpability plans were all designed by a dietician in Raleigh, and she's available to consult as needed."

"So you don't have a degree in nutrition?" one of the women asked.

"No." The question was his least favorite and seemed to come up all the time. Cooper had been the one taking the nutrition courses, while Oliver focused on the business planning. Except now he was sailing the ship alone and making the best he could on half the knowledge and half the savings. Everything was so much harder than they'd said it would be as they'd gone over their plans and projections one more time.

"Just think," Cooper had said, the night before they planned to hand in their resignations. "Tomorrow, we'll be in control of everything. No more bosses. No more soul crushing hours. Just you and me, doing it together."

Twenty-four hours later, Oliver was on his own.

"So you don't have a background in nutrition?" the woman asked again.

Oliver blinked back to the present. He did his best to cover with a charming smile. "No, I don't. But I do have a law degree, so trust me when I say that I'm not going to do anything that might get me sued."

He expected a laugh at that, but the room was quiet. The pause was almost as long as the moment he'd walked into the boardroom, seen Cooper's face, and known something had gone very wrong.

"Why don't you work with one of the nutritionists in town?"

He'd tried that. Not that Seacroft was overrun with nutritionists and dieticians, but in the fall, he'd reached out to a number of local people to see if they would be interested in partnering with him in launching the business. The response had been either resounding silence or a polite no.

"How many of your ingredients come from local farmers?"

This line of questioning was wandering outside of the scope of things he'd planned to talk about.

"Currently not a lot. We're just coming into the growing season, so up until now, there hasn't been the opportunity to use local produce. But I'm at the farmer's market every weekend, and hopefully some of the farmers there will be interested in working with us."

Us. So many of these speeches had been rehearsed, or at least planned out, when Cooper had been part of the picture too.

"Is it true that a cucumber cures hangovers?"

Oliver's gaze swung around to the speaker. Seb, standing at the back of the room, looked smug. Oliver could have kissed him.

"*That* is an excellent question."

The workshop wrapped up on time. The three women Oliver

didn't know and who hadn't seemed all that impressed with his answers to their questions left after a few polite goodbyes. At least Avery signed up for coaching on the spot. Oliver wasn't convinced the kid understood what he was looking for, since he kept talking about "getting healthier" over and over, but a quick sale after the workshop was good, so they'd figure the rest out later.

"Thanks for inviting us," Martin said, once Avery headed out. "That was very interesting."

"I appreciate the moral support." And the body count. The group of six was small. Four would have been depressing.

"So cucumbers really do cure hangovers?" Seb asked.

"About as much as anything does."

———

When Oliver got home, he couldn't sit still. Too early to go to bed and too late to start anything new. He fidgeted. Nights like these, when he'd been busy all day but was alone in the house at the end of it, were the hardest. He was still used to Cooper's company: to debrief on the day's happenings, to strategize their next steps, or, God, to have sex with, even if neither of them really felt like it, to pass the time. Not exactly glamorous, but when you'd been with the same person for a decade, every roll in the sheets didn't leave you seeing stars.

His eye caught the white sheet of paper sitting on the coffee table. His test results. Negative. Nothing to worry about, no difficult conversations to have with Nick.

Oliver's hand shook as he fumbled out a text message.

Hey, Pretty Girl, you busy?

The reply was surprisingly quick, as if Nick had been expecting him.

I asked you not to call me that.

Oliver hadn't been able to help himself. Seb inherited the

largest shit-disturber gene in their family, but sometimes Oliver liked to play too.

Sorry. What are you doing tonight?

Another quick reply. *I have to work in a couple hours.*

Oh. Oliver hadn't considered that. His no-strings pitch had seemed solid, but he hadn't accounted for literally working opposite schedules.

Another message came through.

I could come over for a bit before, though?

Oliver relaxed.

Get over here and get naked.

The only reply that came after that was a thumbs-up emoji.

Oliver flopped down on the couch. This would be good. He was surprisingly calm, in fact. Nick would come over, with his dark eyes and strong body, and there would be some casual fooling around. A great way to cap off a moderately successful night.

In his hand, the phone pinged. He expected another text from Nick. Instead, the little red circle had popped up, indicating he had a new email. When he swiped into the app, his heart skipped.

From: Cooper Parnell.

The subject line said *Hey*.

Oliver stared at it as his skin heated.

Cooper.

They hadn't talked in over nine months. Not since the day Oliver moved his stuff out of their condo. Their plans, everything they had worked for—the shop, the freedom—all in flames, because Cooper had been too scared to let go. Oliver had been left holding the match with no way to save himself. They'd planned to quit their lives and move on to something new—together—and instead, Oliver was moving on alone.

Cooper stood in the hall—looking not nearly guilty enough by half—and wished him well, as Oliver flipped him off.

"I loved you so much. I did this for you." His chest felt like it was going to burst, with too many feelings warring for precedence.

"I'm sorry, Ollie."

That was the last time they'd spoken to each other.

Oliver deleted the email without reading it. Fuck him. Whatever it said, he didn't want to hear.

He had Nick to look forward to.

8

$\mathcal{N}$ick had the weirdest feeling of déjà vu as he walked up Oliver's front steps. He was almost as nervous as the last time, even though, in the broadest sense at least, this time he knew what was going to happen.

He was still intimidated, too, as he stood at the door. Oliver's shiny black SUV was parked in the driveway. A Porsche. Who needed a Porsche SUV? Was off-roading in Europe more sophisticated than in the US? Behind the gleaming black vehicle, Nick's car was ready for scrap.

The front door swung open, and whatever Nick's concerns were, Oliver was a perfect-looking man. If he was interested in getting naked with Nick, then Nick really would have to be a loser to turn him down.

"Hey!" Oliver's eyes twinkled as he smiled. Where every single one of Nick's muscles were tense, like he might still make a break for the car in a minute, everything about Oliver appeared loose. His arms hung at his sides, and his grin was easy.

"Hi." Even Nick's voice was strangled in his throat. Oliver stepped aside, and Nick crossed into the house.

"How are you doing?" Oliver asked as he closed the door.

"Fine. Quiet day at home. Nothing special. You?" Nick had to fight not to twitch or scratch at his scalp nervously.

"Great. I had a great night. There was a workshop at the store. My brother was an asshole at first, but . . ." Oliver's grin spread. "Sorry. Nothing personal, right?"

"Nothing personal."

"Do you want a drink?" Oliver led him up the hall. "Sparkling water again? Or I've got this new recipe I'm trying out for the store. You could be my guinea pig. It's an immune system booster. It's got hibiscus and . . ." He paused and bit his lip with a grin. Heat smouldered behind Nick's ears and spread down the back of his neck in response. "Is that still personal? You're here and I'm still working."

"It's . . ." Nick glanced around the immaculate house. The more Oliver kept talking, the more being here seemed like a bad idea. Nick wasn't cut out for this. Small talk without disclosing anything personal? He was screwed, and not in the way he'd been promised. "We need a code word."

Oliver's blue eyes danced. "A code word?"

Stupid. This was so stupid, but Nick kept talking. "Yeah. At the fire department, there are informal codes, things we'll—um, things *they'll* say if they're at the scene of an accident, and things are going south, but they don't want to alarm the victim."

"We did that. In court or if we were in a big meeting. We didn't have words so much as gestures. If someone on the team put two pens parallel at the top of a notebook, it meant to redirect the question. If a specific person coughed, time to request a break. You mean like that?"

Maybe not so stupid after all. "Sort of." The ones the fire-fighters used were never so sophisticated. They had official codes, of course, but over the years, they developed their own lingo to keep dispatch up to speed on the situation. Brian liked to work in sports analogies. If he referred to the driver in a pileup as "slugger," then Nick was going to be in for a long night.

Oliver scratched at his beard. "So if one of us starts to slide too far into the personal stuff, the other one uses the code word, and we back off?"

"That's the idea."

"What word do you want to use?"

Nick glanced over Oliver's shoulder as he thought about that. The light in the bedroom at the end of the hall was on, and he couldn't tear his eyes away from it. Nerves twisted in his stomach in a way he hadn't felt since his wedding night. Oliver was still intimidating, almost too perfect to actually be real, and now Nick was supposed to have sex with him like it was no big thing.

He stared at the comforter on Oliver's bed, smooth and carefully spread out. By comparison, Nick hadn't made his own bed regularly in more than a decade, and his sheets were a nondescript gray after too many washings. Oliver's sheets had a shine to them and were striped in navy and a gold-brown the color of—

"Caramel."

"Caramel?" Oliver waggled his eyebrows. "That's the code word?"

"No, it's—" Nick's explanation was cut off as Oliver stepped into his space and kissed him. For once, Nick's nerves were enough that he didn't completely lose his self-control. When Oliver pulled back again, Nick exhaled a shaky breath.

"You okay?" Oliver asked.

"Sorry." Nick tried to put on a brave face. "I'm a bit . . ." Old-fashioned? Shit, he wasn't going to be able to do this after all.

"You've never hooked up with someone before?"

Nick could barely withstand the urge to scuff his feet on the hardwood. "I guess that's what the kids call it these days. It's been a while, anyway."

"Hey." Oliver put a hand on Nick's cheek. "We can go slow. It's casual, not porn. It doesn't have to be anything that makes you uncomfortable."

Nick licked his lips and forced himself to nod. He was rewarded with another kiss. This would be fine. Oliver knew what he was doing. Nick's hands were like lead weights, but he lifted them until he could grasp Oliver's hips. The body underneath his palms was hard and strong.

"Tell me what you're thinking," Oliver said as he kissed softly along Nick's jaw.

"I was fantasizing about you," he said.

"When?"

"At the market. The first morning we met."

The admission made Oliver stop and pull his head back. A crease formed between his eyes as he frowned.

"When I had your car towed?"

Nick laughed. "That killed the mood pretty quickly. But before that. You had your back to me." He ran his hands around Oliver's body, gliding them down the muscles on either side of his spine. "You've got a nice back and—" his hands slid farther, over the rough denim of Oliver's jeans, "—a great ass." When Oliver didn't laugh at the cheesy line, Nick caught Oliver's chin gently between his teeth, then kissed over the same spot. The hair of Oliver's beard tickled at his lips, while Oliver's laughter puffed across Nick's cheek.

"See?" Oliver placed his hands over Nick's and squeezed. "You're going to be fine."

They moved to the living room, which helped ease Nick's anxiety further. Why the bedroom set him off, he wasn't sure, but he could handle making out on the couch.

"What do you like?" Oliver asked as he pulled him down.

"Why don't we go with it, and I'll let you know if you start going in a direction I don't want to follow?"

"What about your leg? Anything I need to know?"

Nick snorted. "As long as I don't have to carry you anywhere, we should be okay."

Oliver grinned his movie-star grin. "I'd like to see you try."

Nick raised an eyebrow. So tempting. They didn't call it the fireman's carry for nothing. With the right incentive, he could give it a shot—and Oliver's ass in the air, over his shoulder, would be an awfully good incentive.

"There is one thing, though."

"What's that?"

Nick ran his hands over Oliver's shoulders and around the back of his neck. "I like you better with your hair down." He found the elastic and pulled. He'd meant for the gesture to be hot, but the band snagged, and Oliver winced.

"Allow me."

"Sorry."

Oliver worked the elastic free, watching Nick the whole time he did it. Anya would say something like he had nice highlights, the blond in his hair streaking from brown to gold. Oliver shook it out, closing his eyes as Nick ran his fingers through it. The texture was coarser than he'd expected, and he pulled the ends forward gently until they framed the sides for Oliver's chin.

"I really like your hair."

"Yeah?" Oliver kissed him.

"Yeah."

"Was it part of your parking lot fantasy?" The kiss got more intense, making heat curl over Nick's neck and down his back.

"It may have been."

"Do you want to show me?"

"Do you always talk so much?"

Oliver nipped at Nick's lower lip. "Would you prefer I talk less?"

Nick leaned back on his heels and growled. Oliver didn't seem particularly bothered. His hair was down, lips parted, and he spread his arms over the back of the leather couch, looking pleased with himself.

"You can talk as much as you want," Nick said as he ran a

hand over his chin. "But I have to leave for work in an hour, and I'd like to get some of these clothes off at some point."

Oliver's mouth quirked up on one side, and he pulled his shirt up and over his head. Nick was speechless. Oliver's skin was lightly freckled, his stomach flat. His chest and abdomen were coated in soft swirls of dark blond hair, trailing down below his belt into his jeans.

Nick ran a finger over one of Oliver's nipples, but stopped when Oliver placed a hand over his.

"Don't leave me hanging here."

Nick smiled and pulled his own shirt off. The air in the room was cool on his skin, but he didn't have long to think about it before Oliver was leaning forward and wrapping his arms around him, pulling him tight.

Their kissing stopped being so polite at that point. Opening his mouth, Nick let Oliver's tongue in, chasing it with his teeth and own tongue. Nick buried his fingers in Oliver's hair, loving the way it dragged over his skin. He gripped it, pulling gently, learning the things that made Oliver hiss and what made his hands tighten on Nick's body.

Oliver groaned when Nick ran his tongue down Oliver's throat, then kissed at the point where his neck and shoulder met.

"You can be rougher than that," Oliver said. "I don't mind."

"You said you don't like pain."

Oliver found the same spot on Nick's neck and bit down, hard enough to make Nick throw his head back and moan. All his nerves sparked at once, his whole body reacting to the sharp sting. One of Oliver's broad hands reached around the back of Nick's skull and pulled him upright again so they were eye to eye.

"I meant you don't get to spank me. I said I like toys, but you don't get to use clamps or tie my balls up."

Nick snorted. "I'm not a fancy guy. I don't need all that." He rolled one of Oliver's nipples between his thumb and forefinger, then pulled until Oliver inhaled.

"I like that," he said against Nick's lips. "Show me what you can do."

This time, Nick didn't hold back. His kiss was more like a lunge, pressing Oliver all the way into the couch. He gripped and he nipped, his hands roaming over Oliver's beautiful long body while Oliver explored too, making Nick shudder. It had been such a long time since anyone had touched him like this.

When Oliver cupped him through his jeans, Nick's whole body spasmed. Shit, he was worse than a horny teenager if groping was all it took to get him this hard. He tunneled his fingers deeper into Oliver's hair, close to the scalp, and pulled. He was rewarded with Oliver's gasp, while Nick tried to cover the entire length of his throat with kisses.

Eventually, the couch became confining. Oliver went to sit up, accompanied by a soft ripping sound where his skin stuck to the leather. He grunted, then buried his face in Nick's neck to cover his laugh. "I think we're going to have to move."

"Okay." Nick knelt on the floor. Palming himself in his jeans, he stared at the long outline of Oliver's erection, pressed against the front of his pants. He'd felt it, pressed against his inner thigh, but the sight made his heart race. Oliver was as turned-on as he was. Maybe he even wanted Nick as much as Nick wanted him. Nick's dick ached, and he flipped the button open at the top of his fly, trying to hurry this along.

Oliver watched him for a minute, smile turning crooked.

"As much as I don't need another leather sofa skin peel, you know we're risking some serious rug burn if we get down on the floor, right?"

"Rug burn's no big deal. I know people in emergency services if it comes to that."

Oliver practically tackled him.

The floor was better. More space to move. They wound up

with Oliver on his back and Nick pressing his whole body down on him, their legs twining together.

"Take my pants off." Oliver rolled his hips. Nick was only too happy to oblige. He undid the fly and pulled the zipper down slowly, watching Oliver's face the whole way. His eyes were half shut, and his neck arched when Nick gripped him through his underwear.

"Never mind the pants," Oliver said. "Just do that."

"You really are chatty in bed, you know that, right?"

"Who's in bed?"

Nick pumped him a few more times, loving the way Oliver shifted restlessly, before he sat up and worked Oliver's jeans off. He squirmed and removed his own pants too.

Oliver rolled up onto one elbow to meet Nick as he came back down. His tongue pressed into Nick's mouth while his hand slid inside his boxer briefs. Nick closed his eyes as the wave of pleasure crashed down on him.

"Yes." Not like he didn't jerk off from time to time, but being touched by someone else would always be better.

"Yeah?" Oliver sucked on Nick's lip as he worked him. Nick rolled, taking Oliver with him so Oliver was half on top and Nick lay with his hands behind his head. He'd get back to touching Oliver in a minute, but right now, he wanted to feel.

Oliver kissed all over his body while his hand worked on Nick's cock, making him shudder. How had he gone so long without being touched? Getting here with Oliver suddenly felt so easy.

Oliver pulled him free of his underwear and tapped at his thigh to get Nick to lift his hips. When he was fully naked, Oliver sat back on his knees, still in his own boxer briefs. His hand ran up and down the front of them as he bit his lip.

"You're even better than I imagined," he said as he gazed down at Nick's body.

Nick rolled his head to avert his eyes and hide a blush. "I'm nothing special." But he stroked his cock lazily and let Oliver look his fill.

Oliver spread himself on top of Nick. The fabric of Oliver's boxer briefs on Nick's dick made him groan and rock his hips. Oliver did the same, and they picked up an easy rhythm as they kissed on the floor, grinding in slow circles.

"You are gorgeous," Oliver said in his ear. "Exactly what I hoped for when I kissed you the first time."

Nick was aching and leaking in minutes, thanks to the heat of their bodies and the friction of the fabric rolling over his cock like silk. He tried to shift so he could touch himself, but Oliver's longer body held him in place. If Nick was going to get off like this, he'd need to thrust harder, and then he really would go to work with rug burn.

"What are you doing?" Oliver asked.

"I need more."

"More?" Oliver arched, lifting off Nick long enough to pull his underwear down toward his knees. He kissed Nick, tongue swirling over his lips and teeth. The hard, naked heat of him lined up against Nick made him whimper. Better. They could hump against each other like teenagers, and it would still probably be the best orgasm Nick had in years.

Oliver reached over them, and then something hard and heavy tumbled onto Nick's head, bouncing off his nose. Bright pain burst through his arousal, and tears instinctively welled in his eyes.

"Shit, I'm sorry!" Oliver scrambled off.

"What was that?" Nick rubbed at his face.

"Lube."

"Lube?" Where the hell had that come from?

He must have said that second part out loud, because Oliver chuckled as he leaned down to kiss Nick where the bottle had landed. It would have been sweet, except Oliver's entire body shook with laughter as he did it.

"It was on the coffee table. I was trying to be prepared."

"What are you, a Boy Scout?"

"Lawyer."

"Right." He groaned and rolled his head until he could see the bottle of lube that lay on its side on the carpet. Oliver pumped it a few times into his hand. Then he slid his slicked palm between them to grasp their erections together.

Nick's eyes rolled back in his head at the feeling. The lube was cool to start but warmed up quickly as Oliver worked them. Nick had to bite his tongue to hold back the string of curses as his balls ached, and his toes curled into the rug.

"Better?" Oliver said.

"Mm-hmm." Nick's lips were clamped tight.

"How's your nose?"

"Shut up and come here." Nick wrapped his arms tight around Oliver, crushing them together. He rolled, until he was on top again. Oliver had to pull his hand free to keep from crashing into the coffee table, but that was fine. Nick knew what he needed now. He grabbed the bottle and lubed up his palm before settling onto his knees and taking both of them in his hand. Oliver's cock was longer and cut. The head was flushed purple and leaked against Nick's wider uncut one. He shuddered when Oliver growled underneath him.

"Ready?" Nick said.

Oliver's face was flushed, and his breathing heavy, but his eyes went wide in mock innocence.

"For what?"

Nick thrust again, then stroked them together a few times, letting his hand twist as he came to the end, then slid back down. The innocence vanished from Oliver's face, and he swallowed hard.

Nick placed a hand on Oliver's chest as he started to move, his other hand twisting while his hips rocked. The image was pornographic, almost dream-like, but still better than all of that, because the sound of their heavy breathing and the sight of Oliver's hair spread out around his head were accompanied by the sensation of them gliding together and the sizzling heat in Nick's balls.

Oliver's palm slapped over his chest, fingers pressing into his pec. His tongue darted out to swipe at his lip before he started to pant. In Nick's hand, Oliver's cock pulsed and lengthened farther. Nick was going to come apart, but the fact that Oliver was equally into it fired Nick's blood.

"I want to come like this," Oliver said between gasps. Nick laughed as he leaned forward to kiss him, but the change in their positions made it hard to keep jerking them together, so he settled for a quick peck before he sat up again. His vision narrowed until all he could see was the long blond man underneath him, writhing as the pleasure grew between them.

Nick's orgasm was building, tingling in his lower back, when Oliver shouted and bucked. He groaned, long and low, as come slicked over Nick's hand and out over Oliver's chest. The sight of it, white lines on his skin and hair, was enough to make Nick curl in on himself as his body locked down and pumped hard in his fist. He clamped his teeth shut and grunted through it as his semen landed on Oliver, mixing with what was already there. The moment was messy and perfect, and Nick didn't know why he'd been so nervous before.

He sagged as they both softened in his palm. Beneath him, Oliver was getting his breathing back under control, and he smiled lazily as he lifted his head long enough to glance at Nick.

"Not bad," Oliver smoothed his hair so it lay flat against the carpet.

Nick laughed, still out of breath, and rubbed at the bridge of his nose. "Got a bit awkward in the middle there."

"We don't have to talk about that."

Fair point. Nick rolled off and heaved himself onto the couch, still basking in the warm post-sex haze.

"Watch it." Oliver sat up on his elbows, still beautifully naked and with come on his chest. "Your ass and your bits will stick to that couch if you're not careful."

Nick raised an eyebrow. "My bits?"

"I don't want to mention your balls and my couch in the same sentence."

Nick really couldn't help his laughter this time. "You should get more acquainted with my balls. You might like them."

"Next time." Oliver stood, and his eyes widened. "That's quite the scar."

Nick ran a hand down the scar on his thigh where they'd cut him open to screw his leg back together.

"It's not so bad." He smiled, feeling warm and sleepy. The orgasm was making him dopey, and words were hard to find.

Oliver seemed to take the hint that they didn't need to talk about it more. Instead, he held out his hand. "I'm going to clean up a bit. Want a shower before you go?"

Reality snapped back down on Nick like a board cracking.

Go. He had to go. Work, life, and Anya and Hayden were all waiting for him outside Oliver's front door. For a moment, he'd forgotten, and now guilt tried to swamp him for it.

He shifted. The backs of his thighs, still sweaty from his exertions, stuck to the couch, like Oliver had warned. He tried not to let Oliver see the disappointment on his face as he stood. Nick didn't want him to get the wrong idea. Even though he shouldn't have gotten distracted enough to forget about the rest of his obligations, he already knew he wanted to do this again with Oliver, and soon.

"Thanks." He picked up his discarded clothes off the floor. "Just give me a towel and I'll be out of here in ten minutes."

9

Oliver woke up the next day with an angry red line on his spine from his carpet and a hickey on his chest. His grin was stupid and delicious as he stretched under the covers. Nick had been exactly what Oliver needed, and he already couldn't wait to see him again.

First, though, he had to get to work. The shop was quiet, as usual, and he spent most of the morning with his laptop set up on the front counter, writing a blog post for his website and searching for new networking opportunities in the area. He'd reached out to a lot of the local businesses, and also some in neighboring towns and cities, to see if he could talk to their staff about wellness. His former office had done that occasionally, brought in someone to talk about mental health, ergonomics, or general well-being. Lawyers tended to fall into two categories: chain-smoking workaholics and marathon runners. Whether these guest speakers had any impact on their target audience had always been a bit hazy, since he'd generally skipped them in favor of working another eighteen-hour day, but surely at least a few businesses in Seacroft wanted to wave the work-life balance flag at their staff from time to time.

Except midmorning rolled into lunchtime, and then past it,

and not a single customer came into the shop. After his work-shop the night before, he'd hoped for word of mouth or a return customer or two. Only around midafternoon, when he was in the back, still fine-tuning his hibiscus immunity booster, did the front door open and a tornado with red hair burst through it.

"No, no, that's okay. I know." Avery had a cellphone pressed to his ear. "Yeah, I'll get the changes to you by tomorrow. No problem."

Oliver waited patiently for clarification on why his newest client had decided the best place to make his phone call was inside the shop.

"Good afternoon," Oliver said, once Avery was off the phone. His eyes went wide, and his mouth gaped open, like he hadn't expected anyone else to be there.

"Hey. Hi! I mean, hi! Sorry." He waggled the phone and then nearly dropped it. "Client. I didn't mean—he was very insistent that we had to talk right away."

"No problem. What kind of client was it?"

"It's Mr. Graves who owns the equipment rental company."

"And what kind of work do you do for him?"

"I'm an accountant."

That was not the answer Oliver had been expecting. Every-thing about Avery was young millennial-hip. If he'd had to guess, Oliver might have said graphic designer, copywriter, maybe even a YouTube star.

"An accountant?"

"Yeah." Avery glanced away as he stuffed his phone back in his pocket. "My uncle has a firm in town. We do a lot of personal taxes and stuff like that, and he has me helping a couple of the local businesses too. Hey!" His eyes widened again. "Do you need help with your bookkeeping? I could get my uncle to give you a good price if you did!"

Oliver laughed. "I'm good."

Avery's smile fell. "Oh. Sure. No problem." He looked so

defeated, but laughing at him would be poor salesmanship on Oliver's part.

"So what can I do for you today?"

"Oh!" The smile returned brighter than before. "Yeah! Juice. I need more juice."

Oliver barely resisted an ill-advised joke about not being his dealer.

"More? Sure!" He went to the fridge. "What kind?"

"The same as last night! They were awesome!"

Oliver paused with a bottle of his parsley, carrot, and date blend in his hand. "You drank them all?" He'd sold Avery three different kinds.

"Yeah!" The younger man yawned. "I had a late night. Usually, I'd do energy drinks to stay up, but I was out, so I thought I'd try your juice instead. They were delicious and kept me from getting hungry!"

"It's . . ." He needed a delicate way to say this. "It's also a lot of fiber to consume in a short amount of time if your body isn't used to it."

"Fiber?" Avery frowned as a blush started at the base of his throat and worked its way up to his hairline. "But it's juice."

"Well yes, but it's not like the juice you buy at the grocery store—"

"Oh I know. That stuff is full of sugar. But yours is healthy, right? Do you know Damian Marshall?"

Oliver frowned at the sudden swerve in Avery's verbal onslaught. "The movie star?"

"Yeah!"

"Yes, I do."

Avery's eyes bugged out one more time. "You do? Like really? That's so amazing! What's he like? He's so hot in the movies. I mean—"

"No." Oliver waved him off. "No, I mean I know who he is. I've never met him."

"Oh." Avery slumped. Damian Marshall was the biggest action star on the planet. How the hell was Oliver supposed to actually know him?

"What does he have to do with all-nighters and energy drinks?"

Avery's smile was back in an instant. "I follow him online. He's totally into juicing right now. He says it's the best way to help him get into shape when he starts shooting!"

Oliver sighed. Avery was clearly lacking some research.

"He also definitely has an army of trainers and nutritionists monitoring everything he does. For everyday people like you and me, you can't make wholesale instantaneous changes like that. Your body needs time to adapt to what you're putting into it."

Avery's face clouded over as he clutched at his throat. "What's going to happen to me?"

This poor kid.

"Your first coaching session isn't supposed to be until Monday, but maybe we can do a quick one right now?"

Since opening for business, Oliver only had a few coaching clients. Most had been fairly well-informed when they walked through the door. They'd been looking for ways to enhance their existing lifestyles, so Oliver helped them customize the meal plans, and they checked in from time to time with questions or to pick up juice for busy weeks. But within a few minutes, it became clear that Avery was starting from nowhere.

"I mostly drink energy drinks. I know they're not good for you, but they work. But I thought maybe there was some kind of juice you could make that would work too."

The disappointment on his face when Oliver explained that wasn't really how it worked was almost comical, but Oliver was sympathetic. Energy drinks had gotten him through his last year of law school, and that year in the public defender's office before Cooper had found him a spot with the corporate firm he'd joined after they'd graduated. How Oliver's diet of coffee, cigarettes, and energy drinks hadn't resulted in any serious health effects could only be described as a miracle, and Cooper had finally convinced him to stop.

Cooper, who had dragged him out of his apartment where he'd been working for nearly seventy straight hours. He'd taken Oliver down the block to a diner and forced some food in him.

"You're going to kill yourself if you keep going like this."

Oliver had been too busy trying not to bite his own fingers off while he inhaled his burger to really acknowledge what Cooper was trying to say. He hadn't eaten anything in days.

"Oliver?" Avery asked.

Oliver blinked back to the present. "Sorry, what?"

"I asked how you started this business?"

"What if we gave this up? God knows we've made enough money. What if we did something else?"

"My boyfriend and I came up with the idea a few years ago."

"Your boyfriend?" Avery's eyes widened, and Oliver bit his lip. His newest customer's guilelessness had made Oliver careless.

"We're not together anymore," he said quickly.

"Oh." Avery's eyes turned sympathetic. "I'm sorry. That's too bad."

"Thanks." Oliver said it more because you were supposed to. In the end, Cooper had shown exactly who he was, and the only real shame was how long Oliver took to realize it.

Avery hopped out of his chair like he'd been bitten and then pulled his phone out of his pocket. "It's my uncle. I have to get back to work. I was supposed to go buy us some coffees and come right back." He smiled sheepishly.

"I'm sorry to keep you."

"No!" Avery waved his hands. "You were a big help! I would have bought a bunch more from you today, and based on what you've said, I would've regretted it later."

Oliver couldn't comment on Avery's specific digestive system, but he shuddered to think about it. "Happy to help, then! I'll see you on Monday!"

"You bet!" Avery beamed at him and rushed out of the store. He nearly knocked over the postwoman who came through the front door.

Mail today included a few bills, a lot of junk, and one envelope with a return address from the Seacroft Farmer's Market Board of Directors. Oliver opened it.

Mr. Stevenson,

On behalf of the board of directors, it has come to our attention that your business, Pulpability, *does not meet the requirements under the by-laws of our organization. We work very hard to protect the integrity of the Seacroft Historic Farmer's Market brand, and trust that you can understand the need to ensure it is represented by local producers—*

Oliver paused, not fully understanding what he was reading. He started at the top again.

Mr. Stevenson,

On behalf of—

The letter was horrifically written. If anyone in his office—his old office—had written something like that, they'd have been fired on the spot. While there seemed to be a problem with his position at the market, what the by-law in question was and the reasons his business might violate it was unclear. The writer finished with an obtusely worded invitation to attend the next board meeting, which happened to be the following week.

Well, that was convenient. They sent him a vague letter, invited him to a meeting with almost no time to prepare, and gave him no idea what he should be preparing for anyway. A phone number was listed at the top of the page. He dialed it, but the call went to voicemail.

By the time he got home again, Oliver was restless and frustrated. He made dinner—curried okra and brown rice that turned out to be slimier than he'd expected—and tried to keep his mind off work and the letter, but in no time he was in his office, going through his files on the market. He found the by-laws and read through them carefully. Nothing raised any red flags.

He went to the market home page online next, but it only showed pictures of happy shoppers on sunny days, and farmers proudly displaying truckloads of corn and their bushels of apples.

Weirdly, as he continued to wander the vastness of the internet, he found himself on Damian Marshall's social media feed. Just like Avery had said, Damian was ripped and Hollywood perfect, smiling his movie-star smile into the camera with something green in a glass at the bottom of the frame.

Best #allnatural energy boost there is. #juice #juicing #cold-pressed #bestlife #greengod

Oliver rolled his eyes. Sure, Damian looked all cool and perfect with his nutritionally balanced and carefully calibrated juice blend. But were there any warnings for the Averys of the world about the inevitable intestinal distress when you drank three of those in eight hours?

The juice was the same color as Damian's eyes.

Oliver tended to notice a guy's body and his smile before he noticed his eyes, but he might be developing a thing for Nick's eyes, black-brown and bottomless. And his hands. Strong and rough. Who needed a celebrity when Oliver had Nick's hands on his body and his cock?

Next time, though, they'd find their way to Oliver's bed. The rug had been fine, but the raw spot above the base of his spine had only gotten redder and angrier over the course of the day. He wasn't a kid anymore. He had dignity to maintain.

Somewhere along his internet tour, he must have nodded off, because he woke up in a small puddle of drool on his desk. So much for dignity. Also, he was at half-mast in his pants, because he'd been dreaming of a man with dark eyes and a hard body who pushed him down and did nasty things to him.

His computer screen was dark. His shoulders ached, and his house was too quiet.

He stumbled down the hall, brushed his teeth, and stripped out of his clothes. He fell into bed, still agitated and restless, and waited for sleep to find him so he could go back to his dream.

———

Quiet nights at the station were infrequent but predictable. Nick would arrive and get installed at his terminal. Even a small town like Seacroft had a few calls every night, but on the quiet nights, most were usually false alarms, or a minor first responder call if the fire department was in a position to reach the incident before the paramedics could. These nights were good; they gave Nick a chance to catch up on his reporting and clear his head from the noise and stress at home.

But as it got later and later, and then quieter and quieter, his mind wandered to Oliver. It had been a few days, and while they hadn't said anything about how frequently their little get-togethers might be, or who could contact who, Nick was hesitant to take the lead. For one, he couldn't very well invite Oliver over to his house while Anya and Hayden were there. And even if they weren't, the house was small and cluttered. They'd have to clear out the coffee table and a couple of the chairs from the living room before anyone could roll around on the carpet.

Really, though, Nick mused as he microwaved his mid-shift meal, who needed space? All they needed was a bed and clean sheets, and Nick had those. Still, he was hardly ever home and awake when either Anya or Hayden weren't around, except sometimes midafternoon before Hayden got home from school. But then Oliver would be at work, so Nick still had no solution.

A few hours on Oliver's carpet before Nick's shifts might be the best they could hope for.

As he ate his reheated meatloaf, his phone buzzed in his pocket with a text from Oliver.

Are you awake?

Nick thumbed back a reply.

I better be. I've got five more hours in my shift. Why are you awake?

The reply was quick.

Can't sleep. Insomnia.

Nick grimaced. He'd had his fair share of sleepless days and nights over the last six months.

I was thinking about you.

He forced himself to chew slowly while he waited for a reply.

Oh yeah? Anything specific?

Nick glanced around the empty break room before he typed his answer.

You. Under me.

Like the other day?

Heat started to spread over Nick's chest.

Yeah.

Should we do that again?

His hands were shaking so badly, he had to type the message twice.

I want to, yes. When?

He nearly dropped the phone when it rang.

"Hello?"

"Hey." Oliver's voice held a deep something. Every time Nick heard it, all of him sat up and paid attention.

"Hi."

"Is it okay to talk?"

"For now. I have to go back to work soon. One second." He fumbled in one of the pockets of the heavy cargo pants that were part of his uniform until he found a small pair of headphones.

He plugged them into the phone and put the buds in his ears, the microphone dangling below his chin.

"Okay," he said. "We can talk."

"Hi again." Oliver's voice was soft and scratchy. It made the heat in Nick's chest spread farther, out along his arms and down his stomach.

"Hi."

"When would you like to get together again? Sunday? My place?"

"Yeah." Nick exhaled, glad the option of going to his house hadn't even come up.

"I had fun the other day," Oliver said.

"Me too."

"Have anything in particular you want to do for next time?"

Nick glanced around the empty kitchen again. He'd eaten here five nights a week since he'd come back to work. Most of the guys would be asleep. Tonight, though, would inevitably be the one someone snuck in when he didn't hear them, distracted by the low sounds of Oliver's voice in his ears.

"You want to talk about this now?" Nick asked. "We're not exactly trying to decide between bowling or going to a movie."

Oliver's laugh was evil, and Nick adjusted himself in his pants at the sound.

"Only if you want to. I'm already in bed."

Nick closed his eyes and focused on breathing. Working at SFD wasn't like one of those TV shows where firefighters ducked into hidden rooms for a quick fuck between saving lives. This was his job. His place of work. If anyone found out what he was doing . . .

Against all rationalizations and better judgment, Nick moved to the other side of the table, so he could face the door. If anyone came in, they'd see his embarrassed face, but he'd at least be able to shut up before he got himself into too much trouble.

"I like your hair." *Very smooth.* Nick bit his lip before he said something even stupider.

Oliver laughed softly. "You may have mentioned that."

"I want to touch it." His mouth was dry, but he forced himself to keep talking. "Bury my hands in it. Hold on to it while you—"

On the phone, Oliver moaned. The sound had Nick's pants tightening, and he squirmed in his chair. This was the worst idea. But now that he was thinking about it, he couldn't stop. He needed this.

"Go on." Oliver said, his voice soft and raspy.

Nick kept his eyes glued on the break room door. "I want to hold it, grab onto it with my fists. I want you to suck me off while I hold onto your hair."

"Yeah." He breathed a heavy sigh, and then the sound on the phone changed, growing more staticky.

"Are you still there?" Nick asked.

"Still here." Oliver's voice sounded farther away. "I put the phone on speaker, so I have my hands free."

Nick had to rest his head on the table while he palmed his swelling cock through his pants. This was hot, and he was into it, but coming in his shorts with hours to go before he could get out of his uniform wouldn't be worth it.

"Did I scare you away?" Oliver teased.

"Still here," Nick croaked.

"You want me to suck you off?"

Oh God. Nick sat up again and forced steady breaths through his nostrils.

"Yes. I want to feel your mouth on me."

"Would you be wearing your uniform?"

Nick glanced down at his navy shirt. "How did you know I wear a uniform?"

"You work for the fire department, don't you? I kind of assumed you would have one. Would you wear it while I blew you?"

"I thought you weren't into role-playing." He undid the top button of his shirt so he could breathe.

"Who's role-playing? You're a man in uniform; I'm a man who likes a man in uniform."

"So you want me to wear it?" It could happen. Nick generally preferred to keep his uniform at work, but many of his coworkers took them home.

"I really do. I want you to let me take it off of you."

Breathe in, one, two, three. Breathe out, one, two, three, four.

"Tell me. Tell me what you'd do."

Oliver did. In excruciating detail. He talked about undoing Nick's fly, the smell and the taste as Oliver pulled Nick's cock out. He told Nick about the feeling of his hands in Oliver's hair, holding him down. His words were accompanied by the sound of his body shifting on his sheets. The little hitches in his voice, the strangled whimpers, the moments where Oliver, too, had to pause and breathe, nearly undid Nick. His skin burned, and his dick was so hard in his pants, he didn't know how the seams didn't split.

"Keep talking," he gritted out.

"I can't . . ." Oliver was panting now. He was so close to the edge, and Nick could barely stand it. The quiet closeness of it, Oliver's voice, his heavy moans playing only in Nick's ears through the headset, Nick barely managed to keep himself together. His nails dug into the top of the table, and the tips of his fingers had gone white.

"Ni—" His name on Oliver's lips was cut off when the phone was filled by a shout, followed by his shuddering groan. Nick pressed his lips together and shut his eyes so he could picture it, like it had been the other day. Oliver, laid out on the floor, rocking through his orgasm. Nick gripped himself, forcing his own release back. He'd wanted this, and four hours of blue balls was what he was going to have to pay for it.

"Still there?" Oliver asked between gasps.

"Still here."

"That was—"

"Yeah." The moment could barely be more intimate if they had been face to face.

"Until Sunday?"

Nick had to laugh at that. "If I survive."

"You better. You have to deliver on that fantasy."

The odds of Nick lasting until Sunday were barely fifty-fifty.

"You think you'll sleep now?"

"Undoubtedly. Thanks for that."

They said their good nights, and afterward Nick took a few more minutes alone to collect himself. His dick ached with the need to come, but he'd have to wait.

By the end of his shift, though, Nick was about ready to crawl out of his skin. When Sharon and Dave showed up to start the morning shift, he bolted for the staff room to change out of his uniform.

He was home just as Anya and Hayden were getting ready for their day.

"Hey!" Anya smiled at him brightly. His brain was so consumed by lust, he could barely look at her. He needed them out of his house. He needed to jerk off in the shower, or in bed like Oliver had, and shout his release until his throat and his balls were dry.

"I'm going for a ride."

"A ride?" Anya frowned.

"I'll be back in a bit."

"Nick?" Anya called to his back as he went down the hall to change.

When he'd been younger, Nick had been a runner, but he'd had to give it up after his accident. His leg couldn't take the impact, which should have been his first hint he wasn't going to make it back to firefighting. The physiotherapist had suggesting cycling as an alternative, and Nick still did it sometimes, but he never felt the same high he had when running.

But the alternative today was leaving his sexual frustration to build up at home, so he put on his sweats and got the old bike out of the garage. He could feel Anya's eyes on the back of his neck as he pedaled down the driveway, but he kept going.

Seacroft was quiet. It had rained overnight and was still drizzling. A path system led from one side of town to the other, and Nick followed the trail that wound beside a creek and eventually put him on the boardwalk alongside the beach. Despite the drizzle, the morning was warm and humid, and he picked up a sweat as he rode, which helped to clear some of the Oliver fog from his brain.

He was nearly ready to turn and head for home when he spotted a jogger running along the boardwalk at the top of the beach. Nick coasted to a halt and realized that this guy wasn't a jogger. He was a runner, and he was moving. For Nick, running had been about the cardio and staying in shape for his job. This guy was running like he had somewhere to go or a time to beat. His long legs turned a fast rhythm. His form was good, one foot planting solidly in front of the other. He was dressed for it too, in long tights and one of those nylon jackets with the reflective tape on it.

The hood of his jacket fell back, revealing the blond hair underneath, pulled back to keep it out of the runner's face. Nick groaned. All of his clarity drained away with each thump of Oliver's steady feet.

Oliver must not have seen him, because he turned, leaving the boardwalk and heading out onto the street, long strides eating up the pavement as he went. He was strength and ease, and Nick couldn't take his eyes off him.

He kicked off his bike and followed.

10

The podcast in his ears spoke about moving meditation, except Oliver was feeling anything but mindful. The woman's pleasant voice told him to focus on his breathing, but as he did, the echoes of Nick's ragged breath on the phone the night before dragged him away from the moment again. Not that he was complaining, but he needed to get it together before he went to the shop.

A bike came up alongside him, and he flinched because he hadn't heard it coming. He ran this route most days, and cyclists were rare. He expected it to keep going, but once he was shoulder to shoulder with the rider, the bike kept pace, lurking like a car in his blind spot. Oliver was setting a good speed—he needed it to burn off the sluggishness that resulted in only getting to sleep at one-thirty after coming his brains out in his fist—but a cyclist should have had no trouble passing him.

But this asshole didn't. While the woman in Oliver's ears told him to let go of external distractions and focus on his body, the jerk on the bike stayed at the edge of his vision. No way in hell he could let go of distractions while the bike's front wheel spun fine mist toward his ankles from four feet away. Oliver growled his frustration as he yanked the buds from his ears, ready to hurl a line of expletives. As he turned, he nearly tripped when he saw the expression on Nick's face. His eyes were black, his lips set in a line that said he would devour Oliver the moment they stopped.

Oliver's heart pounded in his chest. "Good morning."

Nick glowered as he kept pedaling.

The night before had been an experience. Oliver hadn't played around like that in a long time. His hand on his cock as he'd talked Nick through the fantasy, while Nick's quiet breathing had echoed through the phone—Oliver hadn't planned for any of it, not really. He'd been unable to sleep and had more or less forgotten that Nick would be at work when he'd sent his text. What had followed after, though . . .

They made the turn back toward Oliver's house, and the whole time he was aware of Nick beside him. The morning was still cool and damp, but the space between them practically glowed with warmth. Oliver had to slow his pace, not from fatigue, but because his body couldn't decide if it wanted to run or be a turned-on horny mess.

On the sidewalk down the last block, Oliver could barely function. Nick had backed off enough that Oliver couldn't see him out of the corner of his eye, but that only made everything worse. The knowledge that he was there left Oliver feeling like he was being pursued, and who knew that was one of his kinks? The shiver of Nick's presence down Oliver's spine kept him centered long enough to make it up the driveway, hands already fumbling for the key in his jacket pocket, while the bike clattered against the side of the house.

They barely made it inside and behind closed doors before Oliver was surrounded, shoved with his front up against the wall in the hallway while Nick pressed his body close. Oliver was warm from the run, but Nick was like a furnace.

"I have to go to work soon," Oliver gasped. "I think I've

figured out the immunity booster formula and there's this movie star who—"

"Caramel," Nick growled, and all of Oliver's good intentions for the day melted. Instead, he whimpered and let himself be plastered to the wall.

"I need you." Nick's voice was rough, and Oliver moaned at the feel of Nick's lips on the side of his neck. The nylon jacket swished between them, but as Oliver tried to create some space between himself and the wall to get it off, Nick pressed in harder, pushing his erection against the crease of Oliver's ass. Nick's breath was hot on his skin as he mouthed at what he could reach, and the only thing Oliver could do was press his forehead against the relatively cool drywall, eyes shut tight.

Nick's hands slid low, forcing Oliver's hips back and grinding them tighter together. Oliver saw white as Nick found his erection.

"Do you want this?" Nick asked. Oliver nodded and gasped while Nick stoked the lust between them, bringing it higher, brighter than the night before when Oliver was alone and could only imagine it.

Oliver turned, grasping Nick's face in his hands, pulling their mouths together, tongues fighting for control. How could Nick ask if he wanted this? How could anyone not want this?

"Tell me." Nick grabbed the base of Oliver's hair where he'd pulled it back, tugging until Oliver had no choice but to wrench his mouth away from Nick's skin.

"I want this. You."

Nick's black eyes gleamed. "It wasn't very nice of you to tease me at work like that."

Oliver grinned as his pulse accelerated. His hands caressed over Nick's hard body, then slipped under the elastic of his sweats, grasping at the hard muscle of his ass. He pulled them together, making Nick moan while he nipped at Oliver's skin.

"It's okay, big guy," Oliver said. Never mind he was taller; in this situation, everything about Nick was dominant. "You show me what you want to do."

"Shower." Nick pulled the zipper loose on Oliver's coat, then shoved it and his T-shirt up over his head. His mouth was on Oliver's skin before Oliver could see again, biting and licking over his nipples and his chest.

Shower was good. Oliver liked the sound of that. They stumbled up the hall, stripping out of their clothes as they went. Nick crowded into Oliver's space the whole time, kissing and stroking any body part he could get his hands on. Oliver nearly slipped and brained himself on the tile as he tried to get the water on in the shower, then yelped as the first cold spray hit his oversensitive skin. Nick was wrapped around him in a second, holding him under the water as it warmed. He pulled the elastic out of Oliver's hair, letting it fall down toward his shoulders, then pushed it aside as Nick kissed the back of his neck.

Oliver planted his hands on the wall as he ground back against Nick. Steam filled the space around them, closing them in.

"What do you want?" Oliver asked. "Do you want me to suck you off? That's what you said, right?"

Nick's hands were on his hips, pressing them tightly together. He thrust, his hard cock pushing up and down between Oliver's cheeks.

"In a minute." He rubbed a bar of soap in his hands, lathering it into white bubbles, before he working over Oliver's shoulders. The sensation was amazing, wet and slippery. He and Cooper had done things like this once, but it had been years, lost in the routine of work and unquestioning commitment.

Except, it turned out only Oliver had been so committed.

Nick's hands washing over his hips, moving down his thighs, kneading at the muscles there with his knuckles, snapped Oliver back from his thoughts. Oliver groaned and might have slipped if it weren't for Nick's other hand pressed against Oliver's stomach, holding him close.

"I want to touch you," Oliver said. He was hard, his cock heavy between his legs, and it was all Nick, his mouth, his hands, his hot breath on Oliver's wet skin, giving him pleasure. "Please, I need to touch you."

Nick turned him, and now Oliver pushed back. The shower was big. He hadn't thought about sex and whether the house would fit a partner when he'd rented it, but now Nick was here, he was glad it did. Nick's back hit the tiled wall, and he hissed, but Oliver was on him a second later, hot and needy. He hadn't been able to the night before, while they'd been on the phone. He needed to touch, needed to complete what they'd started last night.

His teeth grazed over one of Nick's nipples. Nick grunted, and his big hands came down on Oliver's shoulders. They squeezed, massaging again, the sensation working up his neck to the back of his skull. And then the grip changed, pushing down. Oliver knew what Nick wanted. He'd promised to give it to him.

He slipped to his knees on the hard tile. They were out of the spray from the shower, but the air around them was humid and warm. Oliver kissed the line from Nick's navel downward, then raised his head and one hand up.

"Soap?"

Nick's dark eyes bored down at him as he passed him the bar. Oliver lathered his hands and ran them over Nick's flat stomach. The hair on his belly was soft and dark, nearly black, growing thicker at his groin. Oliver watched the suds spill through the dark curls and then down over his thighs, muscled and just as hairy. Cooper had never managed to grow more than the faintest smattering of hair, mostly between his nipples and around his cock. By contrast, Nick was covered in it, and the difference delighted Oliver.

Except why was he thinking about Cooper?

He explored more, cupping Nick's sack, and was rewarded with a deep groan.

"You said I might like your balls." Oliver rolled them in his palm, making Nick shudder above him.

"Quit playing and suck me."

Oliver's confidence gave way to something hot and needy. He was still getting to know Nick, in every sense, but he liked this directness. They weren't here for games. Nick wanted something from him, and Oliver was only too happy to give it to him.

He swiped his tongue over the tip of Nick's cock, tasting salt. Nick groaned again while Oliver licked at the head, his hand moving up and down his shaft. One of Nick's big hands came down to rest on the back of Oliver's head, the fingers tangling into his wet hair, and Oliver went to work.

Nick was big in his mouth. He wrapped his lips around him, letting his tongue explore as he worked his head up and down. Above him, Nick cursed. His skin was flushed, and it seemed impossible that he could be so turned on so easily, but then again, he'd been waiting for this for hours, and Oliver had already gotten off in the middle of the night. Not that he wasn't aroused too. His erection ached for attention, but he had one hand on the base of Nick's cock, and the other braced against one of Nick's thighs.

The fingers in his hair tightened as Nick pushed himself deeper into Oliver's mouth. Pre-come leaked against Oliver's tongue, and he closed his eyes and focused on relaxing enough to take what Nick was trying to give him. He gagged when Nick thrust too far, bumping the back of Oliver's throat, and Nick pulled back immediately.

"Sorry."

Oliver glanced up at him again. Nick's lips were slick and open, his eyes hooded. Oliver focused on keeping his jaw loose as he took Nick all the way in, then another inch farther, into his throat.

The fingers in his hair became a fist, pulling enough to sting, but they didn't fight him as Oliver pulled back to breathe and then sucked Nick down again.

"Oh God," Nick groaned. Under Oliver's hands, the muscles in Nick's thighs jumped. Oliver swallowed him down again, letting his throat work around him, and was rewarded when Nick's hips flexed, pushing himself deeper. Oliver gagged once more, but it didn't matter. He was so turned on, watching Nick come apart above him. His own cock was leaking, and he'd only need a couple quick tugs in his fist to make himself come.

But Nick was going to come first.

His eyes were squeezed tight as Oliver changed tactics again. He tightened his lips around Nick's cock, sucking hard and fast, working with the rhythm that Nick set with his hips. Oliver's neck and jaw ached, but he reached between Nick's thighs to gently roll his balls between his fingers and was rewarded with a stream of hissed grunts and curses.

"So good. Don't stop. Fuck. Please don't stop."

Oliver didn't plan to. He planned to push Nick off the edge and follow him all the way down.

Nick shouted, and then his hands in Oliver's hair twisted, wrenching his mouth off of Nick's cock. Nick took over, jacking himself furiously. Oliver panted and groaned, taking the opportunity to do the same. He was right at the edge, the orgasm gathering in his balls, when a deep groan punched out of Nick's chest as white streaks of come shot out from his fist, landing on Oliver's shoulder and chin.

"Oh my God," Oliver moaned as his own orgasm overtook him. He shuddered and rested his forehead on the crest of Nick's hip, growling and panting. He'd already come no more than six hours before, but somehow this one ripped out of him like it had been months.

When he came back to himself, Nick was pulling him to his feet. He kissed Oliver's throat and cheeks, soft lazy kisses that didn't ask for anything in return.

"Thank you," he said in a raw voice.

"My pleasure."

Nick bent to pick up the discarded bar of soap. Then he turned Oliver to face the water again, supporting his body against his own solid one. Oliver had been trying to blow Nick's mind and now here he was instead, being manhandled like a rag doll, as Nick washed the come out of his chest hair.

"I'm supposed to be taking care of you." Oliver tilted his head back to rest it against Nick's shoulder.

"Says who?" Nick kissed his cheek with a smack.

Said who?

Oliver wrapped an arm backward around Nick's shoulder, pulling them close. He closed his eyes and let himself get lost in the feeling of Nick's hands on his skin again.

Said who? Why did it have to be Oliver who was in charge? He'd been going it alone for months. Maybe he could let go for a morning.

Soapy hands roamed over his body, making no demands, touching and taking care.

He could get used to this. Addicted, almost.

When they finally turned the water off, the whole bathroom was so steamy they could barely see. They laughed and kissed as they toweled off.

"I'd offer to make you breakfast," Oliver said as he walked toward his bedroom. Nick followed, a gorgeous hairy distraction wrapped only in a towel. "But you kind of screwed up my morning routine. I have to open the shop soon."

Nick ran a hand over the back of his head and gave Oliver a smile that was like a punch to the gut.

"I'd say I was sorry, but you screwed up my whole night's

routine. And now I've missed an hour of sleep at home. This makes us even."

What did it say that Oliver was ready to go again? As he reached into his closet, Nick coughed uncomfortably behind him.

"I don't suppose I can borrow some clothes. Mine are kind of sweaty. You run fast."

Oliver went to his dresser and found a pair of sweats and a long-sleeved shirt. Nick was bigger than he was. Anything with buttons or zippers was unlikely to fit.

"I qualified for the Boston Marathon last year," he said, tossing the clothes to Nick.

"Why does that not surprise me?" Nick smiled at him, dark and full of secret thoughts.

"Can I give you a lift home?" Oliver asked as they headed to the front door. Their clothes were still all over the hall, but Oliver left his where they were.

Behind him, Nick had frozen, his confidence vanishing. His dark eyebrows were pulled together, and his eyes filled with hesitation. "You don't have to. I can ride back."

"No, it's not a big deal. How far away can you live?"

Nick made a face, but he followed Oliver silently into the garage and didn't say anything else. He loaded his bike in the back and climbed into the passenger seat of the SUV. Oliver pressed the button to open the garage door and then backed slowly out onto the street.

"This is a nice car," Nick said as they drove away from the house.

"Thanks."

Cooper picked it out. Oliver hadn't wanted something so ostentatious, but Cooper did. And yet, Oliver wound up with it as they'd negotiated their separation. He should sell it. The cash would keep the shop going a while longer.

He forced himself to focus on the drive. He and Nick agreed

to keep their personal lives out of this, and even thinking about Cooper felt like breaking the rules now.

Nick gave short directions to an older part of town that Oliver didn't know.

"This is me here." He pointed to a small but well-maintained bungalow.

"Pretty spot," Oliver said, but Nick only shrugged and wouldn't quite meet his eyes. "I'll see you on Sunday?"

"Sure." Nick unclipped his seat belt and plucked at the shirt he wore, stretched tight over his frame.

Neither of them moved. The space in the SUV felt close, and, for once, Oliver wasn't sure what he was supposed to say next.

Then Nick leaned across the console and pressed a kiss to Oliver's mouth. His lips were soft, and knowing Nick was worn out from their morning antics was gratifying. Every other time they'd kissed was like a gust of wind bringing a fire back to life. This morning, though, it was a kiss.

Nick slipped out of the car, collected his bike from the back, and walked up to the house without a look back. Oliver watched him the whole way.

He had a problem, and not an insignificant one.

If this was Nick's idea of casual sex, Oliver was going to be screwed when it came time to let him go.

11

The next week started out as one of the best in a long time. Nick saw Oliver on Sunday, and the sex was as good as it had been the morning of their run. He ignored the look Anya gave him as he came back home after lunchtime.

"Where did you go?"

"Lumber yard."

"For three hours?"

He nearly told her to stop bugging him, but if Nick let his emotions fuel his words, he'd wind up sounding like Hayden. Except Hayden was on a short leash, whereas for Nick's good behavior, he'd been rewarded with Oliver's careful attention, including his hands on Nick's body and his mouth sucking Nick's brains out through his dick. Nick had brought his uniform. The awkward feeling from the day before, stuffing it into a duffle bag at work and trying to convince himself no one noticed he'd changed his routine, had totally been worth it to see the need in Oliver's eyes when he undid the flat blue buttons of Nick's shirt.

Nick's fast start to the week ended abruptly on Monday when Hayden was late coming home from school again, this time with a bruise under his eye slowly turning purple. He still hadn't been able to give a reason for his lateness or the black eye, other than that he'd slipped and banged his face. No one, familial or correctional, bought that excuse, so now he was no longer allowed to ride the school bus home. Either Anya or Nick had to pick him up right after classes let out, and Hayden was required to check in with the probation officer as soon as he was in the car. The new requirement wasn't easy for anyone.

"Why are you like this?" Anya said, hands in her hair.

"Like what? Why don't you leave me alone if this is such a problem?"

"Leave you alone? So you can go to jail? Is that what you want?"

Hayden rolled his eyes and slumped off to his bedroom. Nick held Anya while she cried.

"I don't understand."

"I know."

"I'm so glad you're here." She gave him a watery smile.

Nick swallowed down the lump in his throat. Lately, he hadn't been around as much as he should. Too busy hooking up with Oliver and pretending everything else was fine.

"It'll be okay," he lied.

Anya hugged him tighter. "If it were just the two of us, I don't know what would have happened. He needs you. I need you."

One of Oliver's texts said the same thing.

I need you.

It had been part of a series of messages sent in the middle of night, something they were doing more and more often while Nick ate his dinner and Oliver did—well, while Oliver was in bed.

I need you so much.

Oliver's message filled Nick with desire. Anya's words filled him with dread. He hated himself for that. He still hadn't told her about Oliver. Who knew how long this thing they were doing would keep going? No sense in making Anya worry he was any less committed to Hayden and their little family arrangement. He was home when he needed to be and had promised to pick up Hayden most of the time after school. What he did in the little free time he had was no one's business but his.

Except Brian apparently missed that memo. Again.

"Did you and Oliver get together again?" Brian asked at work.

"Jesus, would you back off?" Nick snapped before he could stop himself, and Brian blanched. Nick's phone buzzed in his pocket, probably a text from Oliver asking when his break would be. Tonight, for once, it felt like extra pressure he didn't need.

"Sorry," Brian said, moving away from Nick's workstation. "I didn't mean to pry."

Nick sighed. The phone buzzed again, and he turned it off. "It's fine. Sorry."

"Everything okay at home?"

Nick scrubbed at his face. When was the last time anything had been okay at home? "It's exhausting," he said, staring at his palms. "It always feels like we're one step away from the whole thing falling apart. And it's almost like Hayden is trying to make it worse. Like he wants to be caught." Hayden in juvenile detention was Nick's worst nightmare.

"You ever talk to anyone about it?"

"What? Like a shrink?" Anya tried to make them go a few times, but Hayden had been so bored and disrespectful that the whole thing had been pointless.

"It's not a bad idea. Jess and I, we've been talking to one for a few months. It really helps. I can give you her number. Or you know the department would refer you to one if you didn't want to meet the same woman we've been seeing. But I think you'd feel better."

Nick laughed bitterly. He'd told Brian some of it, over the last few months, but talking about it made him angry. Or sad.

"Are you talking to Oliver about it?" Brian asked as Nick's dark mood tried to swallow him.

Nick's hands clenched into fists, and he pushed his chair away from the desk. "Why do you keep coming back to him? There's nothing going on with me and Oliver. Not like that."

"What do you mean? Not like what?"

Nick closed his eyes. Nothing to be ashamed of. He and Oliver were consenting adults, and they had an arrangement that worked for both of them. But talking about it would make it public. He didn't want to share what he had going with Oliver. So little in his life these days was his by choice, but Oliver offered this to him, and he was going to hold onto it with both hands.

"It's just sex," he heard himself say. His voice was raw. "Just casual. You don't need to read more into it than that."

He nearly broke when Brian put a hand on his shoulder. "And you're okay with that?"

Okay? How could he not be okay with it? Even when they weren't together, Nick's brain was full of Oliver. His hair in Nick's fists, the taste of his skin on Nick's tongue. He woke up sometimes, his hand on his hard cock, with the sound, the groan Oliver made a split second before he came, ringing in Nick's ears.

That knowledge, and the ache that came with it, were so much more than his previous exhaustion and numbness. He wouldn't give that up, not as long as Oliver would have him.

"It was my choice." He forced himself to meet Brian's eyes.

The other man nodded, a sad smile on his lips. "You're allowed to ask for more for yourself. You know that, right?"

After that, Nick couldn't look at him anymore.

A tractor trailer tipped over on its side that night, while another lay burning in the ditch on the freeway west of town. The whole department was sent out, and Nick spent most of the shift on the phone communicating with other emergency response teams.

He didn't get around to eating until nearly four o'clock in the morning. Out of habit, he turned his phone on, realizing too late that Oliver would have gone to sleep hours ago, insomnia be damned.

One text message waited for him.

Hey! Want to come by tonight before your shift? You can wear your uniform :)

Fuck Brian. Nick chewed angrily as he read it again. Fuck him for making this text feel like less than the ones sent before. Like it shouldn't be enough for Nick.

He stared at the message a long time before he wrote a reply.

I can't tonight. Sorry.

He left the rest of the meal uneaten.

———

Oliver tried calling the market board office for clarification a few times before his summons. The phone always went to voicemail. In a fit of desperation, he tried emailing the generic *Info* email address on the market website, but that didn't garner a reply either.

The uncertainty made him uneasy.

So did Nick's sudden silence. On Thursday, he made a vague excuse about commitments a few hours before they got together on Nick's day off. Oliver tried calling, but, like the market, all he got was voicemail. So they'd last seen each other almost a week ago.

Finally, with no other option but to be as prepared as possible on zero information, Oliver compiled all his business literature and records. He put on one of his suits, the ones he'd worn like a uniform every day of his old life, but then decided against it and hung it back up. He was going with an open mind. No need to try to intimidate them in his full corporate swag.

The meeting was at Seacroft Town Hall. Oliver ignored the uneasy exposed feeling that slithered through him walking through the building's front foyer. He hadn't gone to a hearing without a team in a while, but he'd chosen this life, so now he would do it alone. How hard could it be?

The market board turned out to have seven members, mostly gray-haired men in polo shirts and khakis, as well as two women, both also in late middle age. None of them smiled when he pushed open the door.

"Mr. Stevenson," an overweight man who sat at the end of the table said. "I'm Richard Polson, the board chair. Have a seat."

Oliver would have liked to shake some hands, or possibly pass out some literature, but starting off as nonconfrontationally as possible was critical, so he did as instructed.

The man to Richard Polson's left leaned over to whisper something while the rest of the group watched Oliver silently. He had to bite down a laugh. Someone had watched bad lawyer TV. Next they'd be scribbling covert notes on a legal pad and sliding it surreptitiously between one another like they were negotiating his settlement.

They should know that Oliver never accepted the first offer.

"Mr. Stevenson," Richard said again.

"Yes."

"Thank you for joining us. You received our letter."

He didn't say it like a question, and Oliver grinned. He knew how to play this game. "I did, yes, thank you."

"So you understand why we asked to meet with you?"

Here was his step up. Make them explain, instead of Oliver answering all the questions.

Richard continued before Oliver had a chance to reply. "And as a result, I trust you understand why we have to revoke your license as a market vendor?"

It took all of Oliver's training not to twitch. "If you don't mind," he said. "I'll need you to break it down for me, in layman's terms."

"It's come to our attention," the man sitting to Richard's left said, "that your business does not meet the minimum criteria to sell your products at our market."

"That seems unlikely. You reviewed my products when I submitted my application. You approved them then. Nothing has changed."

"The goal of the market is to promote locally grown and sourced products to—"

"I'm sorry." Oliver held up his hand. "What did you say your name was?"

"Barry Boudreau. Mr. Stevenson," he continued, frowning impatiently, "new market permits are highly competitive. Our goal is to highlight the best of Seacroft's businesses, farmers, and vendors. We approved your application based on the understanding that you would be selling a local product."

Oliver kept his temper locked down behind a wall of ice. "It is a local product. I don't know how it could be any more local. I make my juices in my shop, which can't be more than three blocks from here."

"But you don't buy your produce from local farmers," Richard said. "In fact, we've heard you've been highly dismissive of some of our other vendors."

The ice began to melt. "Is this about—" he struggled to remember, "—the orchard? Is this about Marsha and . . ." He remembered her but could not bring her husband's name to mind at all.

"It's about protecting the integrity of our brand." Barry glanced at Oliver over the top of his glasses.

"You're going to punish me because most of the ingredients I need aren't in season yet?"

"The by-laws are very clear. You presented yourself as a local producer when you made your application last winter and—"

"I *am* a local producer." He kept his hands clasped tightly in his lap. A board of farmers and self-important businessmen could not break his control so quickly.

"There is also the concern that you're making dubious health claims, without having a scientific or medical background to support them."

Oliver's undergraduate degree was actually a Bachelor's of Science, but pointing that out would be petty and pointless. "All my meal plans are developed by a licensed nutritionist."

"And the juices?"

Richard lifted a paper and read from it. "Enhances mental clarity. Supports immune system function."

He swallowed and, like a coward, wished Cooper were here. Cooper would have these answers. That had been his part of the plan. "All of my products contain vitamins and minerals that have been *scientifically* proven to do those things." It was half an answer—the true half—but even he could hear the way his voice wavered.

"And if someone drank one of your juices before going for a late-night drive? Or if a mother gave her sick child one instead of taking them to the doctor?"

"I would never suggest anything I sell could be a substitute for proper medical care." He couldn't stop himself from running a shaky hand over his hair. He was angry now. To suggest he wasn't playing by their rules was one thing. To say he was negligent was a completely different matter.

But then again, hadn't Avery thought what Oliver sold could substitute for one of his energy drinks? What if someone else did the same, but then tried to do something more dangerous than a night of video games?

This was his fault. He'd gone off-script, off-plan. He'd rushed into signing up for the market when he knew better than to rush into anything. After making a whole career by being the most prepared person in the room, Oliver had improvised, and now he was on his heels.

"Mr. Stevenson." Richard shuffled his papers. "We received a number of applications from new vendors this year. Spaces rarely become available at our market, and we liked what you had to offer. We are always looking to support innovative entrepreneurs in Seacroft."

But only if they fall in line and scratch your back and your buddy's. These self-important bastards were going to try to take away his business. They had no idea how much Oliver had given up to be here.

How long had Marsha and—dammit, he still couldn't remember her husband's name—waited until they'd lodged their complaint with these people?

Richard gave him a smug smile, the same one Cooper gave him while carrying the last of his things to the SUV, as his apologies turned to anger. The same one practically daring Oliver to drive away into an uncertain future just to prove he could.

"We're willing to give you a grace period. I understand it can be difficult to make connections when you're new to the community." He paused and leaned toward Barry. They whispered theatrically. Oliver was still waiting for the legal pad with their best offer to appear.

Barry straightened in his seat. "You have a month to either find a new local supplier for your products, or to find additional products you can sell that would allow you to work with Seacroft farmers. We'll review this at our next meeting and make a decision then."

Oliver could practically hear the invisible gavel bang off the table, along with another nail in his coffin. "I'll keep you posted on my progress."

He'd told Cooper he'd succeed without him, and now he'd do it in spite of the people in front of him too.

12

"*F*uck 'em," Seb said as he took another drink.

Oliver chuckled and lifted his glass. "I can't. I'm in a relationship."

"With who?"

Oliver waved him off. "With no one." What he and Nick had was an agreement, not a relationship. They didn't do relationship things. For example, when Oliver stalked out of the market meeting on what felt like wooden legs, he'd texted his brother, not Nick, that it was time to get roaringly drunk. You didn't get roaringly drunk with your fuck buddies.

Well, you did. Sometimes. He and Cooper had started that way. Or, actually, they'd started the other way. They'd been well on their way to completely wasted, celebrating a big win—or was it a big loss?—the first time Cooper kissed him. And the second, and the third. It took a year of drunken hookups before they finally admitted they didn't need the alcohol to be together.

"Fuck Cooper." Oliver needed two tries to get the glass to his lips.

"I'm not sure what brought that on, but I'll drink to it." Seb saluted him.

"He was an ass."

"But he *had* a great ass. I can say that now."

Oliver snorted. "That's the nicest thing you've ever said about him." Cooper had been so vain about his ass. All the waxing and bleaching. The endless squats and workouts. He and Seb had never liked each other, but he'd be pleased to hear Seb still recognized a work of art when he saw one.

"So are you going to tell me what happened between you two now?" Seb chewed on an olive and squinted at him.

Oliver shook his head. He'd lost track of how much he'd had to drink after the fourth dirty martini, but he was still with it enough to know he wasn't going to talk about that.

"Come on," Seb said, signalling a server for another round. "The longer you hold out, the more I come up with better and better things in my head. Did he climb back in the closet? Is he living some morally gray double life with his stepbrother?"

"That's disgusting. Don't be a pervert."

Seb rested his head on Oliver's shoulder and smiled a big toothy smile. "But I'm your pervert."

Oliver sighed, letting the alcohol do its thing. "I'm not supposed to be drinking."

"Part of your holistic lifestyle makeover?"

"It spikes your blood sugar and depletes your electrolytes."

"You know it's all horseshit, right? It's people afraid of dying, so they fill their bodies with kale and seaweed like it's some magic elixir. I mean, who wants to live forever anyway?"

Another pair of martini glasses appeared between them, and Oliver saluted his brother with one. "I'm really glad you're here."

"Of course I'm here. You said the first five rounds were on you."

"No." Oliver pressed a hand to Seb's shoulder. Stringing the next sentences together took some work. "I'm glad you're in Seacroft. It would suck a lot if I were here by myself."

Seb laughed. "I was here first."

"Well, I'm glad you're still here! And I'm sorry about before."

"When?"

"Before." Oliver waved a hand over his shoulder, then had to grasp the back of his chair to keep from falling off it. "Before. Everything. I haven't been a very good big brother."

Seb jabbed a finger at him, but missed the mark and wound up gliding past Oliver's ear. "Do not get sappy on me. We cannot start crying all over each other in the middle of this bar."

Oliver wrapped an arm around his younger brother and gathered him up in a hug. Vodka and olive juice splashed against his neck. His drink or Seb's, it didn't matter. "I should go home." He should call Nick. Assuming he was accepting Oliver's calls again. A little quality time would be the perfect way to finish his mission to forget about his stupid meeting with the board.

Oliver stepped down from his chair. The bar spun pleasantly around him.

Seb grabbed at his sleeve. "It's still early. You need to stay."

"I have to work tomorrow. At the market." The fucking market. Where Marsha and Whatshisface would stare daggers at him from across the way and plot their revenge, because he didn't think Ponce de Leon would give two shits about their apples.

"Fuck the market!" Seb said it louder than he should.

"Stop. I have to work there!" Oliver laughed as he shushed him, pressing his hand to Seb's mouth.

They helped each other out the door, wobbling the whole way. Another half martini, and they probably would have been singing.

"I should call a cab," Oliver said as he pulled out his phone. He'd driven downtown for his meeting. He'd have to get his car sometime, but he was in no condition to drive.

"Want me to wait with you?"

"No. I'll be okay." Oliver waved him off as he tried, and failed, to dial the number for Seacroft's one lonely taxi service. If the farmer's market succeeded in running him out of business,

Oliver was going to look into starting up Lyft in Seacroft. A little healthy competition for the cab company that hadn't updated its sedans in a decade or more couldn't hurt.

"Sounds good. Martin is probably wondering where I got to. He worries about stuff like that. Did I tell you he thought I was a ghost when we first met?"

Oliver laughed as he continued to fumble with his phone. "You did. Spooky Seb. Oooo!" He raised his arms, floating on his toes while Seb laughed along with him.

Seb gave him a smacking kiss on the cheek. "We should have done this months ago. When you first got here. I'm sorry I was a terrible little brother."

Oliver squeezed him until Seb gasped. "You're a great little brother."

Seb stumbled away, down the street toward his apartment.

Oliver turned his attention back to the phone, trying to find the number for a cab. Instead, the phone shook in his hand as a call came in.

Incoming call

Cooper Parnell

He nearly threw up when he saw the name.

Frantically, he tried to reject the call, but his thumb slipped and picked it up instead. Oliver stared in horror as the counter started to tick away the seconds.

"Hello?" The voice was faint and tinny as Oliver held the phone away from himself like a bomb. "Hello?"

He lifted the handset to his ear, while his vision blurred and his stomach twisted.

"Ollie?"

The voice. Fuck, the voice. The name. His name on Cooper's tongue.

"I'm so sorry, Ollie."

He could do this.

"Ollie, are you there?"

"Hey, babe. Fancy meeting you here."

"Ollie?"

"That's my name, don't wear it out." God, had anyone said that in the last twenty years? *Smooth, Ollie. Very smooth.*

"I didn't think you'd take my call."

"Yeah, well, I'm full of surprises." He thrust his hands up like a cheerleader, and the phone slipped from his grasp, clattering onto the pavement. He swore, bending, nearly falling, to pick it up. He wobbled on the street corner and laughed.

"Ollie? What are you doing?"

"I'm talking to you. What are *you* doing?"

"Are you drunk?"

"Might be, a little." He squinted his eyes and pressed his thumb and forefinger together, then laughed again. "Sorry, you can't see that, can you? One second, let me put the call on video." Let Cooper see what a good time he was missing.

"Maybe I should—" Cooper started to say, but whatever he should maybe do was lost as Oliver fumbled with the phone. Trying to bring up the video so he could see Cooper's lying face for the first time in months, he managed to disconnect the call instead.

He stared down at the screen for a long time, expecting a return call.

It didn't come.

The world spun in a haze of vodka.

Finally, he turned to his texts. A text would be better. It would last longer. He scrolled past his text to Seb, past Nick's weird excuse for not coming over. He scrolled and scrolled until he realized that Cooper wasn't there. It had been too many months since Cooper had been a part of his life. He had no reason to butt in now. They were over.

Oliver went back to the answered call and flipped through the screens until the number connected to a new text. With shaking fingers, he typed.

Don't ever call me again, you bastard.

———

The hangover the next morning almost negated the value of Oliver's sibling drunkfest the night before. Almost. His stomach was rancid, and his skull felt two sizes too small for his brain.

He tried to make a home hangover remedy—cucumber, celery, watercress, ginger, fennel—but the sound of the juicer was like a chainsaw through his head, and then something jammed in the blades, making it shriek and emit a burning smell. Oliver's stomach twisted hard. He left the thing half-finished on the counter, settling for a mass-produced sports drink from a convenience store instead.

Somewhere in the middle of the night, he'd sent a bunch of sloppy texts to Nick. He'd asked, practically begged, him to come over. To call. The messages got increasingly incoherent. Oliver could barely look at them in the light of day. He sent a pointed text to Seb about being a bad influence so his messages to Nick wouldn't be at the top of the list.

He could practically smell the vodka in his pores as he set up his stall. Since he'd had to get a cab back to his SUV, then drive over to the shop to pick up his supplies, it'd already been a long morning. Of course he'd been out of ice at the shop, so he detoured to buy some at the nearest gas station. He nearly asked the sleepy-looking guy behind the counter if the ice had been made from locally sourced water, because heaven forbid he get docked for not supporting Seacroft's ice-making industry too, but his stomach cramped as he was about to unleash his snark, so he threw down a few dollar bills and left.

As Oliver loaded the tubs and juice onto the table, he really wondered if this was all worth it. The market should have helped increase visibility and make Pulpability feel accessible. But with all these hoops to jump through, did the perks outweigh the hassle? Maybe having the store open on Saturdays and drawing weekend shoppers there would be better.

Maybe he should give up altogether.

"You're new!"

Oliver glanced up from where he was setting his bottles at the woman standing in front of the table. She was petite, with dark hair that gleamed burgundy in the sun.

"Good morning." He tried to smile, but barely managed a squint.

"What are you selling?"

Many of the vendors around him were still setting up, and for the first time since he'd started this business, Oliver struggled to be gracious. He could easily tell her he wasn't open for business yet.

The market board had spies everywhere, though, and maybe this woman was one complaint away from his permanent blacklisting in the Seacroft business community.

"I've got a number of cold-pressed juices. The cold-pressing helps to maintain the nutrient value of the fruits and vegetables."

"Like antioxidants and things? They look so good. Do you want one?" She pulled a bottle out of the ice and turned to a dark-haired teen standing behind her. How Oliver had missed him earlier, since he stood a full head and shoulders above her, was a mystery, but Oliver wasn't really firing on all cylinders.

The boy grunted something noncommittal, and the woman put a patient hand on his arm, towing him forward. "It's going to be hot this morning. You'll get thirsty. Pick one."

The boy pointed at one of the bottles of *Mango Tornado*.

"I haven't made it down here yet this spring," she said as she dug through her purse. "I usually work on Saturdays, but I always mean to do my shopping here instead of the grocery store during the spring and summer. So much better to buy things locally than fruits and vegetables shipped all the way from California. I mean, who knows what they put on those things to keep them fresh and—oh Hayden, there's your dad. Go grab him. Nick! Hayden, go! He didn't hear me. I don't want him to leave without me." She pushed at the teen's shoulder, and he shuffled away at a pace completely at odds with the urgency on her face.

She handed Oliver some money and then waved at someone down the aisle. A dozen bracelets on her wrist jangled together. Oliver flinched away from the sound, but followed her gaze.

The hangover tightened around his brain like a vise.

Nick walked up the aisle next to the boy, making it impossible to doubt that they were related. The same dark hair and black eyes. The boy was nearly as tall, although he hadn't grown into Nick's frame yet. Where Nick was bulky, the kid was all gangly limbs, but they clearly shared DNA.

Every step they took made it harder for Oliver to breathe.

"There you are!" the woman said, oblivious to Oliver's distress. "I was dropping Hayden off and saw this new stall here." She leaned back and frowned at the sign. "Pulpability. That's kind of cute, isn't it? Sounds like 'possibility.' Anyway, we were buying some juice. Do you want one?"

Nick's features were like granite. "I'm okay."

"Suit yourself." She turned back to Oliver. "Did you have my change?"

Oliver jumped and dropped the coins in his hand. They clattered on the table, and he apologized as he gathered them up and woodenly handed them to her.

"How long have you been here?" she asked. Oliver couldn't look at her, not with Nick lurking like a silent mountain behind her.

It couldn't be what Oliver thought. This couldn't happen again. He'd been through it already with Cooper. The whole point of keeping things casual with Nick had been to protect himself, and now . . .

He hadn't answered her question. "Not long. This is my first season at the market. I've got a shop open on Front Street during the weekdays."

"Well, this looks delicious." She smiled and reached over the bottles, bracelets rattling, to shake his hand. "I'm Anya. This is Nick, and that's our son, Hayden." She gave the teenager a squeeze, and his face said he wanted to be anywhere but there.

Oliver knew the feeling intimately.

He risked a glance at Nick, whose dark eyes met his. The guilt, panic, and fear there made Oliver's stomach turn. He'd seen the same expression on Cooper's face that morning in the boardroom.

Nick should be very afraid. *The cheating bastard.* He had no idea what Oliver was capable of when he was pissed. It would be meticulous, and it would be painful.

Oliver turned back to Anya and said, "I'd love to see you again." He handed her a flyer. "We have weekly workshops on wellness and self-care. They're totally free. You should come."

She smiled, poor woman. Did she know the joke was on her too?

And yet, was it really? Oliver was the one who got to stand there, smiling blandly, while Anya looped her arms through Nick's and the boy's and wandered away. A happy family on a Saturday morning market tour. They were picture perfect.

And Oliver was alone.

13

*N*ick white-knuckled the steering wheel all the way home. The bottle of juice rocked in the cupholder like a silent reminder, or an accusation, almost as if it was spying on Nick. Anya carried on a stream of oblivious conversation the whole way home, and he could barely stand it.

He'd been unable to take his eyes off Oliver's face, and so he'd seen it all. The hurt. The sadness. The color seeped out of his skin, and his bloodshot eyes said so many wordless things. And Nick could only stare at him like a statue as his heart beat so hard in his chest, it left no room for his lungs.

The arrangement was over. With nothing said between them, their little secret was outed, and the private space they'd built shattered.

He slammed the car door so hard the whole vehicle rocked and marched toward the house.

"Are you okay?" Anya asked from the driveway. He didn't reply. His shift had been a shit show of false alarms, drunk drivers, and two stupid teenagers who had gotten high and set off old fireworks that had nearly burned down a cottage on the northern beach road. Now that seemed like the least of his problems.

He poured himself a glass of water and stared out the kitchen window, waiting for his heart to slow or his whole body to stop shaking like it wanted to rattle him to pieces.

"Nick?" Anya stood in the door.

"You're going to be late for work."

"What's wrong?"

"Nothing. Go on."

"Nick." She put a hand on his back, and he bowed his head over the sink. How could he be so upset over something that had only ever been casual sex and wasn't even that old?

But he couldn't mistake the betrayal in Oliver's eyes.

"Babe?"

"Don't call me that!" He turned, the water in his glass splashing a wide arc, as she danced back.

"Then tell me what's wrong! You can't give me the silent treatment. We get enough of that from Hayden. You can't do it too. I couldn't take it."

He sagged into one of the kitchen chairs, his whole body exhausted. Anya sat next to him, and he shuddered when she touched him again, but she didn't pull away. He took his phone out of his pocket, opened his text messages, and showed it to her.

Oliver's texts from overnight had been different. Nick didn't know what had changed, and by the time he'd been able to reply to them, it was too late to expect Oliver to still be awake.

I want you.

When can I see you?

I can't wait.

It needs to be now.

Soon.

Please. I need to see you.

Anya scrolled through them. "What are these?"

"I've been seeing someone."

"Seeing someone . . . like you're dating someone?"

He shrugged.

She studied the phone screen. "You've been seeing Oliver. That's his name? You've been seeing a man?"

He nodded and slipped the phone back into his pocket.

Her smile nearly tore him in half. "But that's so great! Is it serious? How long? Why didn't you say anything?"

He didn't deserve her enthusiasm. "I didn't—I couldn't tell you. Because of Hayden."

"You don't want him to know you're bisexual?" She sounded confused.

"I didn't want to tell *you.* I didn't want you to think I was getting distracted. I promised you we'd do this together. The thing with Oliver—I didn't want you to think I'd forgotten what I'd promised."

Anya tilted her head to one side. "Babe." Nick flinched at the old pet name. "I would never think that. You're here every day. You're more patient with Hayden than I am most of the time. But that doesn't mean you can't have something for yourself too."

He didn't cry very often, but the tightness in his chest constricted, squeezing his throat until the tears had nowhere to go but out. Anya cradled his face in her hands gently, like his mother would have, and waited for him to get himself together.

"It was the guy at the market," he finally said.

It took a second for his words to reach her, and then she leaped out of her chair like the kitchen was on fire.

"The hot juice guy? The hipster with the beard? Holy shit! You're dating him?" She waved her hands around in a weird happy dance.

Nick couldn't return her excitement. "Not dating. Not exactly. We're—We fool around sometimes."

"Holy shit, you're *having sex* with him? What's it like? How did you meet him? He's so hot! You know how hot he is, right?" Her eyes were bright, and she was breathing so hard, he worried she might pass out. Nick guided her back to the kitchen table.

"It's not serious. You don't have to worry about him getting in the way of me being here." She seemed to be taking this better than he expected or deserved, but he still needed to make sure she knew Hayden's situation was the priority. He'd had his fun, and now Nick would come back to reality.

"Is that where you've been going? When you leave in the middle of the day?" Her eyes widened. "You had someone else's clothes here last week. Were they his?"

"It doesn't matter. It's over."

"What?" Anya's smile faded so fast, he could practically hear the needle scratch.

"It was a casual thing and it's over."

"Why? What happened?"

He did not need couples counseling from his ex-wife. He had Brian for that. "He—We agreed that we'd keep our personal lives to ourselves. Nothing serious. No problems. But you guys have met him now, and if I see him again, he'll want to know about you and Hayden, and that wasn't part of the deal."

Anya slapped him.

He didn't even see her hand move, but he couldn't miss the sting across his cheek. Anya was wide-eyed, hands over her mouth, like she couldn't believe she'd done it.

Their marriage had had its failings, but they had never been abusive with each other.

"What was that for?"

"You do not get to be ashamed of us."

"I'm not! I don't—" He was ashamed of how much he needed to get away sometimes. What kind of father did that make him? But he'd never been ashamed of them. "What Hayden did, and what we have to do for him . . . That's not something I want to talk about with most people."

She exhaled slowly. "And that is understandable. But if it's someone you care about, and someone who cares about you— those are the people you *have* to talk about it with."

Did Oliver care about him? That had never been part of the agreement.

I want you.

When can I see you?

I can't wait until Thursday.

It needs to be now.

Soon.

Please. I need to see you.

Nick assumed his texts had been about sex. But Oliver's expression at the market hadn't been about losing a simple sexual arrangement.

"I'm sorry I slapped you." Anya was tiny on her chair.

He pulled her close to him. He'd always loved the way she'd fit against him, her head under his chin. When they'd been in school, holding her there felt like she was his to protect.

Except now she didn't want it. Hadn't wanted it in years. His sexuality didn't even figure into it, although she'd known about it since high school, maybe even before Nick knew for sure. But despite all their history, they'd still been too young when they'd gotten married—or Nick was, anyway. He hadn't been mature enough to realize their marriage only worked with both of them committed. Sulking and passing blame instead of working for it had been so easy, and this—this impossible situation—was the result.

"I'm sorry I didn't tell you," he said.

"You're lucky I didn't see him first. Is he bi too?"

Nick laughed softly, and it made him feel better. "I don't think so."

"You don't think so?" She leaned back so she could see his face. "What the hell have you been talking about? You better go see him. I'm sorry if I made it complicated for the both of you."

Nick kissed the top of her hair. "It was bound to happen. I'm sorry I upset you. I've never been ashamed of you." He'd never been anything but proud to be in her life, in whatever way she'd let him. She'd tried to be Nick's friend and ally, but being rational enough to accept it for the gift it was took him years.

"I'm going to be late for work. Give me a lift. You'll have to pick up Hayden from community service."

Nick's nerves hadn't settled, but he followed her to the door. Whatever else happened, he was on sure footing at home again, and that was a good place to start.

Now he just had to see where things stood with Oliver.

―――――

The knock had Oliver's hair standing on end. He almost didn't hear it, as he tried to clean up the mess from the half-finished hangover remedy he'd started that morning, but then it came again.

He glanced out the front window and hesitated at the sight of Nick's old car on the street.

He didn't have to answer. If he stayed out of sight, Nick would eventually leave.

"Oliver." Nick's voice was as quiet as his knock had been, muffled on the other side of the door. "Please. I don't have to stay long but let me tell you about what you saw."

Cooper had tried to explain once, but it had been too little, too late, and Oliver had wound up with a Porsche full of his stuff and a broken heart.

At least this time, Nick would be the one to go.

He opened the door and stepped aside. Nick slipped into the hall quickly, like he was afraid Oliver might reconsider and slam the door in his face.

"Thanks." Nick hunched in his jacket. The hospitable thing would be to offer to take it, hang it in the closet, but Nick wouldn't be staying that long, so why be polite? Nick hadn't used any of his manners when he'd chosen to cheat on his wife.

Oliver went back to the kitchen and resumed his clean up.

Nick slid onto one of the stools by the breakfast bar, hands folded on the counter.

"I told you I was divorced," he said.

"You didn't look all that divorced this morning." Oliver regretted it as soon as he spoke. Showing that much emotion put him at a deficit.

"I wasn't aware there was a particular divorced look. Is there a shirt I'm supposed to wear?"

Oliver glared at him, and Nick sighed. "Sorry."

Something was jammed in the juicer. Oliver stabbed a knife into the opening in an effort to dislodge it.

"You might want to unplug that thing first."

Oliver went to snap out a reply, but then his eyes followed the cord from the back of the juicer to where it was still plugged into the outlet. He scowled at Nick as he yanked the cord out. "We had rules," he said. "Rules that were there to protect us both."

"And I didn't break any of them!"

Wrong move. Arguing technicalities would never help Nick's case, but Oliver was willing to play along, just to see how far Nick would dig himself in. "All right. I specified if you started seeing anyone new that you had to let me know. I guess technically your wife isn't new—"

"Ex-wife."

"You two were awfully cozy for ex-anythings."

"It's not—"

"You lied to me!"

"Will you please let me talk?" Nick's dark eyes flashed.

Oliver let his knife clatter to the counter. This was a bad idea, but the irrational part of him, the one that had wanted to believe Cooper too, led him to the living room again. He folded one leg underneath him as he sat on the sofa, forcing a casual facade. "So talk."

Nick followed him, still hunched into himself like he wanted to appear nonthreatening. If only that were the problem. "Anya is my ex-wife. We have been divorced for almost eight years. We have a son, Hayden, who you met. He's fifteen."

"I knew who he was as soon as I saw you two together. He looks exactly like you."

Nick smiled, but then it disappeared just as quickly, and he continued. "I told you Anya and I got married young."

Oliver did recall that, yes. "College sweethearts?"

"And high school. She was my best friend. My dad died when I was sixteen, and she helped me get through it. I never wanted to be with anyone but her."

Oliver reached his arms over his head to stretch. "This is all very sweet and completely supports your happy family routine at the market, so if there is a point you're trying to make, I suggest you get to it."

Nick's eyes narrowed. "You said no personal stuff. But I saw your face this morning. This isn't casual for you, and it isn't for me either. I don't know if it ever was."

Oliver fought to hang onto his anger at Nick's admission while a tiny bubble of hope struggled to come to the surface. He couldn't allow himself the space to consider Nick might be feeling even half of what Oliver had. Anger was easier. "But you—"

Nick cut him off. "You're going to walk away from me, and we agreed that you can do that, but do it for the right reasons, not because you don't understand what you saw."

Nick was playing with the hem of his jacket, big fingers moving along the stitching back and forth. Nothing about his posture or his gaze spoke of dishonesty.

Oliver sighed and motioned for him to continue.

"We were kids when we got married, and we were still kids when Hayden was born. I was the man, the husband. My job was to provide, or that's what I thought. But it's never that easy. It felt like I was never enough. I didn't earn enough money. I wasn't there when Anya needed help with the baby. I couldn't give her the life we'd planned in college. I didn't know what to do, so I got angry and blamed everyone but myself. The fire chief, for not giving me enough shifts. My dad, for not living long enough to tell me what to do. Eventually, I started blaming Anya for not being happy with what I could offer her. It was her fault we never had enough money. Her fault we lived in a shitty house in the oldest part of town. Then, one weekend, she said she was going to visit her sister with Hayden, and they didn't come back."

"She took your son away?" Oliver had never thought seriously about having kids. He and Cooper had always been too dedicated to their careers. But the idea of Nick's wife taking his son away in the blink of a weekend was unsettling.

"She gave me lots of chances to work it out. She didn't even leave town, just rented an apartment near the salon. I'd stop by when I could, but I worked a lot of night shifts, and . . . That was an excuse, to hide how much I'd failed them. I told her she'd known what she'd signed up for when she married a firefighter, because it was easier than admitting I'd fucked up. She said she wanted Hayden to have his father in his life, but . . ." He shifted uncomfortably. "I was angry at her for a long time. So I made excuses not to see them. And by the time I finally got over myself and tried to make it better, it was almost like I wasn't his dad anymore. Just some uncle he had to see on holidays and in the summer. Like he was marking time until he could go back to her."

Oliver's mouth went dry as he listened. Nick was so subdued, and his sincerity so plain. His words weren't about pity or covering his ass. Oliver's own insecurities had led him to believe Nick would break his heart—and maybe Anya's too—but the truth wasn't nearly that simple.

"Come here." Oliver motioned to Nick, who hesitated for a second before sitting on the couch, as far from Oliver as he could. Oliver went to move toward him, but Nick tensed, so Oliver sat back again.

"There's more." Nick stared down at his hands.

"What happened?"

"A couple years ago, Hayden started getting in trouble at school. Real trouble. He was talking back to his teachers, skipping classes. Anya started calling me. She was worried. He'd always been a boy, doing stupid boy stuff, but it was getting serious. It went from detentions to suspensions. He missed an assembly, and they found him in the parking lot getting stoned with some of his friends. He got arrested for stupid things like stealing *Playboys* at a gas station, although he was never charged. Anya said I needed to be more involved, that he needed a role model."

"And you stepped in?"

Nick shrugged. "Tried to. But we didn't have the kind of relationship that meant he'd listen to me, and now the kid I knew was gone. He used to be really close with Anya, but even she couldn't reach him by then, and most of the time, I felt like all I could do was tell him to do his homework and listen to his mother. We tried the usual things: grounding him, extra chores, no friends over on the weekends. But he didn't seem to care. He'd spend all his time in his room, and when the chores didn't get done, what were we going to do? Tell him he had to do more on top of the ones he already hadn't finished?"

Oliver could imagine how well that worked. He'd never had the kinds of problems Nick was talking about, but Seb had. So many nights in high school, their father had loomed over the heavy wooden table in the kitchen, demanding that Seb concentrate and do his homework, or there would be "consequences." Seb had been Seb, all teenage sass and dramatics, and their father had been infuriated.

"I failed him, I think," Nick said. "Or maybe we were never going to stop it."

143

"Stop what?" This time, when Oliver slid over the couch cushions, Nick didn't shy away. Oliver wrapped an arm over his broad shoulders, and Nick sagged against him.

"He got arrested again, last fall. He was harassing another boy in his class online. Anya said Hayden and the kid used to be friends, but . . ." Nick shrugged, settling further against Oliver's chest. "Anyway, the records the police showed us said it had been going on for a while. The kid was gay, and Hayden was threatening to out him to their classmates, and . . ."

Oliver didn't need to hear the specifics. He'd heard about enough cases like that to know. Schools had zero tolerance policies on bullying, and especially on cyberbullying, where the records were so easy to track. And if the victim was gay, it hit all the red flags for harassment.

"So they charged him as a juvenile."

"The lawyer we hired said the court would probably go easy on him, but, I don't know, something happened, and the next thing we knew, the lawyer was saying Hayden was going to jail and we didn't know what to do."

Professionally, Oliver was curious what the "something" was. Personally, he wanted Nick to stop telling this story because the distress in his expression was etching lines that didn't look like they'd ever go away.

"It's okay." Oliver ran his fingers over Nick's prickly scalp.

"No." Nick wiped at his face. "No. You need to know this. When he got arrested, we didn't have any idea what to do. Anya was hysterical, and Hayden wouldn't help himself. He wouldn't give a reason why he'd done it, or anything that might make it easier for him. And the lawyer said normally Hayden might get something like probation, or probably house arrest, but since Anya was by herself, and no one would be able to monitor and vouch for Hayden during the day, the judge might not think that was an appropriate sentence."

Or the judge had seen a blue-collar kid with a single mother and decided to make an example of him.

"But he's out now? He was at the market today."

Nick shook his head. "I moved them back in with me. I told the lawyer that Anya and I had gotten back together, for Hayden, and now they could put him on house arrest because we could both vouch for him."

The world rocked around Oliver. He staggered under the magnitude of it.

"How long has it been?"

"Six months. Originally, it was supposed to be three, but Hayden..."

"They've extended his sentence." Oliver swallowed, then asked the question he didn't need the answer to anymore. "So you're all there, at your house. You, Hayden, and Anya?"

Nick turned up toward him. His eyes were black in the dark living room, and they were bright with unshed tears. "I told her about you, after this morning. I thought it was better to not make a big deal about it with her before, but that was wrong. So I told her. And now I'm telling you. I'll tell you anything you want to know." His voice took on an edge of desperation. "Anya sleeps in the guest room. She has since they moved back in. Everything we're doing is for Hayden. When they finally take the tracker off his ankle, I don't know what Anya will do, but..." He sniffed. "We both love our son as much as we know how to, but we don't love each other. Not the way you think."

Oliver didn't know what to think. Accusing Nick of cheating was petty in comparison to the reality of it all.

"I'm sorry," Nick said. "I should have told you sooner, but this thing with Hayden... It's not only the last six months. It's been going on for years in one way or another, and ... Our arrangement—I needed it to be easy. Oliver, I'm so sorry."

Oliver wanted to do so many different things at once. Hold

him. Tell him it would be okay. Ask to see Hayden's file and double check every detail.

Oliver chose the easy path and kissed him. Nick groaned under his mouth, the sound full of need and relief.

"Stay tonight?" How long had Nick been here? Oliver had been ready to tear the whole thing down less than an hour ago, and now he couldn't make himself let Nick go.

Nick kissed his chin. "I'd really like that."

14

*N*ick couldn't believe he'd done it. He'd nearly turned around ten times on the drive over, and even as he knocked on the door and asked Oliver to let him in, he was terrified. He could have left details out, focused only on his divorce and skipped over the rest. But once he started talking, it all came out. Maybe he wanted forgiveness. Maybe he needed a pep talk.

In the end, he found himself watching TV with Oliver. For almost everyone, it would be such a normal thing, almost boring. Except, for Nick, the TV was the last place anyone in their house wanted to be in the evenings. The charging station was the worst of Hayden's confinement. So many nights, Nick's old sofa was the site of a stand-off.

Oliver's body was warm where Nick rested against it. The couch here—firm, leather—had obviously been bought by a tall man trying to find something comfortable, because they fit together well on it. If they'd been at Nick's, there would have been limbs sticking off every side.

"Does Hayden know you're bi?" Oliver asked softly.

Nick trembled. "No." Theirs hadn't been the kind of father-son relationship for important talks. Maybe someday, if they survived.

"Do you think he'd—I'm mean, if he was bullying a gay classmate . . . If he knew about us, would he—" Even Oliver looked afraid to ask, and Nick couldn't make himself answer.

This question lived in the blackest, most terrifying parts of his mind. He'd asked himself a similar question only once, not long after Hayden had been arrested. Not about Oliver, necessarily, but about Hayden's reaction to Nick's own sexuality. He had no idea where Hayden's hatred for his classmate came from —Anya certainly didn't believe those things—but if it was legitimate, if he felt the same way about Nick . . .

He pressed closer to Oliver, seeking comfort and maybe distraction, and Oliver seemed to know exactly what he needed.

Their kiss was like the night at the restaurant. Gentle at first, and then Nick reached for him, fingers burying in Oliver's hair as his mouth opened to let Oliver inside. Warmth filled his chest, pouring over the rest of his body. Nick shifted, sliding over the soft leather, until he was lying against the arm of the sofa.

Oliver followed with a soft laugh. "Remember we have to move somewhere else before we take our clothes off. Don't want anything important sticking to the cushions."

Nick frowned, even as he fought back a grin. "That's really disgusting."

Oliver pushed against him, sliding a thigh between Nick's. "Trust me on this."

It could have been weird. They'd agreed to keep it casual, nothing personal. Today, Nick set fire to that understanding, and the change could have made things awkward. But Oliver's body on his was already familiar, the brush of his beard on Nick's chin an easy distraction. His own body heated and started to harden, forgetting the stress and the sadness.

Oliver's hair fell forward, brushing over Nick's cheek. A strand of hair tangled in his mouth. He tried to pull it out, but another one followed.

"Wait." He pushed at Oliver's shoulder, winding up with

more hair in his face as Oliver lifted his head.

Oliver grinned and straightened, shifting to straddle Nick while he pulled his hair back into its usual messy bun. The movement—sitting upright, head tipped back, hands raised behind him— only served to show off his body. The strong width of his chest, the narrow V of his hips. Nick surged up, pushing at the hem of Oliver's shirt to kiss his belly button and flat stomach, then moved up through his chest hair to his nipples. Oliver laughed. The rumble vibrated through Nick's lips, encouraging him to explore further.

Oliver sighed and lifted Nick's face to kiss him, mouth crushing against his. Nick wanted to show him how much relief he felt that this wasn't the end.

"I was so mad at you this morning," Oliver said as his kisses moved along Nick's jaw.

"I know."

"I was mad that you didn't follow the rules." He groaned as Nick gripped his hips, pressing them together.

"I know."

"I was mad that I'd let myself get so caught up in this, and that I was going to miss you once you were gone."

Nick paused, lips a fraction from Oliver's. Their breath filled the space as too many words tried to get out of Nick's mouth at once.

"I don't have to go anywhere," he finally said.

Oliver licked his lip and smiled. "I know. I'm glad." He ran a hand over Nick's scalp. "But let's get off this couch, because we're going to get naked."

Nick laughed, bigger than he had in a while. "Oh, are we?"

Oliver pulled his shirt off, tossing it to the floor. He stood, hands on his belt, eyebrow arched, and Nick leaned back, splaying his legs wide while he spread his arms along the couch. No sense in rushing this if Oliver wanted to put on a show.

Shaking his head, like he'd caught on to Nick's invitation for a strip tease, Oliver bit his lip as he pulled the belt from its buckle.

"Do we need music for this?" He wiggled his hips.

"Depends on how long you're going to take."

It took about three flicks of his wrists, and then his pants were open and he was pushing them down his thighs in a rush of khaki. His underwear followed, but this part he did painfully slow. His body was amazing, all hard lines and ridges. Nick's throat went dry as the thatch of Oliver's pubic hair became visible, then the base of his dick. He stopped there, glancing up at Nick with laughter in his eyes. Nick grumbled, then surged to his feet, nearly knocking Oliver over as he wrapped around him, pushing his clothes off. He sucked at Oliver's Adam's apple, and the growl that purred in Oliver's chest had Nick's cock straining inside his jeans.

His hands were heavy as he fumbled with his own clothes, and in the end, Oliver had to peel Nick's shirt off and shove his jeans and boxers down to his ankles. Nick was pressed against Oliver's front, Oliver's thick cock nestled in the crease of Nick's ass. His knees wobbled as Oliver grasped Nick's cock, hand sliding lazily up and down while he spread kisses over Nick's bare shoulder.

"Come to bed," Oliver said, voice rough in Nick's ear. Nick twisted his head so they could kiss. He buried his hand in Oliver's hair, holding them close while Oliver continued to pump his cock with easy attention.

"Come on." Oliver rocked his hips, making Nick's cock jump. When Oliver pulled away, Nick whimpered at the loss of contact. Stumbling, he turned, tangled in his pants around his feet, but getting free of them gave him a chance to watch Oliver's amazing ass as he walked down the hall.

The bedroom was like the rest of the house, tidy and modern. The sheets were the softest Nick had ever felt as he crawled over them toward Oliver, their slick coolness making him shiver. He didn't have long to worry about it, though, because Oliver was reaching for him, pulling them together, until their bodies were lined up, their legs tangled.

"What should we do?" Oliver asked. He always asked. At first, it had made Nick uncomfortable, but he had a very clear idea of how he wanted this to play out tonight.

"I want you in my mouth, and then I want you on your knees with me inside you."

Oliver bit at Nick's lip, hard enough to sting. "A man with a plan is such a turn on for me."

Nick nuzzled at the musky, warm, tender skin on the inside of Oliver's thighs before he grasped Oliver's cock, jacking it slowly a few times to bring him fully up to attention.

Pre-come beaded at the tip, and Nick licked it off. Oliver rewarded him with a strangled groan, cut off when Nick wrapped his lips over the head and sucked him down.

"You don't waste time," Oliver said. Nick replied by sliding a hand between them to grasp Oliver's sack, gently rolling his balls between his fingers.

He sucked, taking Oliver deep, using his tongue and his cheeks to hold him tight and make him twist. Oliver's hands shifted over the covers before finally settling on the back of Nick's head, holding him in place as Oliver's hips rocked. Nick let him have control for a moment, enjoying the heavy weight of him in Nick's mouth. Letting all the emotions of the day wash off, his mind went blank. Nothing else mattered except what they were doing here. The world outside could slip away for a while.

Oliver's thrusts picked up, his hands pressing Nick's head down. He'd come if Nick let him, but that wasn't the plan. Nick tapped at the back of Oliver's hand and was released immediately.

"What?" Oliver gasped, lifting his chin. His eyes were glazed, and his hair was slipping loose of its band again.

Nick slid off his cock and licked gently at the head, eyes locked on Oliver the whole time, to let him know everything was okay.

"You were getting ahead of me." He moved down a bit farther, so he could mouth at Oliver's balls. He sucked one, then the other, between his lips.

Oliver laughed, setting his head back down, one hand coming to his chest. "I was excited."

Nick ran a finger down the thick vein of Oliver's cock, making him inhale. "I could tell." Nick traced the finger farther down around his sack, to stroke at the smooth skin of Oliver's taint.

"Yes." Oliver groaned as he planted his feet, spreading his knees to give Nick access.

"You don't want to rush this."

"Hell yes I do!"

Nick massaged at the spot gently, before moving on toward the tight ring of Oliver's ass. The muscle was pink, and it flexed as Nick approached. He sat up on his heels so he could see Oliver as he explored, watching for the little signals that would tell him what Oliver liked. They hadn't gotten this far before. There'd been groping, touching, mouths and fingers, but it had always been quick, focused on jerking or sucking each other off until they came. This, though. Oliver said at the beginning he was fussy about cleanliness when it came to butt play. They hadn't talked about other limits, so Nick was going to take this slow.

He toyed at Oliver's entrance, circling without getting too close, spurred on by his heavy breaths and whispered encouragement. Nick pressed small kisses to the inside of Oliver's knee, dragging his teeth along his thigh.

"Please," Oliver said. "I know you're having fun, but you need to move faster. I need you."

I need you. Like his texts the night before.

"Lube?" Nick asked. Oliver rolled, scrambling up the bed. He pulled open the nightstand drawer and blindly tossed a bottle and a couple condoms toward Nick, who had just enough time to get his hands up before he took a bottle of lube to the face for the second time. "You got those quickly."

"I was a Boy Scout."

"I thought you were a lawyer."

Oliver came back across the bed on his knees, stopping only when they faced each other. "I was a Boy Scout first. Then I was a lawyer. Both taught me a lot about careful preparation." He brushed his nose against Nick's, then laughed as Nick pulled him in for a kiss, their chests bumping together.

Nick's hard cock brushing against Oliver was a delightful distraction, and he had to focus on steady breaths to keep from wrapping his fist around them both and jacking them off until they blacked out. Instead, he gave Oliver a solid shove, and the taller man went over easily, laughing as he hit the mattress. The laughter died quickly as Nick popped the cap on the bottle and smeared lube over his fingers. "Ready?"

Oliver turned, pulling himself up to his hands and knees, and the sight made it hard to breathe. His ass was still perfect, the muscles at the base of his spine a tight triangle that created two small dimples as he settled into place.

"Jesus, you're beautiful," Nick said, smoothing his unlubed hand over the small of Oliver's back, unable to tear his eyes off the muscles shifting and bunching under his touch.

"Flattery will get you—" Oliver's reply was cut off by a yelp as Nick drizzled lube along his crack. "That was cruel!"

Nick laughed, pressing a kiss where his hand had been. "I gotta get my fun somewhere."

"If that's the most fun you're having, then I'm doing something wrong." He bent his head between his shoulders as Nick ran a slick finger through the lube, circling his anus, then pressing inside.

"Oh fuck!" Oliver gasped, and Nick retreated, waiting a moment before pushing again to the knuckle. Oliver clenched around him.

"Breathe." Nick kissed him again. His skin smelled like sweat and the faint chemical of the lube. "Or tell me if you change your mind."

"Not going to change my mind," Oliver growled as Nick slipped in farther.

Going slow was the best kind of torture. Oliver was so responsive, alternating between cursing and begging as Nick worked him open. His body bowed and flexed when Nick crooked his fingers, stroking over Oliver's prostate.

"Come on. Please." He squeezed around Nick, pressing back against his hand.

When Nick had three fingers moving back and forth comfortably, he pulled out, watching as Oliver's hole clenched. "You're ready."

"Of course I'm ready." Oliver glared at him over his shoulder. "You don't have to treat me like some breakable virgin."

Did he not know how nervous Nick was? He was turned on, sure, but this seemed big. They'd crossed so many lines, and fucking Oliver felt like the last one. There would be no coming back after this, no more distance to keep.

He ripped open the condom and rolled it on before applying more lube. He stroked himself, eyes on Oliver's ass.

"I might—" He bit his lip. "This might be fast. I haven't done this in a long time." He walked himself forward on his knees, lining himself up.

"That makes two of us—oh God." Oliver gasped as Nick pressed in. Nick went to ask what he meant. How long? But then the tight heat of Oliver swallowed him up, and it didn't matter. He didn't get more than the first inch before he had to pause and withdraw, pushing in again, even slower.

"You're so tight," he said.

Oliver shuddered. "You're so big. Jesus. I didn't know you'd be this—" The last word was choked off as Nick shifted, moving closer so he could press in deeper.

"That's nice of you to say." A guy never minded having someone compliment his equipment, but in this case, Oliver's tight grip on him spoke as much about someone who hadn't done this in a while as it did about the size of Nick's cock. "Do you need me to stop?"

"I need you to stop asking me that!" Oliver's growl turned from arousal to anger, and Nick drew slow circles on his back, humming and shushing like he might do with a nervous animal. When Oliver's muscles relaxed under Nick's hand, he started again.

Nick gritted his teeth as he eased in, trying to stay patient. His knuckles were white where he gripped Oliver's hips. They both groaned when he bottomed out, his pelvis pressed against Oliver's ass.

"You feel amazing." Nick fell forward, wrapping an arm around Oliver's chest as he kissed his shoulder. He pulled his cock back, then thrust in again. His eyes nearly rolled back in his head at the sensation, and Oliver trembled underneath him. Nick pumped his hips, adjusting to the range of motion, listening to the way Oliver's breaths turned ragged.

"So amazing," Nick said again. He traced wet, open-mouthed kisses on Oliver's skin as his hips found their rhythm.

"More," Oliver gasped. Under Nick's weight, he wouldn't be able to move very much, which left Nick completely in charge. The realization made his heart flutter, and he bit at the heavy muscle on Oliver's shoulder, making him moan.

"You want more?" He shifted, sitting back enough that he could thrust harder. When Oliver tried to take charge, pushing back, Nick slipped a hand in his hair and the other one over his shoulder, pulling tight so that Oliver's head was forced back.

"I didn't think you'd be like this," he said as he rocked inside Oliver, the heat melting his brain.

"Like what?" Oliver twisted his head so they could see each other. His hair hung loose around his face, and his blue eyes were dark, his mouth open. He looked . . .

Needy.

Nick's hips slapped against the back of Oliver's thighs as he pounded into him. He grunted with the exertion, but Oliver laughed as he fell to his elbows. The change raised his hips, and Nick found another fraction of an inch he didn't know was there, plunging himself deeper inside Oliver with every thrust.

"Yes," Oliver chanted it. "Yes, baby. I can take it. Yes."

"Don't call me that."

"Have to call you something."

Nick covered his body, really fucking him. The name didn't bother him as much as he thought it might. When Anya said it, he felt like he hadn't aged in twenty years, and not in a good way. *Babe. Sweetie.* The names they'd called each other at seventeen and trying to be grown up.

Coming from Oliver's mouth, it was different. A plea, like Oliver was claiming him. Welcoming him, even. Nick would let him have the name while Nick took control of everything else.

His thighs ached, and their bodies were slick where they pressed together. Nick drove Oliver into the bed, the pleasure trying to drown him. He hadn't known how much he needed this, and now he didn't know if he'd ever be able to stop.

Oliver's orgasm was a surprise. He bucked and clenched underneath Nick, who rode through it, feeling his own climax starting to build.

"You're so good," Oliver gasped beneath him. "So good. Come for me, baby. I want to hear it."

Fireworks. The orgasm rocked out of him, spilling into the condom while he shouted, clutching at Oliver's shoulders tight enough that there might be bruises in the morning. It seemed to go on forever, and then all his muscles forgot how to work at once. He flopped to the side, barely remembering to keep track of the condom as he pulled out of Oliver.

"You okay?" Oliver rolled over beside him. His hair was spread out all over the place, his chest heaving as he gasped for breath.

Nick thought about that question a long time before he answered. "Yeah." He gave Oliver a smile—the only thing he had left to offer. "Yeah, I'm good." So good. Just like Oliver had said. Nick didn't remember it ever being so good before. He didn't know if he'd be able to walk again anytime soon, and even if he could, he wasn't sure anything would ever convince him to leave this bed.

Later, hours maybe, the room was dark when Nick jerked awake. He wasn't certain how long he'd been asleep, or really what woke him up. He was warm, sprawled out in Oliver's big bed, the sheets still soft on his skin.

He was also alone. When he rolled, Oliver's body wasn't there for him to settle against. The spot where he should have been was cool.

Nick slid his hand over the mattress, until it connected with something solid.

"Hey." Oliver's voice was soft. "Go back to sleep."

"You okay?" Nick opened his eyes. The room was dark, but he could make out the shape of Oliver's tall frame, sitting at the edge of the bed.

"Fine."

"Insomnia?" Nick sat up and moved over the bed until he was wrapped around Oliver. He placed a hand over Oliver's chest and kissed his shoulder as Oliver laced their fingers together.

"I have to tell you something." Oliver tipped his head back to nuzzle at Nick's cheek.

"Yeah? What is it?" He leaned to the side to flip on the bedside lamp, but Oliver pulled him closer.

"Leave it off. I . . ." He lifted Nick's palm to his lips and kissed it. His beard tickled Nick's wrist. "Just leave it off."

This was serious. It had been the craziest day, and Nick prayed silently that whatever Oliver wanted to talk about wouldn't burst the bubble that had formed around them.

"Okay." He ran a hand through Oliver's hair, pulling it back over his shoulder. "I'm listening."

Another squeeze of his hand, then Oliver let out a shaky breath.

"I was with someone. For a long time."

"Like a boyfriend?"

"Like a . . . like a partner. His name was Cooper."

———

Oliver shivered. Just saying Cooper's name made his stomach twist.

But he needed to do this. Needed to tell someone, and Nick had done everything today but bare his soul, so it had to be now.

Sitting in the dark helped. Nick's warm, big body wrapped around his helped more.

I'm listening.

"We'd known each other forever."

"More high school sweethearts?" Nick's voice was a low rumble settling deep in Oliver's belly, grounding him.

"Not really. Family friends. We went to the same schools, all the way until we were called to the bar. Then I thought I was going to change the world by working at the public defender's office, and he thought he'd buy the world instead by climbing the ladder at a big corporate firm. We kept in touch, though, because he was like my brother except—well, you haven't met my actual brother but—"

Seb never liked Cooper. The familiarity, the years Cooper and Oliver had known each other, made it so easy when they first got together. But maybe those years also blinded Oliver to Cooper's flaws. He should have trusted his brother.

"You're not together anymore, though, right?"

Oliver nearly laughed at Nick's question. He'd accused Nick of the same thing, and knowing what he did now about Nick and his family, the idea was ridiculous. But waking up in the middle of the night to tell your new lover about your old partner was even more unheard of, so Nick's was a reasonable question.

"He broke up with me. Cheated on me, actually."

The words made his stomach turn again. He hadn't spoken them out loud, not in the ten months since that bullshit day when everything blew to pieces.

Nick's lips on his skin made him shiver, and he pulled Nick's arms tighter around his body.

"A long time ago?" Nick asked.

"Last summer."

August first. Eleven-thirty in the morning.

"What happened?"

Where did he even start?

"Oliver?"

"He was supposed to be here." His voice cracked.

What an awful thing to say. He'd just had some of the best sex of his life, and now he was telling the man who gave it to him about the man who was supposed to be in his bed.

"It's over between us," he said quickly. "Even if he showed up tomorrow with a hundred apologies, it would still be over." What Cooper broke between them could not be rebuilt, but it surprised Oliver how much it still hurt.

Nick rolled away, and Oliver nearly crumpled under the rejection, but then a strong hand gripped at his bicep, pulling him back down to bed, and he was wrapped up in Nick's arms. Oliver nearly cried with relief. Nick had cried, earlier, when he'd talked about his son. He might have thought Oliver hadn't seen him, but he had.

"We used to work so much. Eighty hours, a hundred hours, it didn't matter. It was the job, and we were good at it, and we got paid well to do it. And then, one night, we were up late, again, working on this case that we were never going to win. And it was enough. Too much. We'd been so successful, but it was only a matter of time before the job killed one of us." Nick's hand was stroking through his hair, and the motion kept him from spiraling too hard out into the sadness and regret that always filled him when he tried to piece together how he hadn't seen Cooper's betrayal coming.

"We made a plan. We worked so hard for it. Took two years before we decided we were ready. We took courses, built the business models. He wanted to call it Habeus Juice Us, but I said that was a terrible name." He laughed, then tilted his head to glance up to Nick, whose black eyes were bright in the dark room.

"I don't know what that means, but it doesn't sound very good."

"Lawyer puns. So is Pulpability, but it's better, if you ask me, and it's my business now, so . . ." He choked on the end of the thought. "We had a plan. We had leases signed and resignation letters written. And then . . ."

He trembled, walking into the board room where they'd agreed to meet afterwards. Turning in his resignation was one of the scariest things he'd ever done, but as soon as he walked out of that office, an incredible sense of lightness came over him. He'd set himself free. He and Cooper were free, finally, and they would—

"He changed his mind." Oliver traced circles in the dark hair on Nick's chest as he laughed bitterly. "Or, I guess, he got a better offer. Better job. Better boyfriend."

Cooper's face was miserable, but it didn't help the numb sensation spreading through Oliver's limbs. "I didn't know how to tell you. I've met someone. He . . . We're moving to San Francisco. There's a firm there, a job—"

The sick feeling in his stomach might have been real, or it might have been a memory of that moment.

"But . . ." Oliver's tongue felt too big in his mouth. "You're telling me now? You couldn't have told me yesterday, or this morning while we were driving to work? I just quit my job for you!" His career, the one he'd spent the last ten years building—he'd turned it to rubble.

"It's okay!" Cooper's smile was bright, like he believed his own bullshit. "It's okay. You can come work with us! I've already told the partners about you. They want to meet you!"

The knowledge that Cooper planned it all out, right down to the best way to soften the blow, hurt the most.

Nick pulled him close and kissed his forehead. "So he left you?"

"I loved you so much . . . I did this for you."

"I'm sorry, Ollie."

"Fuck off. I can do it on my own."

"I left him. And came here."

And met you.

He didn't say that last part aloud. It would mean too much.

Nick rolled them so Oliver was on his back and Nick was pressed on top of him. The intimacy in Oliver's dark room was a comfort. He hadn't felt this in a long time.

"I don't believe in violence," Nick said. "But if I ever meet him, I will beat the living shit out of him for you."

"I appreciate that. I know a good lawyer to represent you if it comes to that." Oliver kissed him, memorizing his taste. Before, when Nick pressed into him, his heavy cock stretching Oliver open, he'd nearly panicked. It hurt, but no more than it ever did, and it would go away if he could relax and let Nick in. But he hadn't bottomed in more than ten months and hadn't had sex with anyone not Cooper in nearly ten years. He hadn't expected letting someone new into his body to be so terrifying.

"I'm sorry he hurt you," Nick said, brushing a thumb over Oliver's lower lip.

No one had ever said that before. Mostly, Oliver had been met with questions, or Seb's endless poking. Nick hadn't known him before he'd come to Seacroft, but, more than that, no one else knew the whole story. Telling it had been too much for Oliver, an admission of failure. Amidst all the questions that followed when he quit his job and announced his holistic lifestyle makeover, he couldn't admit his plan had fallen apart before he'd even packed up his desk at the firm. Better to soldier on like he'd always meant to go it alone. Except now he was here by himself, with no option but to succeed and fewer and fewer ways to make it happen.

He pressed himself closer to Nick, seeking comfort. How could he have thought he was going to let Nick go? "You should know it might be hard for me, sometimes. I want to trust you. I want to find out what this thing is between us. But sometimes—like today—it might be hard for me, and I need you to know why."

Nick kissed him again, deeper this time. His hands were in Oliver's hair. He hadn't considered this element when he'd let it grow, but Nick's fascination was exciting. Cooper had never touched him like that—the opportunity hadn't been there—and now he was glad to have something that was theirs. His and Nick's.

"We'll take it slow." Nick's kisses moved to Oliver's throat, and his body responded.

"Not that slow." His hips shifted, his cock coming to alertness like he was still in his twenties, and he laughed against Nick's lips.

Letting someone new into his body had been difficult. Letting someone new into his heart would be even harder.

For Nick, though, he was willing to try.

15

*O*liver's whole body dragged by the time he set up for the next workshop at Pulpability. Nick had spent the rest of the weekend with him, and, well, neither of them got much sleep. Letting Nick go had been hard as he put his clothes back on—again—and left for his shift. Oliver crashed early and slept through the night—something he almost never did. He woke in the morning to find a series of grumpy mid-shift texts from Nick about how tired he was and why he blamed Oliver for all of it. Oliver only felt guilty long enough to get to the store where he found Nick hanging out by the door.

"What are you doing here?"

"Wanted to see you. It'll be a few days now until we can really see each other, but I've got to drive Hayden to school in another hour, so there's no point in going home too soon. I'll want to fall asleep." He followed closely behind Oliver, who let them into the store.

Inside, when Oliver expected to be mauled after twelve hours of not being together, Nick was gentle. Soft touches, brief kisses. Oliver blended him a kale and coconut water smoothie, which he raised an eyebrow at but drank.

"That wasn't bad." Oliver kissed away the pale green smear

on his lip. "I could have made you something nicer than this," he said, a hand on the wobbly bar chairs that Oliver and Seb had assembled.

"You could?"

Nick gave him a shy smile. Oliver was falling so hard for Nick's odd dichotomy: the imposing man who loomed and could use his size to intimidate if he needed to, and the soft-spoken person inside who did everything he could for his family. And made chairs, apparently.

"I've got a workshop at home." Nick said. "It's not fancy, but if you needed something, I could probably make it."

Oliver wanted to say yes. He wanted to take Nick up on his offer. But the chairs he had were fine, more than fine considering how little use they got. And he'd want to pay Nick for his work, and that wasn't an option at the moment.

He settled for a kiss at the corner of Nick's mouth, one that slowly moved to the center and turned fiery. Never mind that they were standing in the middle of the shop, in full view of anyone who might walk by. No one was around this early in the morning.

"I should go," Nick said eventually. He trailed his hands in Oliver's hair.

"I'll see you later?"

"I'll text when I'm going on my break tonight."

That was barely enough, but still the best they could do.

The shop was always quiet on Mondays, but today seemed especially so. Oliver tried to stay productive. The market issue was still in play, so he made some calls and sent some emails to other vendors to ask about sourcing new produce. It largely came to nothing. He needed organic sources, which were rare in the area.

At three, the shop phone rang. Oliver almost jumped out of his skin. He'd nearly forgotten he'd had a landline hooked up since no one ever called it.

"Good afternoon, Pulpability!" He tried to sound upbeat, even though he hadn't spoken to anyone in hours.

"Ollie?"

He froze, grip tightening on the handset.

"What do you want?"

"Are you sober?" Cooper's voice was flat, and Oliver kept silent, rather than rising to Cooper's easy bait. "Are we going to have a reasonable conversation this time?"

Oliver needed a cigarette. He'd quit in the fall, but maybe it was time to start again. "Probably not."

"How have you been?"

"Fuck you." He slammed the phone down in its cradle. With no one to see how he shook, he braced himself on the counter. He needed to get beyond this. Cooper was his past. Nick might be his future, but even if Oliver was on his own again by the end of the summer, he had to get his emotions under wraps.

And why the fuck was he calling anyway? They'd said everything that needed to be said months ago.

He turned the sign on the shop door over at six, which seemed pointless because no one appeared to care that he'd been open, and also because he was going to turn it back over again in an hour. He'd scheduled another workshop that night, but he wasn't optimistic about the attendance. On Saturday, he'd been too worked up over Nick and the sudden appearance of his family at the market, but he'd managed to hand out a few flyers.

Seb and Martin weren't even coming for moral support. Martin texted midday to say Seb had a line on someone selling old books, and they were going out of town for a few days.

In the end, the full and total attendance of Oliver's workshop was Avery. He sat, hands clasped on the counter, eyes wide in anticipation, bright red hair sticking up in fiery tufts from his head.

"You didn't need to come," Oliver said with a smile. "I was planning to give the same talk as last time."

"Oh, I don't mind!" Avery wiggled in his seat like a puppy. "I'm sure there was stuff I missed." He rummaged through a satchel at his feet and pulled out a tablet and a small keyboard. He sat, shoulders square, fingers poised on the keys, like a stenographer ready to take Oliver's testimony.

"You really don't need to do that." Oliver had handouts for anyone who came and wanted something to refer back to, but then again, Avery probably laminated his from last time.

Oliver sighed and pulled a few bottles of juice from the fridge. He popped the top on his and clinked the side of Avery's. "Cheers. It's on the house."

"Really?" Avery smiled at him like he'd given the kid a medal.

"Sure. Why not? You made the effort to be here. Normally, I'd pass out small samples to everyone, but since it's you and me, might as well go for the full meal deal, right?"

Avery frowned. "But you said I couldn't use this as a meal replacement."

"What?" Oliver swallowed his *Beet the Rap*. "No. I mean. Yes. You can't use this as a meal replacement. That's not what I meant, I—" He smiled. "I'm glad you're here. Thanks for coming."

Avery gave him another wide smile, then took a sip of his juice. He set the bottle down on the counter, turning it slowly in his hand. "How many of these do you need to sell a day to cover your costs?"

Oliver snorted. He gestured at the still largely full fridge. "More than that."

"Do you have other revenue streams?" Avery asked, flushing when Oliver turned his attention back toward him. "Sorry. Accountant. It's hard to shut my brain off sometimes."

"The coaching packages are supposed to be where we make the money. The juice was meant to act as a sort of loss leader, but . . ." Admitting Avery was his only current coaching client was embarrassing.

"They're expensive for a loss leader."

Oliver shrugged. He could have explained about the cost of organic produce, or the limitations of cold-pressing, but the projections he and Cooper had put together were sound.

They hadn't accounted for the general apathy the town felt toward their offerings. All of Oliver's research said the demographics in Seacroft were right for a small business like this, and he still didn't know where he'd gone wrong. The market was a gamble, but even there, he hadn't expected to have his knees cut out from by the board before the season even got into full swing.

"If you've got any suggestions, I'm all ears."

That bright smile flashed again, like flipping on a light in a dark room. Avery turned back to his tablet, pulling up a new program. He typed, fingers moving quickly over the keys.

"This is rough, but based on standard utility rates in town, and average rents—you know the rents are so much cheaper if you're a block north of here right? I mean, this is where the tourists hit first in the summer, but if you wanted to manage your costs better—" His words were punctuated by more vigorous typing. "And the cost of an industrial juice press." He glanced up at Oliver, his freckles disappearing under splotches of red. "I looked it up. Thought about buying one for me, but dude, those things aren't cheap!"

Oliver was very aware. Finding a model he and Cooper liked at a cost they could afford slowed down their original plans to start the business. They'd argued for a long time over how much to charge to make the investment back—and that was before the first press died in a month. Pulpability's price point reflected the product he was offering and costs to make it, but anyone who wandered in expecting an alternative to mass-produced iced tea walked away disappointed.

"Do you ever think about making anything else?" Avery asked as he continued to run numbers.

"Like what?"

Avery rummaged in his bag again, pulling out a few crumpled pages. He set them on the counter, smoothing out the wrinkles. "If there was time, I was going to ask you if you thought these would fit in my meal plan. I saw them on Damian Marshall's Instagram yesterday. He says they're totally the best thing to make for a quick snack. Maybe you could make something like this and sell them here? It would be cheaper than the juice. Might get people to buy more."

Was making something from a movie star's Instagram considered a celebrity endorsement? That was pretty well what he needed to get more people to come into the shop, but Oliver leaned over Avery's shoulder to read what he'd brought, recipes for what appeared to be vegan baking.

"What's a flax egg?" he asked.

Avery shrugged and turned his head, the top of his hair brushing against Oliver's arm. He had to step back so they could see each other at a better angle. "But what do you think? This one is for chocolate chip cookies. People like cookies! And cocoa energy balls. Those sound good, right?"

"I'm not much of a baker."

"Well, you're going to have to do something." Avery's eyes turned into saucers as soon as he said it, and he slapped a hand over his mouth. "Sorry," he said between his fingers. "Sorry. I work with a lot of businesses in town, though. I know the signs when one is struggling and . . ." He gestured around them at the empty chairs.

Oliver eyed him. "How old are you?"

"Twenty-five, why?"

That was unexpected. With his uncombed hair and scruffy jeans, he really looked like he was barely out of college.

Oliver read over the recipes again. He pulled out the ones for the energy balls and the cookies. "If I got together numbers for costs of raw materials and give you better information on my fixed overhead, could you run some projections for me?"

Avery clapped his hands, whole body shaking. "Definitely! When do you need them by?"

Oliver laughed. "Let me get the numbers first."

"Yeah, of course! But, I mean, I could do them tomorrow! You could be running by the weekend! And you can pay me in juice!" Avery lifted his bottle.

"And energy balls?" Oliver fought against the excitement. Wait until Nick heard he was getting into the baking business.

———

The week stretched on endlessly. Hayden missed his second period class on Tuesday, so the school decided to pull him out of his classes, and he was now working independently in the guidance counselor's office instead, the equivalent of solitary confinement. The sentence made him even more miserable to be around in the evenings.

Anya's birthday was coming, and she and Nick arranged she would take a few days away with girlfriends while Nick spent all weekend at home with Hayden. He was happy to do it for her, even if he wouldn't get to see Oliver. So who could blame him if he nearly tore the door off its hinges when he showed up at Oliver's house on Thursday evening?

"Is that you?" Oliver asked, somewhere further inside.

"It's me."

"How's it going?"

"Caramel." The code word was a bit redundant, now their cards were all on the table, but despite the weekend before, Nick found he still didn't want to talk too much about Hayden. Maybe they'd get there one day, or maybe Hayden would finally get his shit together, but right now, Nick wanted to be with Oliver.

He shrugged out of his jacket and hung it in the closet, then pulled off his shirt. Oliver had sent seriously distracting texts the night before on Nick's break. The pent-up frustration was burning him from the inside out, and he needed relief now. "I want you to take your clothes off if you haven't already."

Oliver's warm laugh came down the hall. "I'm a bit busy right now."

"Doesn't matter." Nick undid his belt as he came into the living room. Oliver was at the far end, in the kitchen, with his back to him. "Whatever you're doing, it can wait."

"It really can't. I don't want these balls to dry out."

"These what?" Nick wrapped his arms around Oliver, pushing aside his ponytail to plant a kiss on the back of his neck.

Oliver turned his head to nuzzle at him, but didn't stop working, his hands turning in tight circles. "Energy balls. Or that's what they're supposed to be, anyway."

Nick rested his chin on Oliver's shoulder. Oliver didn't acknowledge his touch, instead growling as something brown and lumpy like a small turd fell out of his hands and landed on the counter, breaking apart into clumps.

"I hate to tell you." Nick slid an arm around Oliver to poke at it, watching as it crumbled even more under his finger to reveal tiny bits of coconut. "But these don't look like something a person should eat."

Oliver sighed, sagging back against him. That part, at least, Nick could get on board with. He rubbed his hands over Oliver's stomach as he kissed from the base of his skull around to his ear. His cock hardened in his pants, and whatever Oliver's cooking plans were, Nick wasn't in the mood to be patient.

"They're energy balls. Cocoa, dates, ground cashews, some other stuff, I don't know. They're supposed to be these little things you can pop in your mouth, but they—" He gathered up the remains of the one he'd dropped, squishing it together.

When he placed it back down, it fell apart again. "They just disintegrate."

"Worry about it later." Nick slipped his hands lower, gratified when Oliver groaned and arched against him. He turned, cupping Nick's face as he pulled him into a kiss. Oliver's texts last night included detailed descriptions of everything he would do with his mouth if Nick were there. Looked like he hadn't forgotten about that. Nick certainly hadn't.

Oliver pulled back, and then his eyes widened. "Oh no!" He laughed, stepping all the way back so he leaned against the counter.

"What?" Nick frowned. Oliver pointed at him, but then doubled over, howling. "What is it?" Nick's erection was fading at the sudden interruption, and he was not happy about it.

Oliver straightened. He went to wipe tears from his eyes, but then stopped, howling louder.

"What's so funny?" Despite his irritation, Nick was fighting laughter at the glee on Oliver's face.

Oliver shook his head. He tried to speak, but it came out as a snort, so instead, he held up his hands, palms out.

They were brown, dark brown. The color of chocolate.

Or cocoa.

"No!" Nick slapped a hand down his face and ran down the hall. Sure enough, his reflection in the bathroom mirror showed more or less hand-shaped smears of brown on both his cheeks.

Somewhere behind him, Oliver let out a weak giggle. "I'm so sorry. I didn't know they'd make such a mess."

Nick growled. "You are in so much trouble." His belt was still open, so he undid his pants and stripped out of everything.

"I'm sorry!" Oliver said again, but then his eyes widened as Nick came out of the bathroom, naked and horny.

"You're sorry?"

Oliver licked his lips and gave him a once-over. Nick didn't even bother to hide his preening. His dick was getting back with the program, and Oliver was going to do the same very soon.

Nick stopped when they were inches apart. Oliver's eyes crinkled at the corners as he smiled. Nick had noticed his hair first, but Oliver's smile would always be impossible to resist.

"You're making a mess." He lifted one of Oliver's hands and sucked a finger into his mouth, tongue circling around it. Oliver gasped and stepped the remaining distance between them so their bodies were pressed together.

"I can get a—" He didn't get to finish the sentence because Nick swallowed it in a brutal kiss. He had waited too many hours for this, and he was done.

Their mouths together tasted like cocoa and sweetness.

"Been sampling as you work?" Nick asked as he ground against Oliver's hip.

"I was going to try selling them at the shop. I needed to know if—oh." Oliver gasped as Nick put two more of his fingers between his lips, licking, eyes on Oliver's blue ones the whole time.

"Later." He took Oliver's hands in his and dragged them over his bare chest. They left brown streaks over his skin and hair. "You've made a mess, and I need you to clean it up."

"I'll get a cloth." Oliver didn't move, instead choosing to go back to kissing. Coming to this man's house and having this— taking this—was so hot. Nick pulled Oliver's hair loose, grabbing thick fistfuls and pulling until Oliver released his mouth. His lips were parted, his breathing ragged.

"I think we're past cloths." Nick was working fast, undoing Oliver's jeans and pushing them down. "The only way to fix this is a shower, and fortunately, you have a big one."

"Room for two." Oliver's hips bucked as Nick cupped him through his boxer briefs. He slipped a cocoa-coated finger in his mouth one more time, loving the way Oliver hissed and flexed against him.

"Better get started."

Later, cleaner, they lay wrapped around each other in Oliver's big bed. Nick's edge was gone, thanks to Oliver's expert hands and the sweet heat of his mouth.

"I'm going to be busy this weekend," Nick said.

Oliver lifted his head, the wet tips of his hair tickling at Nick's skin. "All weekend?"

The disappointed tone made something happy bubble up in Nick's chest. "Anya's going away for the weekend. It's her birthday. The last few weeks have—she needs some time away. But it means I'm going to be home all weekend supervising Hayden."

Supervising. What a stupid word. Hayden would probably spend the whole weekend in his room.

"Do you—" Oliver hesitated, tracing kisses down Nick's chest. He paused at the bottom of his sternum, then glanced up. "I could look at his case, if you want? See if there's anything that you could use in his favor at the next court date. It's been a long time since I did a criminal case, but I could—"

Nick silenced him with a kiss, then ran a hand through Oliver's hair, cool and slick under his fingers. The room was dark, but he hoped Oliver could see his smile. "That's really good of you. I'm not sure there's much point, though. Hayden isn't doing anything to help himself. He's still having problems at school. It's hard to argue against that. If anything, his behavior is getting worse."

"Is there a reason?"

Nick shook his head and pulled Oliver up to kiss him. No one had offered to help them in such a long time. "He's fifteen? He thinks everyone is out to get him. I don't know. Can we not talk about this right now? I just needed you to know I'll be busy this weekend."

Oliver rolled them so they were spooned together and then pulled the blankets up around them. The house was quiet, and Oliver's hands running gently over Nick's body made him relax.

Behind him, though, Oliver pressed his hardening cock against Nick's ass.

"Again?" Nick groaned, but he couldn't help his body's response as he rocked back.

Oliver tweaked one of Nick's nipples before pushing a leg between his thighs.

"Better maximize the time we have tonight then, don't you think?"

16

*O*liver dreaded the market that Saturday. His experiments in vegan baking had been an epic disaster: the energy balls dry and crumbly, the cookies hard enough to sharpen the blades on the juicer.

He set up the tables, the bins, the bags of ice, and tried to ignore the anxious feeling telling him this exercise was becoming increasingly pointless. It didn't help that Nick's car was nowhere to be seen, and Hayden wasn't among the volunteers directing parking. Oliver didn't know what he would have done if they were there; he had to work, and he and Nick couldn't exactly make out at his stall. He was still trying to smooth things over with the market board. Flaunting his gratuitously homosexual life and his hot boyfriend in front of them wouldn't help.

Except that was precisely what he wanted to do. The morning wore on, and fewer and fewer people stopped by. He offered workshop flyers with less than his usual enthusiasm, and he didn't flinch when not many people took them. It didn't matter. He wanted to see Nick.

This couldn't be healthy, right? They'd only known each

other a little while, and though the sex was great, Oliver was getting very attached.

"Hey there!" A familiar voice made Oliver pop his head up. Deep circles sagged beneath Avery's eyes, and his hair was plastered to his forehead in greasy streaks, but his smile was, as always, electric.

Oliver returned the smile as he set his phone down. "Good morning! Late night?"

Avery frowned, but then started like he'd been shocked and scrubbed his fingers in his hair. "Yeah, I guess you could say that. There's a tournament this weekend."

"A tournament?"

"E-sports." He waited for a reply, but Oliver shook his head. "Video games! It's the world championships of *Winterlands* this weekend!"

Oliver had heard about those kinds of things, but didn't know much. "And you're playing?"

Avery laughed. "No! I'm good, but I'm not that good. Maybe someday, though."

"So you were up all night watching someone play video games?"

"Not just someone. Kevin Chan! He's the champion! Undefeated for the last fourteen months!"

"And they play all night?"

"Well, I do. Sometimes." Avery laughed self-consciously. "But no. The tournament's in South Korea this year, so the time is weird. It's totally worth it, though! How's it going here?"

"Good!" He forced a cheery expression. "Bit quiet, but they don't know about my new product line."

Avery's eyes widened. "So you're going to do it?"

"Just working out a few recipe tweaks." Like how to make the energy balls ball-shaped and how to make the cookies more chewable than cinderblocks.

Avery clapped his hands as he did a happy dance on the

spot. "That's amazing. You're totally going to let me help you with the pricing and the financials, right?"

"Absolutely." Oliver was pushing the optimism so hard, his face felt like it might crack.

Avery gave him another happy hop. The enthusiasm radiating off him was contagious.

Oliver could still succeed.

But when the market wrapped up for the day, Oliver found himself staring down the barrel of twenty-four hours at home alone. He'd made plans to have brunch with Seb and Martin the following day, but didn't want to tread on their hospitality more than that.

Oliver didn't know why being at loose ends bothered him. He had work to do—in particular he promised the market board a progress report, but so far his progress had all been backwards —and he'd spent plenty of weekends on his own since coming to Seacroft.

But that had been before Nick.

By six o'clock, he gave it up for a hopeless cause. Nick was stuck at home all weekend, and Oliver wanted to see him, so he'd have to go there.

He shouldn't go empty-handed, though.

By seven o'clock, he pulled the SUV into the driveway behind PRTYGRL. He had a pizza and six-packs of beer and soda on the passenger seat. Showing up like this was presumptuous, but a food-based peace offering had to help and, worst case scenario, they ate the pizza, and Oliver went home.

Nick's eyes widened when he opened the door.

"Hi!"

"Hi."

"What are—" He glanced over his shoulder. "What are you doing here?"

Uncertainty gripped at Oliver's heart, but he was here; he might as well bluff his way through it. He lifted the pizza and drinks. "I brought dinner. I hope that's okay." Behind Nick, Oliver caught a glimpse of a small messy kitchen, but no sign of anyone else.

Nick's frown broke into a grin, and the tension in Oliver's shoulders relaxed.

"Yeah. Yeah, that's great! We were just debating what to have for dinner." He pulled the door wider, and Oliver stepped inside. He leaned in to kiss Nick, but paused when Nick made a soft, strangled noise. Embarrassed, he stepped back again.

"Sorry. That was a bad idea. I . . ." He dropped his voice even lower. "I wanted to see you."

Nick studied him, then exhaled slowly. When he spoke, he was just as quiet. "It's fine. I'm glad to see you too. I—" Another check over his shoulder. "Hayden's charging and it's not always his finest time of day." He squeezed Oliver's shoulder, the touch making him relax even more. "But come on in! Hayden!"

"What?" The question came from another room, farther back in the house, and rang with adolescent boredom.

"Dinner's here!" He grabbed a few plates from the cupboard, then led Oliver down a narrow hall.

Hayden was in the living room, sprawled on an old green and beige couch. He looked exactly like the weekend before, except for the wire trailing from the heavy black device strapped around his ankle to the floor and behind the leg of the couch. When Hayden's eyes met Oliver's, Hayden straightened and pulled down the cuff of his sweat pants to cover the bracelet.

"Who are you?" He had dark eyes like Nick's.

"This is my friend, Oliver." He hesitated for the smallest moment before he said *friend.*

Oliver grinned. "Hey there! We met at the market."

Hayden's expression didn't show any recognition.

"And he brought pizza." Nick put the drinks and plates on the coffee table.

Pizza got his attention. Oliver tried not to be insulted. He'd been fifteen once.

Hayden appeared to realize Oliver was still watching him and puffed out his chest. "What kind of pizza?"

"I didn't know what kind you guys liked, so I got a meat supreme, half with mushrooms."

Nick, who had gone back to the kitchen and returned with paper napkins and a bottle opener, snorted. "You know, for a guy who was making energy balls and sells beet juice for a living, I don't think a meat supreme pizza fits the lifestyle." He handed Hayden a soda and took the spot on the couch next to him.

"Everyone is entitled to a cheat day from time to time."

Hayden rolled his eyes, but he didn't complain when Oliver flipped open the pizza box. Instead, he slid across the couch, the leg with the tracking bracelet dragging behind him, and grabbed three slices, dumping the first two onto a plate and putting the third one in his mouth before he'd even gotten back to his seat.

"Hey," Nick said. "Oliver is our guest. You should have let him take the first slice."

Hayden side-eyed his dad hard.

"It's fine." Oliver took a slice and grabbed a beer, then settled himself in the faded blue armchair.

"We were twenty minutes into this movie." Nick used his own pizza slice to gesture at the TV. "But we could put something else on."

"No, we can't!" Hayden said mid-bite.

"No, I've seen this. Keep watching, I don't mind." Oliver hadn't actually seen it, but he was just glad to be there and not at home alone for the evening.

Nick gave him a grateful smile, whether he knew Oliver was lying or not. They settled down to watch.

The situation was trickier than expected. Oliver hadn't taken the time to plan out what might happen once he showed up unannounced at Nick's. Obviously, he had things he'd *like* to have happen, but most of them involved nudity and Nick's hands in his hair. He'd known, of course, Hayden would be there, so the X-rated stuff would have to wait, but he hadn't considered that Hayden would literally be tethered to the couch, unable to give them any kind of space or privacy. And why would he? As far as Hayden knew, Oliver was some weird guy his dad knew from the market who randomly showed up with pizza.

Being in the same room as Nick and not touching him was almost painful. Oliver considered texting him, like they did when Nick was working, but that would be unfair. And Hayden was probably one of those kids as tied to his phone as to the thing on his ankle. If they started sending dirty texts to each other, separated by only a few feet, Hayden would notice.

The movie took forever, and Oliver was nearly ready to crawl out of his skin, but then suddenly, as mutants were about to destroy New York City, a beep sounded on the other side of the couch, and Hayden shot to his feet like he'd been bitten. He scrambled, hopping on one foot, and flung the cable away from his leg. Oliver and Nick were silent as he stumbled out of the living room, and shortly afterward a door slammed farther down the hall.

On the TV, the Empire State Building collapsed.

"Guess he wasn't enjoying the movie," Oliver said.

Nick's mouth quirked up on one side, and he nodded. "He doesn't like being told what to do, and the tracker basically tells him what to do all the time. The two hours it takes to charge are the worst." His head lolled on the back of the couch, and he rolled it lazily toward Oliver with a smile that made his heart speed up.

"I'm sorry if I made it awkward tonight," he said, at the same time Nick said, "I'm glad you're here."

They sat, smiling at each other like a couple of lovesick

idiots, until footsteps stomped back up the hall. Hayden lurked in the doorway, hands on hips.

"I need to make a phone call."

"To who?" Seeing Nick in his role as a father was disconcerting. His tone of voice held an authority that made Oliver shiver.

Hayden did not appear to be as impressed, instead sighing dramatically. "To Carson. I have to ask him about some homework."

Nick raised an eyebrow. "You're doing homework on a Saturday night?"

"What else am I supposed to do?" Hayden shouted. Nick glared at him until his gaze dropped. "Sorry. Please, it's important."

Nick pulled his phone out of his pocket and handed it to Hayden. "Five minutes."

Hayden sighed again, but he took the phone and stomped back up the hall.

Nick winced as the door slammed. "Sorry. It's one of the terms of his house arrest. He can't use the internet without parental supervision, and he's not allowed to own a phone. Anya and I are responsible for every call he makes, so we try to keep them short."

That was all fairly typical in a cyberbullying case. "So he's discovered a passion for reading?"

Nick laughed. "It's amazing how little there is to do when you're fifteen and can't use the internet. He used to be a pretty good artist. Anya bought him a bunch of pencils and sketch pads for his birthday this winter, but I don't think he uses them much."

"What happened to the kid he was bullying? There must have been a restraining order when they're at school."

"Anya said the kid's parents sent him to a private boarding school." He stretched his arms over his head. "Sometimes I think we should have found a place like that for Hayden too, somewhere with more structure and control, but it's not like we could afford it, or like any of those fancy places would take a kid with a record." Nick stood, checking his watch. "In any case, we're wasting time."

"For what?" Oliver grinned as Nick crawled into his lap.

"He'll milk every second out of that phone call he can. I usually have to go knock on the door and tell him to wrap it up." Nick bent to kiss Oliver, tongue demanding entrance. "He's technically only got four minutes to go, but I'll look the other way if he stretches it to six."

Oliver laughed, hands settling on Nick's hips. "That's very generous of you."

"Dad of the year." He made quick work of the band in Oliver's hair.

"I missed you."

"I'm glad you came."

———

Nick should have been considered a superhero for the strength it took to drag himself off Oliver before things got too far along. They were both panting, and Oliver's hands were twisted in Nick's shirt when he finally pulled back.

"Time's up."

Oliver narrowed his eyes. "Did you do that on purpose?"

"No, I accidentally fell on top of you with my mouth."

"You know what I meant." Oliver shoved at his chest, and Nick stumbled to his feet, laughing. Oliver turning up at the door had been a shock. Nick had actually forgotten that Oliver knew where he lived. And then came the unexpected panic that *my boyfriend* was somehow tattooed on Oliver's forehead in an invisible ink that only Hayden could see. Of course, Hayden didn't appear to notice or care one way or the other. He'd inhaled more than half the pizza and disappeared into his room as soon as the charging was done.

Just a typical Saturday night at their house.

"Do you need to go get your phone?" Oliver asked. His lips were puffy, and he smirked as he pulled his hair back into place.

"What?" Nick adjusted his pants. If that had been six minutes of kissing, he'd gotten worked up embarrassingly quickly.

"Your phone? You said time's up. If you were kidding—" Oliver stood and tugged Nick forward by his belt loops, "—then I'm happy to pick up where we left off."

Nick laughed, stepping back again, and Oliver let him go.

"One sec." Nick went down the hall and knocked on the door.

"Yeah?"

"Are you off the phone?"

"Almost."

Nick glanced down the hall. The routines of Hayden's confinement had become everyday to Nick, but having Oliver in the house made him self-conscious. The empty hallway behind him was a relief. Whatever Oliver thought about their situation, he was at least giving Nick some privacy by staying in the living room. "Come on, buddy. Time's up. You know the rules."

Hayden yanked the door open and shoved the phone through the opening wordlessly. Nick took it, met with another slamming door before he had a chance to say anything else. Out of habit, he checked the call log. One call, lasting five minutes. He added the contact as "Carson," in case the probation officer did a spot check on his next home visit.

Oliver was on the couch when he came back to the living room. Nick sat next to him, careful to leave enough space that if Hayden walked by on his way to the kitchen, nothing would look suspicious.

"Everything okay?" Oliver asked.

"Fine. Yeah." He stuffed the phone in his pocket.

"You know I'd be happy to help you guys, right? When is his next court date?"

Nick waved him off. "I don't want to talk about that. Let's talk about something else. How are you? How was the market today?"

Oliver watched him for a second longer, but Nick held his ground. He appreciated Oliver's offer, but only Hayden falling in line would get his family out of this.

"It was fine." Oliver's smile was tight, like he was disappointed Nick had turned him down. "There's this guy, Avery. He's turning into my best customer, and I think now he wants to be my business partner too."

Nick growled. "Do I need to be jealous?"

"Of Avery?" Oliver laughed. "Not in the slightest. He's sweet, but he doesn't hold a candle to you."

"Thanks." Nick didn't get a chance to say much else, because Oliver was up and on Nick's body to kiss him. Nick groaned under Oliver's lips as their kiss got wet and messy. It should have been such a turn-on, to have his man spread across him, but up the hall . . .

"Stop," Nick whispered, pushing at Oliver's chest.

Oliver slunk back to his side of the couch and tugged at an earlobe. "Sorry. I'm not used to having to behave myself around you."

"Trust me." Nick focused on breathing slowly as arousal continued to burn through him. "I know the feeling."

"Do you want me to go?"

Not at all. Anya had left first thing that morning, and Nick hadn't expected how housebound he would feel once she and her friends pulled out of the driveway. Suddenly, everything he wanted to do involved leaving the house. Having Oliver here was a welcome distraction, even if behaving themselves for the sake of the teenager was nearly impossible.

"Come on." Nick stood and pulled Oliver to his feet.

"Where are we going?"

Somewhere with no couches and no beds.

"I'll give you the tour."

The tour was brief at best. The house wasn't very big, and Hayden and Anya's rooms were off-limits. The tour of Nick's bedroom was further limited for the sake of his paper-thin composure. Before he knew it, they were back in the kitchen.

"I keep meaning to refinish the cabinets." He ran a hand over the old oak doors. They had been there since he and Anya had moved in, and the finish was chipped and peeling around the edges. He mentioned it mostly to draw Oliver's attention away from the dirty dishes stacked up by the sink.

"Is that something you know how to do?" Oliver said.

"The cabinets? Sure. Sand them down, apply some stain. It would only take me a weekend."

Oliver's forehead wrinkled. "I've never been very handy. I come from a family of artists and intellectuals. I can change a lightbulb and empty a lint trap. After that, I hire a professional."

Nick grinned. "I come from a family of carpenters and construction workers. We are the professionals. You'd think someone with those skills would have a nicer house." With Oliver in the space, Nick was so aware of every deficiency, every corner and surface that could have been repaired or replaced over the years.

Oliver squeezed his hand. "I like your house. It feels settled. Lived in."

"It's a far cry from your place. Nothing's been upgraded here in ten years at least."

"I don't care about that. I care about the people who live here."

Nick bit his lip. He cared about Oliver. So much. Having him in this house, so close, was almost painful, because Nick couldn't have him, not like he wanted, while Hayden was here.

"You told me you could have made me stools for the shop. Were you serious about that?" Oliver ran a hand over the back of one of the old spindled chairs at the table. His strong fingers slid around the curves like they slid over Nick's body sometimes, and just the sight of it made him shudder. Whether he knew it or not, Oliver was doing nothing for Nick's self-control.

What if...

"Come with me." Nick linked a finger around Oliver's pinkie, because touching more of him than that ran the very real risk of Nick cracking right there and pawing at Oliver's clothes like an animal.

Oliver followed willingly, his smile growing like Nick's. "Where are we going?"

"The basement."

Oliver's voice dropped to a whisper. "For a little privacy?"

Was Nick that transparent? "Keep it together. I want to show you my workshop."

"You know I have a thing for Santa, don't you?" Oliver said, not as quiet this time.

"Shh!" Nick could barely control his laughter as he pulled Oliver toward the stairs. "I do not need to know about your weird fetishes."

Oliver caught him as they hit the landing and kissed him hard. "I really think you do."

Nick shook his head and continued the rest of the way downstairs.

———

The basement was damp and largely unfinished, with concrete walls and floors. The ceilings were low too, especially for Oliver. Nick's head was only a few inches below it, and he seemed to know exactly where to duck to avoid beams and exposed pipes. Oliver wasn't quite that lucky, but he only managed to hurt himself once, on the doorway that led into a small room in the back.

"You okay?" Nick asked.

"I'll be fine." He blinked a few more times to clear the tears from his eyes, and then blinked more as he took in what he was seeing.

"What do you think?" Nick picked up a long smooth piece of wood and flipped it between his fingers. As it settled in his hand, Oliver realized it was a spindle, like the kind in the backs of the chairs upstairs.

"You made that?" Oliver reached for it. The wood was nearly soft under his fingers, unvarnished, but sanded so fine it hardly needed it.

"It's my dad's old lathe." Nick rested a hand on a heavy piece of machinery mounted on a workbench. "All his stuff, actually. It's been down here since we moved in, but I only started playing around with it again in the last few years."

"What do you make?"

"Nothing much. I made new spindles for the kitchen chairs last winter. And the desk in Hayden's room. You didn't see it, but I made that last year, before they moved in." He smiled, a bright unrestrained smile. "The drawers nearly killed me. Took me four tries before I could get them all to sit flush."

"You made your son a desk?" Oliver couldn't explain how impressed he was. Nick said he was still figuring out how to be a father to Hayden. A handmade desk didn't build a relationship, but as a gift, it was precious.

"It was the only room it fit in when I was done." Nick scratched at his chin. "I wish I could say it motivated Hayden to work harder at school, but ... " He shrugged.

It always came back to that, didn't it? The workshop went quiet, and between the low basement ceilings and the stuffy air in the windowless room, the whole weight of the house and its inhabitants silently pressed down on Oliver. He hadn't realized it before, but Nick's little refuge made it clear how much he—and probably Anya too—was on house arrest, right along with their son.

"Do you ever think about making things to sell?" Oliver asked, trying not to dwell on the other thought. Nick didn't like talking about it, and while Oliver was still sure he could help, he wanted to be what Nick needed more, even if that was someone to admire his furniture.

Nick shook his head. "No. I did, once, a few years ago. I started with a few small things, Christmas ornaments and stuff like that. But I'm not very good at the selling part, so . . ."

"But handmade items are so trendy!" Oliver couldn't help his enthusiasm. All the pieces in this small workshop were unfinished, but three other spindles on the bench near where Nick stood had been sanded until they nearly shone.

"I'm not trying to be trendy." Nick put the spindle down. "It gives me a place to come. To relax and think sometimes. I'm not doing it to make a career out of it."

"But you could." Oliver came forward to rest his hands on Nick's chest. He grinned as a sudden thought occurred to him. "We could get you a stall at the market next to mine. They'd love you! Local boy, local products." He didn't mention his own problems. He'd nearly blurted the whole thing out when Nick had asked him about his morning at the market before, but he didn't want to saddle Nick with his difficulties on top of what Nick was facing at home.

Nick's hands were warm over his, and his thumb stroked the back of Oliver's knuckles. "We'd get into a lot of trouble being so close to each other."

Oliver knew a come-on when he heard one, and that, coupled with the way Nick's pupils widened, was definitely a come-on. He stepped forward until his feet were between Nick's, so he could press him against the workbench.

"What kind of trouble?" He circled his hands over Nick's

chest. The thick hair under Nick's shirt crinkled beneath Oliver's palms, and he licked his lips.

Nick rumbled, deep in his chest. He let go of Oliver's hands and gripped his hips, holding them together. Oliver sighed as he nuzzled at Nick's jaw

"We should go back upstairs," Oliver said. Every electron in his body screamed this was a bad idea. He needed to be respectful of Nick and his boundaries, especially with Hayden in the house. He should be good.

"He won't hear us down here." Nick squeezed Oliver's ass, his erection grinding into the crease of Oliver's groin.

"I'm trying to be honorable." For another ten seconds, anyway.

Nick let him go and pushed past him, making Oliver sigh in relief. At least one cooler head was going to prevail. But then Nick closed the workshop door and turned, his back pressed to it. The look on his face, the need and the determination, had Oliver standing to attention, even while his knees wobbled.

"Here's what we're going to do," Nick said as he closed the small space between them.

Oliver swallowed hard. "I'm listening."

Nick pulled their mouths together, his tongue pushing in brutally, his fingers tangling in Oliver's hair. Oliver groaned under his control. Whenever Nick got like this, Oliver had to fight not to turn into a puddle. He needed Nick to take control—of him, of his pleasure. All of it.

"Do you want this?" Nick ran a hand over the front of Oliver's jeans.

Oliver went to nod, but Nick still had a tight grip on his hair, and the pull when he tried to move brought a few bright tears to his eyes. "Yes."

"You want me to make you come? Here?"

Oh God. Oliver would always want that.

"It's going to be fast." Nick pressed against him so he was pinned to the workbench.

"Okay." The feeling of Nick's hand on Oliver's dick made it hard to concentrate.

"And you need to be quiet." Nick punctuated his point with his tongue in Oliver's mouth, swallowing his agreement. "If you make too much noise, I will stop. Do you understand?"

Oliver could only whine against Nick's lips while his hips jerked in the man's grip.

Nick wasn't kidding about fast. One second, they were devouring each other. The next, Nick was on his knees, with Oliver's pants undone and pushed around his ankles.

Oliver's cock bobbed, free from his boxer briefs, and he stroked himself while Nick kissed his thighs. He only had a second to prepare himself before Nick took over, jerking him hard and rough. Oliver gasped. Just as suddenly, Nick's hand was gone, leaving Oliver feeling exposed. He shivered as he glanced down. Nick, his perfect face turned up, was watching him. When their eyes met, he pressed a silent finger to his lips in a warning, and Oliver nearly came on the spot. He gripped the bench, the rough wood biting into his hands and nodded, then nearly lost it all over again when Nick opened his mouth to take in Oliver's cock.

Nick's mouth was perfect. And hot. Wet and tight. Oliver squeezed his eyes shut to block out the image of his cock disappearing between Nick's lips, but it didn't matter because the sensation alone would set him on fire.

He bit his tongue to keep from shouting when he bumped against the back of Nick's throat. Nick choked and slid off him, going back to working him with his hand. The friction was hard, but Oliver wouldn't ask him to stop, not in a million years. He arched back, focusing on staying quiet and also on staying upright.

"You're so beautiful," Nick said. "So fucking beautiful. Do you know what you do to me?"

He sucked Oliver back down, head bobbing to nearly the same pace as his hand. Oliver clenched his lips shut, mesmerized. His breath came in heavy gusts, while his hand came down on the back of Nick's head to hold him in place. Nick gagged as Oliver thrust, hitting his throat again, but he didn't pull away. He braced one hand against Oliver's hip and kept going.

So good. You're so good. Keep going. More. Oliver chanted it silently in his head.

When his cock slipped deeper into Nick's throat, he stuffed his remaining hand into his mouth to smother the choking sob threatening to burst out of him. He glanced down, and Nick's eyes were watching him intently as he sucked, taking Oliver all the way to the base of his shaft.

Oliver bucked when a single finger pressed against his ass, circling the tight muscle. Tears leaked out of the corners of his eyes, but he fought down the moans as Nick continued to tease him.

More please. Fuck me. Please.

There wouldn't be any fucking tonight, but that didn't keep Oliver from picturing the deep concentration on Nick's face as he pushed himself into Oliver's body. It didn't keep him from shuddering at the remembered sting of Nick's thick cock taking possession of him.

He nearly fell as his orgasm erupted out of him. He definitely had to let go of Nick's head to clap both his hands over his mouth, muffling his shouts while his cock pumped itself dry down Nick's throat. The neon tube lights above them dimmed, or else Oliver was trying not to black out as he panted. Despite it all, he heard Nick's grunt, even while Oliver was still in his mouth, that said the other man was coming too.

Oliver needed a long time before he was sure he wouldn't embarrass himself when he uncovered his mouth. So many things he wanted to say all at once. He wanted to praise Nick, call him a million dirty names, or pour all the softest and most desperate things in his heart all over the basement workshop. The depth of it terrified him. So he kept silent.

His cock went limp in Nick's mouth, and Nick released him, head resting against Oliver's thigh. His pants were open—though when he'd had time, Oliver had no idea—and his fist was slick with come.

"You're so beautiful," he said again, nuzzling above the line of Oliver's pubic hair. He groped blindly on the workbench until he found a rag, which he used to clean them both up as best as he could before he sat back, tucking himself into his pants.

Oliver ran a shaking hand over Nick's skull, then froze as the small room was filled with the sound of stomping feet upstairs. Nick pulled himself to his feet, and they stared wordlessly at the ceiling. Above them, Hayden made his way to the kitchen. There were a number of muffled banging noises—cupboards being opened and closed—and then the feet marched back up the hall.

They stayed still for a minute longer, but with no further noise upstairs, Nick planted a kiss to Oliver's temple. "Stay here tonight?"

Oh God yes. And yet— "I should go."

Nick grasped his hand. "Don't worry about Hayden. He usually shuts himself in for the night around nine, so that was probably his last round for the evening. And he's fifteen, so the only way he gets out of bed before noon tomorrow is if I make him." He squeezed him. "And I don't have to make him if we don't want to."

Oliver pressed their foreheads together, fighting back a shiver. "Nick."

"Please."

Such a bad idea.

"Okay."

Nick smiled against his lips. "Yeah?"

"Yeah."

They made their way out of the workshop, but their progress was slow and messy as they laughed and fumbled. Oliver kept having to push back the thought that swirled in his head.

He was falling for Nick.

Falling so hard.

So fast.

Oliver caught his toe on the top step, crashing into Nick, who caught him with a grin.

"All right?" he asked, kissing Oliver's cheek.

"Wanna kiss it better?"

"You'll have to show me where it hurts."

Oliver wrapped his arms around Nick's waist, holding him close.

"Why don't you find out?" he said.

Nick ran his tongue over Oliver's throat. "Here?"

"Not quite?"

A nip at his earlobe. "Here?"

Oliver hummed. "Closer."

"What the hell are you doing?"

The world went dark for a second, fear flooding Oliver's system at the new voice. Nick was already pulling away, pushing Oliver behind him like he needed protection, and Oliver stumbled into place because he didn't know what else to do.

Hayden stood at the end of the hall. His eyes—his father's eyes in his face—were narrowed and his expression was furious. "What the fuck are you doing?"

"Hayden," Nick said. He still had one hand behind him, holding Oliver close. "I thought you were in your room."

"Well, you were wrong." The last word sounded like a curse. "Now tell me what the fuck is going on!"

17

When Anya called that awful day last fall, her words nearly drowning in her own tears, Nick had been scared. She could barely speak, and Nick was so sure Hayden had been injured, maybe even killed, and any hopes he had ever had for rebuilding a relationship with his son were gone. He'd been terrified that he'd missed his chance in his years of hurt feelings and distance. And then Anya managed to get out that Hayden had been arrested, that the police had come to the house and taken him away, and the fear was overtaken by a new mix of confusion and anger. His son? How could they arrest his son? The police had made a mistake.

But the mix of emotions he'd felt that day were nothing to the battle banging inside him now. Oliver stood behind him, and Hayden loomed in the dark hall ahead of them, and Nick didn't know where to start.

"I thought you'd gone to bed." He spoke without any real thought.

"Answer my question."

Nick flipped on the light with shaking fingers, then flinched back at the fury in Hayden's eyes.

"I can explain." Nick raised his right hand. His left one was still in Oliver's, and he was afraid to let go.

"Tell me what is going on!" Hayden's voice cracked on the edge of hysteria.

"So you may have seen Oliver and—"

"You were kissing!" Hayden pointed a finger beyond Nick's shoulder. "You were kissing him!"

"Yes." Nick tried to keep his voice from shaking. "I was kissing him. He's . . . He's my boyfriend."

Oliver's hand squeezed his, but any relief Nick might have felt was wiped out by the twist of Hayden's face. "Your boyfriend? You have a boyfriend?"

"Yes."

"You're gay?" Hayden's eyes narrowed.

"Bisexual. But Hayden—"

"Does Mom know?"

"Hayden."

"Does she? Does she know you like dick?"

"Hey!" Nick's shout was loud enough to echo off the narrow hallways. "Watch your language."

"What? I can't say dick? Because that's what you are. A dick."

Nick skipped over the next retort. "Your mother knows."

"She does? If I called her right now, she'd know that you were screwing around with some long-haired wannabe hipster."

"She knows." Calling Anya would be about the worst thing Hayden could do. Not because Nick was worried about what she'd say, but because she deserved twenty-four hours without Hayden and his chaos crashing into her.

"You're some—" Hayden bit the sentence off. "You both knew. You let us move back in here, you both knew about this, and you didn't tell me?"

"Who I date has nothing to do with the two of you living here."

"But you didn't tell me!" Hayden's voice was shrill and his

posture stiff. Either he was about to run, or he would start breaking things soon.

"Did you think your mom and I were going to get back together?"

Hayden snorted. "Fuck no. She's too good for you, you piece of shit—"

"That is enough!"

"Should I—" Oliver started to say, but Nick pulled him closer.

"Hayden, apologize."

"Fuck that." Hayden stared at them both like they were a disease.

"Apologize. You don't get to criticize anyone else's behavior in this house."

"What?" Hayden folded his arms over his chest. "Now you're going to be my dad? Want to give me another lecture about responsibility? You think I give a fuck about anything you have to say?"

He took a step forward. "Let's talk about this. Oliver and I— there's nothing wrong with what we're doing."

Hayden also came forward, his lips pinched together tight. He shoved at Nick's chest much harder than a kid his size should have been able to. "No!" He shoved again, and Nick stumbled, his feet tangling with Oliver's. "Get away from me!"

"Hayden. Let's talk about—"

"Talk? You never listen to me! You never even ask!"

"Hayden."

"No. Why should I listen to you? I hate you! You're not my dad. You're a liar! Do you hear me! I never want to speak to you again." Hayden spun and stormed down the hall, slamming his bedroom door behind him. Nick went to follow, but Oliver wrapped strong arms around him, holding them in place.

"Let me go." Nick strained against him.

"Give it a minute." Oliver's voice was calm in his ear.

"Let me go!"

"Calm down first."

"I have to talk to him!"

"Not like this. Breathe. Come on, breathe." His held on tight, and his extra height and strong body meant Nick couldn't break out.

"I have to talk to him." He said it with less conviction this time. He was breathing, but his breaths were coming too fast, and he couldn't slow them down. "I have to—" he gasped.

Oliver pulled him back, turning them, and used his weight to move them both to the floor. Nick collapsed into his lap. His chest was on fire, like his lungs were filling with water or his heart was about to burst.

"Nick. Calm down."

Nick swung his head. "I can't—I can't breathe."

"I know." Oliver ran a hand over his head, pressing Nick against his chest. "I know. You need to relax."

"I think—I'm having a heart attack." His dad had been a little bit older than Nick when his heart attack killed him. Had it felt like this?

Oliver kissed his temple. "It's a panic attack. Please, baby. Follow me, okay? Breathe."

Beneath his cheek, Oliver's chest rose and fell steadily. Nick closed his eyes and tried to focus on the feeling. "I can't." His face was a mess of snot and tears.

"You can. Come on. In, one, two, three, four. Out, one, two, three, four. That's it."

Getting back to normal took a long time. When they were done, Nick sat there, held against Oliver's strong body like a child, while Oliver petted his head and murmured soft words in his ear.

"You're okay. It's okay."

Eventually, he sat up, blinking and wiping at his face with

his shirtsleeve. "I have to talk to Hayden," he said again, calmer now.

"Do you think that's a good idea?"

The thought made him want to throw up, but he'd fucked up pretty badly. "I have to." He stood and pulled Oliver to his feet. "You should go."

"I'm sorry." Oliver kissed him.

"No." Nick shook his head. "It's not your fault."

"It is. I should have behaved myself. It wasn't fair to you. I—"

"It's my house and my son. My responsibility." Nick kissed him, hard, and then, when he paused to breathe, said, "I love you."

Oliver froze beneath his lips, and Nick trembled. If Oliver backed away from him now, he'd probably collapse again, right there on the floor.

Outside, a crash shattered the stillness, and a car alarm sounded, high and piercing, close to the house.

"What—"

Another crash.

They rushed to the kitchen, and the car alarm got louder. Nick pulled the front door open and nearly tripped on Anya's welcome mat as he struggled to understand what he was seeing.

The passenger side window of Oliver's SUV had been smashed.

And Hayden stood next to the vehicle with a baseball bat in his hands.

"What are you doing?"

Hayden's eyes widened at Nick's shout. He stared at them with a vicious smile before he hefted the baseball bat and slammed it against the SUV's door. Despite the black vehicle on the darkened street, Nick could make out the size and shape of the dent in the metal.

"Hayden! Stop it!" He ran across the yard as Hayden wound up for another swing.

"Fuck you!" The bat connected with the sideview mirror, sending pieces of plastic and glass flying.

Nick caught him before he had another chance to swing. Like Oliver had done with him, he wrapped his arms around Hayden's torso, hauling him backward. The kid thrashed, and his head clipped Nick's chin. Blood filled in his mouth, but he pulled, hauling Hayden away from the SUV.

"Fuck you!" Hayden fought and kicked the whole way back to the house. Somewhere along the way, he'd dropped the bat, because Oliver had it when they were back inside, the three of them all wild-eyed and gasping.

"Sit down," Nick said quietly, then spat red-tinged saliva into the sink.

"No." Hayden kicked at a chair.

"Sit down!" His words were a roar, and Hayden blanched as he dropped into the chair like he'd been punched. "Apologize to Oliver."

Hayden eyed them both, and Nick braced for more hatred and slurs, but then Hayden slumped in his chair, suddenly the same bored teenager as always. His fight was gone. "Sorry."

"Stay there." He pointed at the table, then glanced at Oliver, who nodded silently. He must have set the bat down because it leaned against the kitchen counter, out of both their reaches.

Nick went down the hall. Hayden had gotten out, and Nick needed to know how. He turned the knob on Hayden's bedroom door, but when he pushed, the door held tight. Nick removed the lock when Hayden moved in—another condition from the court— so he glared back down the hall.

"What did you do?"

Hayden didn't look up from the kitchen table. "I jammed a chair under the knob."

Nick rolled his eyes and put all his weight against the door, leading with his shoulder. It took a few tries, but eventually the door gave way. Nick's momentum burst him into the room, and cool air hit his face.

The window was open.

He slammed it closed, the glass rattling in the frame, and stalked back down the hall. Hayden shrank into himself, but Nick kept walking, past him, to open the front door. He motioned to Oliver to follow, and Oliver slipped past him and stepped outside.

"Don't move," Nick said over his shoulder. "I'm leaving the door open, and if you're anywhere but at that table when I come back inside, house arrest is going to feel like a birthday party. Do you understand me?"

Hayden nodded without meeting his eyes.

Oliver was standing with his hands on his hips, staring at the wreckage of his car, when Nick joined him.

"You need to go."

"Yeah."

"This time of night, the police will be here in another minute or two because he can't be outside." He was surprised they weren't here already. "I know you could press charges, but I'd appreciate it if you didn't. I'll pay for the damages."

Oliver kissed his temple, and Nick shuddered.

"Please." His throat hurt. If Oliver stayed any longer, Nick would start sobbing, right there in his front yard.

Oliver left. His tires crunched as he backed over the shattered glass on the asphalt.

Wordlessly, Nick went back to the kitchen and got his keys. Hayden flinched when Nick picked up the baseball bat, but he went back outside. He was numb and exhausted, feeling like someone else was in his body as he turned the key in the old sedan's ignition and pulled it down the driveway. He got out and went to the passenger side, picking up the bat.

It took a few swings. He had to give Hayden credit for taking out the SUV's window in one go. Anger and homophobia gave him special powers.

As the glass cracked and shattered, filling the night with another crash, and sirens started to echo down the street, the only thing Nick heard was an absence.

He tossed the bat into the trunk.

Later, when the police left and Hayden was in his room again—but with the door open, the policy going forward—and Nick was alone in his bed . . . when his heart finally stopped slamming in his ribs and the last shivers of his crashing adrenaline faded, he heard a quiet voice in his head. It reminded him —softly, gently, painfully—of the thing he hadn't realized in the chaos, the thing he almost needed to hear the most. The words that would have given him hope for more in his life than the furious boy whose eyes matched his, who looked at Nick like dirt on his shoe.

Nick buried his head under a pillow, but the insidious voice persisted.

Oliver hadn't said he loved him too.

18

*B*y noon on Sunday, Oliver was teetering on panic. He hadn't slept much the night before. Nervous energy had kept him awake for hours, and then worry for Nick occupied the rest until the sun came up.

He shouldn't have gone over there. Shouldn't have treated it like some kind of booty call when Nick clearly had deeper responsibilities and commitments than Oliver could have anticipated. He'd stopped defending the petty criminals and first-time offenders who got off with house arrest so early in his career that he'd never given its wider ramifications much thought. And he'd rarely defended juveniles, so the impact that sort of sentence would have on immediate family had hardly crossed his mind.

Nick was trapped. The terrified look on his face as Hayden smashed Oliver's car made it all clear. So did Nick's heaving body in Oliver's arms while he tried to breathe through his panic attack. He was as trapped as his son, but he'd taken the sentence on voluntarily, trying to do the right thing for his family.

Oliver was desperate to talk to him, but Nick would need room to deal with Hayden's legal fallout. Oliver had already muddied the waters too much. He needed to give Nick space and time, but the waiting made him pace tight circles in his living room, and it hadn't even been a day.

Oliver drove downtown to meet Seb and Martin for brunch, although he really didn't feel like going. He'd taped up the window on the SUV with plastic sheeting. Neither Seb nor Martin had a car, so Oliver would have to get a recommendation on a body shop from someone else. Fuck, he should probably sell the stupid thing. He should have sold it as soon as he'd left Cooper, but he'd been so caught up in plans for the business that shopping for something new hadn't seemed important.

Seb and Martin were waiting in front of the building that housed their gallery and apartment. Seb whistled as Oliver stepped out of the car.

"What the hell happened there?"

Oliver grunted. "I was moving stuff around in the garage and knocked over a shelf."

The lie was better than the truth. *My boyfriend's juvenile offender son nearly caught his dad deep-throating me in the basement and took his frustration out on my Porsche with a baseball bat* didn't quite trip off the tongue. And while the bookshelf story could only lead to more questions, Oliver could lie his way through them.

"A shelf?" Seb raised a blond eyebrow.

Bingo.

Oliver muttered responses as they walked down the street. By the time they arrived at the diner, Seb had either bought Oliver's explanation or gotten bored.

Oliver ordered a black coffee, sausage hash, and an extra side of bacon. He ignored the nervous glances his brother and Martin threw each other and scalded his tongue on the coffee.

"Everything okay?" Martin asked.

"Yeah, you said sausage hash, but you meant egg white omelet with a side of hay, right?" Seb smiled, then flinched after Martin must have kicked him under the table.

"Everything's fine." Oliver downed the rest of the coffee and leaned back to flag their server for more.

"You're sure?" Seb asked.

"Why wouldn't it be?"

"Well, we could start with your German pimp-mobile looking like it wound up on the losing end of a street fight. Or the fact that you just ordered a heart attack on a plate after living on cauliflower and air for the last six months. Or really, we could skip all that and go with the fact you look like toasted shit on a cracker."

"Thanks." Oliver fidgeted with his flatware.

"You really do," Martin said.

Oliver snorted and thanked the server for the fresh coffee.

"We're not buying your stupid act," Seb said. "What's going on? Is it the veggie shack? Did you make too many celery smoothies again?"

"It's not the business." Oliver stared down into his coffee. "The business is fucked."

"It's what?"

"Fucked, okay?" Oliver's voice raised over the din of the brunch crowd, and he hunched down in his seat, running a tired hand over his face. "It's all fucked. The market is going to kick me out, which is fine, really, because, it's not like anyone ever does anything but take free samples and flyers for workshops they never actually show up to."

"It can't be that bad," Martin said.

"Not that bad? Not that—I have one client. One." He thrust his index finger between them. "And lately I've been giving him juice for free too because it's going to spoil in the fridge. So I'm keeping the lights on with willpower and savings to prove a point to an asshole who isn't even here to see me kill myself over this thing that was supposed to be ours."

They were silent. Seb and Martin stared at him, open-mouthed. Oliver slurped at his coffee, and it dribbled into his beard. He glared at his brother, daring him to try some kind of snarky comeback.

"But you have a plan to fix it, right?" Seb said.

"What about the people? The ones who came to that workshop we went to?" Martin asked.

"They never came back. Not one, except for Avery."

"The ginger twink with all the questions?"

"He's an accountant."

"And he can't help you figure out the money?"

Oliver laughed. "Believe me, he's trying."

More silence. Their breakfasts were delivered. Oliver dug into his hash like he'd been starving for weeks. It tasted hot, greasy, and salty, almost too much so. So many flavors he'd hardly tasted in months. He scarfed it down in huge bites, barely pausing to breathe, only stopping when he nearly choked on a potato.

He glanced up as he finished another mug of coffee. Seb and Martin were staring at him like he was a *Men in Black* alien in an Oliver suit.

"What?" he said as he resumed eating.

"You're joking, right?" Seb said.

"I don't think he's joking." Martin poked at his eggs.

"I'm not."

"Is it really that bad?"

Oliver shrugged. He wasn't in the mood to detail his failings. He didn't need Seb's sarcasm or his judgment.

He needed Nick.

Shit, he was trying not to think about that. Nick would call if he needed help, but otherwise, Oliver was going to stay a few steps back, out of the way, where he wouldn't cause any more trouble.

I love you.

He nearly choked on another potato.

Specifically, that was the thing he was not thinking about.

Nick's soft words, rough with fear and anxiety. Nick's warm body, clinging to him, desperate for comfort.

Oliver had loved Cooper, and it hadn't been enough. Nick loved him now, but if another shoe dropped with Hayden, Oliver didn't doubt for a second where he'd fall on Nick's priority list, regardless of what he thought he felt now. And it would be the way it should be too. Telling Nick Oliver loved him would make it all harder.

"Hey!" Seb snapped his fingers right in front of Oliver's nose. He started, blinking rapidly. Seb was half out of his chair, and Martin was twisting his hands in his shirt. They had both moved beyond concern into actual worry.

"Sorry."

"What the hell was that? One second, you tell us you're going out of business, the next, you're having an out-of-body experience."

"I'm not going out of business, and I wasn't—" Oliver sighed. "It's fine. The business will be fine. I got off course somehow. I have to go back to the plan and figure out how to fix it."

"I can help you, if you want," Martin said. "A lot of my tutoring work is going to be quiet for a while with school wrapping up for the year. I learned a lot when we were getting the gallery up and running. I could help you reevaluate."

Reevaluate. Oliver gritted his teeth. He didn't want Martin's help. He'd only accepted Avery's because he needed Avery's business, but letting family step in was admitting he couldn't do this on his own. He wasn't ready.

"It's fine." His fork scraped at the bottom of his empty plate. "Sorry. I'm tired. It's not as bad as all that. I appreciate the offer, but I'll be okay."

He had to be. He needed to be okay so when Nick called, he was ready to be what Nick needed.

Sunday at Nick's house was tense, to put it nicely. The cops hadn't looked fully convinced the night before when he'd told them Hayden heard someone vandalizing Nick's car and ran outside to scare them off. But with no one else around to confirm or deny and nothing stolen, the police took their statements and left.

Needless to say, Nick didn't sleep much, but at seven o'clock he pulled himself out of bed and made a pot of coffee. He gave Hayden another half-hour, mostly because Nick needed the time to tape up the window on the car. At seven-thirty, though, he went to Hayden's room and pulled open the blinds.

"Hayden. Come on. Time to get to work." Nick didn't actually expect it to be that simple, and Hayden proved him right when he didn't move.

Nick sighed. After last night, he was already doomed as far as Hayden was concerned, so nothing would damage his reputation. He leaned over Hayden's sleeping body, wrapping him up in the comforter. "I'm sorry about this," he said. Then he heaved the blankets back, yanking them and Hayden off the bed.

Hayden hit the floor and came awake with a shout, sitting up and glaring at Nick. "What the fuck!"

"Get dressed. There's coffee in the kitchen, and then we're getting to work."

"Work?" Hayden was gasping like a fish.

"You have five minutes." Nick left him there.

Hayden could have told him to fuck off or—worse—smashed a few more windows. Instead, he was at the kitchen table in six minutes. He wouldn't meet Nick's eyes as he drank his coffee, but that was okay. They didn't need to socialize for what Nick had planned.

Before eight o'clock, they were in the garage. Nick pulled a couple rusty shovels and other tools from the back of the garage. He tossed a shovel to Hayden, who caught it.

"What's this for?"

"You're going to pay Oliver back for his car."

"I don't have any money." Hayden smirked as if he'd found the magic escape card.

"I know that. So you're going to earn it in labor, and I'll pay him for the car."

"What?"

"Come on. We're digging up a flower bed for your mom." He led the way out of the garage, and Hayden followed behind him, grumbling. He let the shovel drag, clattering on the driveway.

"This is stupid. We're not—" The last of his words were drowned out by the rattle of the shovel.

"What was that?" Nick turned so fast, Hayden nearly ran into him.

"I said we're not staying. Me and Mom. It's stupid to make her a garden because we're not staying."

Normally, comments like that would have hurt. Another rejection. Today, though, he was still too angry to be hurt.

"You're certainly not helping your case to get that thing off your ankle."

Hayden rolled his eyes. "Whatever."

"Hey!" Nick stepped in front of him as Hayden went to push past. "I don't care what you think about me and my life—"

"Your boyfriend." More eye rolling.

Nick didn't let himself react at the mention of Oliver. "You have put your mom through hell. And every time you screw up again, you hurt her more. She needed this weekend away, and we are not going to let her come home to a smashed-up car and this shitty yard."

"You smashed the car, and the yard was shitty when we got here." Hayden jabbed the shovel toward him, but backed down when Nick stepped into it, letting the blade poke him in the chest.

"She'll be back this afternoon. By then, I want this flower

bed dug up, and then we're going to go buy some plants to put in it."

Hayden gaped at him.

"Do you want some gloves?" Nick held out a pair of heavy work gloves. Hayden stared at them for a moment before turning his back and jamming the shovel into the dirt.

The work was tough, and Hayden moved slowly. Nick tried not to criticize. The point was to get him working, not turn him into a landscaper. Nick hadn't worked on his yard like this in years. When he and Anya moved in, there had been a pretty little flower garden, but after she'd left, he hadn't bothered to keep it up. It went to weeds, and eventually he dug it up and filled it with grass.

Undoing his work now felt good. The morning warmed up, and his shoulders ached from the digging. Too late to piece his family back together, but maybe if he brought back this garden, it would mean he hadn't fucked everything up completely.

At eleven, Hayden threw his shovel down with a shout.

"What's wrong?" Sweat trickled down Nick's spine.

"This sucks!"

"So does having your boyfriend's son wreck your car with a baseball bat. Do you know how much a Porsche costs?"

"So what? If he's got a Porsche, he can afford to fix it. You can't make me do this!" He balled his hands into fists and then winced, unclenching them. Hayden kicked the dirt, picking at his palms. They were red and cracked.

"Did you hurt yourself?" Nick reached for him, but Hayden jerked his hand away.

"It's fine! Can we please stop this?"

Nick grabbed his wrist. Angry blisters had formed on both hands, and a few were torn and bleeding.

"You should have worn gloves."

He hadn't meant to hurt him. He hadn't really been sure what he'd meant to do, but Nick had been so angry and confused ever since Hayden found them. He needed some space, some time, with his son, to sort out what the problem was, and how they were going to fix it. His relationship with Oliver couldn't be what finally drove Nick and Hayden apart forever. It couldn't. Because Nick couldn't face the prospect of letting Oliver go.

Nick loved him.

He pushed the thought away. Today was about Hayden and trying to find common ground again. "Go inside and put some Polysporin on those blisters. I'll call the probation office and let them know we're going out."

On the drive across town, Hayden was subdued. He'd wound his hands in bandages like a burn victim and stared out the window the whole way to the nursery. He followed two steps behind Nick, a sulky shadow answering only in grunts when Nick pointed out plants.

"Do you think your mom would like these?"

"I guess."

Nick knew as much about gardening as he had about energy balls, so in the end they chose flowers in a few different colors and drove home. Hayden picked at his bandages the whole way back. By the time they pulled into the driveway, he had unraveled them completely.

"We've still got some work to do," Nick said as he turned the car off.

"I know." Hayden slammed the door behind him and walked into the house, but he came back a few minutes later with fresh Band-Aids over his blisters and a pair of gloves in his back pocket.

Planting flowers turned out to be a lot easier than digging up the yard. And faster. What took them three hours to dig only took an hour to plant. When they were done, Nick couldn't stop his pride at what they had managed to do. "Looks pretty good."

"I guess."

That was as good as it was going to get.

They went inside. Nick poured them a couple glasses of water, and they sat at the table, slipping back toward awkward silence. "How are your hands?"

Hayden flexed his fingers. "Fine."

The old house creaked, and the sink dripped.

"Do you . . ." Nick squinted down the hall. "Do you want to talk about last night?"

"No." Hayden's glass hit the table hard.

"You seemed pretty upset."

"You didn't seem too worried about upsetting me when you were sucking on your boyfriend's face."

Nick bit the inside of his lip to keep from speaking too quickly. The spot he'd bitten the night before was tender and metallic-tasting under his tongue. "You met Oliver at the market, the last time your mom dropped you off for community service. Do you remember?"

Hayden shrugged.

"He runs a store downtown. He makes juices and does workshops about healthy living."

"And he's gay."

"That doesn't really have anything to do with his business."

"But he *is* gay." Hayden crossed his arms over his chest.

"He is."

"And so are you."

"No. I'm bi."

"Whatever. You're still with him."

I love him. "Yes."

"You're dating a man."

"Is this about your mom?" Nick's skin crawled at the way Hayden was staring at him. "Because she's known about Oliver since that morning you guys met him at the market and—"

"Why do you keep talking about the market? I don't

remember him, okay? Was I supposed to notice you guys eye-fucking and figure out my dad is queer?"

Considering Oliver had nearly broken off their agreement that day, there hadn't been much eye-fucking.

"Does it bother you that he came over?"

"Gee, Dad. Does it bother me that you've been lying to me about your sexuality for my whole life? What do you think?"

"I didn't—" Nick's resolve threatened to break. Hayden was trying to get a rise out of him, make him yell again. "You're currently under house arrest for bullying a gay classmate. So I think it's only fair that we talk about—"

"Why didn't you tell me?"

"About Oliver? Why does it matter?"

Hayden popped up from his chair, but he didn't go far. Instead, he gripped the back, his knuckles white, and bent over it. His cheeks were pink, and he was breathing hard.

"Is this about school? Are you afraid your friends will find out your father is involved with a man?"

"Like I have any friends left there? Everyone hates me." Hayden glared at him.

"I don't want to push you on this. You've never explained why you were bullying your friend."

"He's not my friend!"

"But I would hope you understand you don't get a say in my sexuality. It doesn't work like that."

Hayden shook his head. He was in motion, taking short steps back and forth on the opposite side of the table. "Fuck you. You're disgusting. You disgust me, do you understand that?"

"I'm sorry you feel that way." Nick's heart was breaking. Since the moment they found out what Hayden did, he'd been afraid it would come to this. He'd been a coward. While they'd talked about homophobia and prejudice, Nick had never been brave enough to use himself as an outright example, because what if Hayden finally rejected him completely? But now, with no way—and no desire—to hide who Oliver was to him, it turned out his son wasn't going to accept him.

They'd never been close, and that was Nick's fault, but this was always going to be between them.

"Why didn't you tell me?" Hayden's voice was small.

"Would you have felt any different if I had? Less disgusted?" He couldn't help the edge in his words. The hurt chewed at his insides.

"Fuck you."

"Less ashamed? Less embarrassed to be seen with me?"

"Fuck you, fuck you!" Hayden bowed his head.

Nick was barely holding onto his temper. He needed Anya to come home. He needed to get out of here.

He needed Oliver to hold him like he'd held him last night.

"I'm sorry I'm such a disappointment. I'm sorry that who I am is so unacceptable to you."

"Fuck you! Why didn't you tell me?" Hayden raised his head. His face was red, and tears streamed down his cheeks.

"Why would I? So you could spit in my face?"

"Because!" He collapsed into the chair again, blistered hands in his hair. "Because I'm gay too!"

19

*N*ick was falling. A hole had opened up in the rippled linoleum of his kitchen floor, and he had dropped into it. He fell and fell with no way to stop.

Far away, Hayden was crying. Screaming. A chair scraped, and feet ran across the floor, and Nick kept falling.

The sound of vomiting broke through his fog. The falling feeling stopped as suddenly as if he had slammed onto the floor. His heart was pounding in his chest, and his vision spun.

Hayden was at the sink, throwing up. His whole body heaved with it.

"Hayden." Nick's feet were like lead weights.

"Fuck you." The same words. So much sadder now.

"You're gay?"

"Go away."

"Are you sure?" The question was stupid, but it was all Nick's stumbling brain could come up with.

Hayden laughed, then spat into the sink as he turned the water on and let it run. The kitchen smelled sour.

"Are *you* sure?" Where Hayden's face had been blotchy before, he'd gone pale now, all the color gone. Nick nodded, and Hayden shrugged. "There you go."

"But—" Nick struggled. "Why didn't you say anything? Why didn't you tell me? Or your mom?"

Hayden's face crumpled, tears tumbling down his face in fat drops. He shook his head. Nick dragged his feet across the floor, but when he was close enough to touch Hayden, hug him, tell him all the things a father was supposed to say in this situation, Hayden scrambled back, until he could get a chair between them again.

"Why didn't *you* tell *me*?" He gasped out wet sobs. "Huh? You're so out and proud, why couldn't you tell your own family? Don't you think it might have helped for me to know something like that?"

Nick shook his head, his own throat going tight.

"You're a shitty father, you know that? You're supposed to be an example, a role model. And where the hell were you when I needed you?"

Every word cut at him, and he couldn't stop his own tears. "I'm here now."

What a stupid, useless thing to say.

Hayden laughed, and then his eyes widened. He stumbled back from the chair, banging against cabinets. A car pulled into the driveway.

"You can't tell her," Hayden said.

"What?"

"Mom. You can't tell Mom."

He turned back to the kitchen. "Hayden. She'll understand."

Hayden shook his head, hands on his cheeks. He backed away, toward the hall. "Please. You can't tell her. She'll want to talk about it, and I can't . . . Please." He was halfway to his room.

Nick's stomach twisted, and he glanced out the window again. Anya stepped out of the car, then pulled a suitcase out of the trunk. She waved and smiled at the driver, and the falling feeling started to come back.

She couldn't see them like this.

Hayden was ahead of him, the door to his bedroom slamming.

She couldn't. Whatever Hayden was afraid of, she'd take one look at them, and know something had happened.

Nick took the coward's route. He ran. Before Anya was at the door, long before she entered the kitchen, he was gone, into the basement. The workshop was silent and close. Less than a day ago, he'd been on his knees in front of Oliver. Less than a day ago, everything had been safe, separate.

Where the hell were you when I needed you?

Nick put his face in his hands and waited for the shaking to stop.

———

By Monday, Oliver could only try to stay busy at the store. He had stock to replenish—mostly old stock to throw out—and he was up to his elbows in Swiss chard when the bell over the front door chimed.

"I'll be right out!" he called over the buzz of the juicer. The reply from whoever had come in was muffled.

Oliver's eyes widened when he came out to see who it was. "Avery?"

"I'm okay." Avery sat at the counter, head buried under his arms.

Oliver crossed to him and put a hand on his shoulder, and Avery flinched away with a whimper that made Oliver take a step back.

"What's wrong?"

"I need—I need . . ." Watching him try to get the words out was painful. His voice wobbled with every sound. "I'll be okay in a few minutes. Unless I puke my guts out again. Do you have a garbage can close by?"

Oliver scrambled to find one. Never mind Avery vomiting in

his store would do nothing for business. Right now, Avery was his *only* business.

"Seriously. Can I call someone? What's wrong?"

"Migraine. It's not a bad one. I just needed somewhere quiet for a minute before I go to my next client."

"Client?" Oliver was fretting like a nervous mother. "You're not going to any meeting. Please. I think you need to go home." Or else Oliver needed to call a doctor.

Avery held up a hand to hold him off. Slowly, so slowly, he unwound himself from his arms. He looked awful. His freckled skin was the color of wet putty, and his eyes were barely open.

"My uncle is away. I'm in charge. I can't go home. Please." He crumpled back to the counter. "Just give me a minute."

Cooper used to get migraines, and the pain would break Oliver's heart, back when he still cared about Cooper's suffering. Watching Avery, hunched and hurting, Oliver felt useless. After two days of silence from Nick, here he was, failing someone else.

He went to the fridge and pulled out a *Green Monster*. Celery, wheatgrass, spinach. Even he had to admit it tasted like dirt, but maybe that was what the doctor ordered. He pulled a chair around to the other side of the counter, careful not to let it drag on the floor, and poured the juice into two glasses. He slid one toward Avery, then silently sipped his own.

After what felt like forever, Avery lifted his head again. His eyes were bloodshot, but some of the color was back in his face. He blinked when he saw the juice, then gave Oliver a weak smile. His hand shook as he lifted the glass, but he took a sip and then smiled wider as he set the glass down again. "Thanks."

"Are you okay?"

Avery gave him a wobbly nod. "I will be. It's better already. I needed to get out of the sunlight."

"Do you get migraines often?"

"Once or twice a month. Usually, I can call in sick or meet

with clients over the phone, but since my uncle's away, there are a few I had to go see in person."

Oliver smiled sympathetically. "You're kind of a mess. You know that, right?"

"My uncle will be back tomorrow. Maybe I'll stay home."

"You better. I'll call you to make sure you do."

After they finished their juice, Avery shuffled out of the store, looking steadier, but still not great, and Oliver called after him to get some rest. Where his momma bear instinct came from was a mystery, but clearly no one was looking out for Avery, so Oliver was going to have to.

The rest of the day went as expected. A few walk-ins came by around lunch, a couple more before he closed. Only one of them actually bought anything. He was supposed to be holding a workshop again that evening, but he wasn't optimistic. Clearly, Avery wouldn't be there, and even if he did show up, Oliver would tell him to go home.

He was in the back, finishing his evening clean up, when the door out front opened again, and disappointment flooded him. He'd almost resigned himself to no one showing up and had half formed a plan to see Nick before his shift with the available time.

"Grab a seat!" he called, forcing himself to sound positive. "We'll get started in a minute."

"Start what?"

The deep voice, low and confused, nearly had him slice his hand on one of the knives he was carrying to the sink as they dropped into the basin.

Nick stood in the middle of the store, wearing his navy uniform shirt and cargo pants. His hair had been trimmed to a black haze on his scalp. Dark circles sagged under his eyes, and his smile was tired. He was the most beautiful thing Oliver had ever seen.

He nearly turned it into a Hollywood moment, nearly ran to

close the space between them so he could throw himself in Nick's arms. After almost two days of silence, the relief at seeing him made Oliver shudder.

Nick moved faster. Oliver had barely opened his mouth to say hello, and he was already being pulled into Nick's big arms. Nick's kiss was like the last moment of drowning: Oliver couldn't breathe, and he didn't even care anymore.

"I'm sorry. I know you're busy." Nick was kissing his face, squeezing him so hard. The last of his air really was leaving his lungs.

"It's okay."

"I can't stay long, I have to go to work."

"It's okay. I'm glad you're here."

"I needed to see you."

Their words were all breathless. A little desperate. And now Oliver hoped no one showed up for the workshop, not while two guys made out in the store. Not while they said stupid things, real things, that needed time and privacy.

"It's a mess," Nick said into Oliver's neck.

"I don't care about the car. What happened with the police?"

"Nothing. I said I was asleep and Hayden had to chase off some kids who were trying to break into the car."

"I should have stayed."

"No, you shouldn't have. Nothing you could have done. It's over. Just another fuck-up on Hayden's list." He shook his head, and it drooped. Oliver lifted his chin and kissed him. Nick's lips were soft under his, restrained. So many times, they dove right in, letting the need take over. It had always been so easy, and the desire still burned, under the restraint. Oliver could lock the front door, turn off the lights, and drag Nick to the back.

Only one thing stopped him.

I love you.

That needed to be addressed. Nick had been so desperate, so

sincere. It hadn't been the right time, and they'd agreed they didn't want it from each other. But now—

"Hayden told me he's gay."

Time slowed. Oliver was suddenly aware of so many little details around him all at once. The red-yellow-green stoplight of the bottles in the fridge. The hum of the lights overhead. Nick's unshaven jaw and the tiny silver hairs in his dark scruff Oliver had never noticed before.

"What?"

Nick's eyes were puffy, and the whites outside his irises were bloodshot. His lips were pinched tight and trembled almost imperceptibly. "My son came out to me."

"When?"

"Yesterday."

"What did you do?"

"Nothing. I—" Nick ran a hand over his scalp. "I blanked out for a second. And then he was throwing up. And then Anya came home and—" He buried his hands in his face.

"Did he tell Anya?"

Nick shook his head.

"Did you?"

"No."

"But you're telling me." A sour feeling turned in Oliver's stomach. This was it. This was the part where Nick said he needed space and time, where he needed to be a father and couldn't be Oliver's boyfriend. Not forever, he'd say. But for now. And Oliver would have to let him go because what else could he do?

"I don't know what to do. He won't talk to me."

Oliver blinked back his growing fear. "It's a big thing." His own coming out had been a long time ago now, but the memory still made him anxious. The only other time he'd been so terrified of disappointing his dad was the night he announced he'd left the firm. That had been a classic Stevenson family shit show, with Seb as the ringmaster. Coming out, though, he'd done on his own. "He's scared."

Nick's eyes widened. "Of what?"

"You. Himself. All of it."

"And what do I do? I've failed him almost every way I can. What do I do?"

Oliver wanted to hold him. Better, he wanted to take Nick back to his house and hold him all night. But Hayden needed a father more than Oliver needed a boyfriend.

"Do you want me to talk to him?" If he couldn't have Nick to himself, then he had this to offer. "Maybe having someone not quite so close to the family will sit better with him."

Nick shook his head and wiped at his face. His laugh was bone-tired and dry. "I don't think he likes you very much."

Oliver laughed too. "We didn't make a very good first impression, did we?"

"No." Nick groaned and rested his head on Oliver's shoulder. "No, the only way it could have gone worse would have been if he'd found us with your pants around your ankles and your dick in my mouth."

Oliver pulled Nick tight against him and kissed his throat, letting Nick's coarse stubble scrape over his lips.

"We'll figure this out." Oliver's throat was tight, and his muscles ached from the tension of not reaching for Nick. But he couldn't resist when Nick reached for him, when his coarse stubble scraped over Oliver's lips and Nick's body moved restlessly against his.

"I wish this weren't so complicated." Nick's grip on him tightened.

"We tried that," Oliver said.

"I want you." Nick's voice was rough in his ear. "I want you so badly. Just to forget, for a bit. We could go back to your place. Take a shower. You on your knees. Me inside you. Oh god, I—"

Oliver cut him off with a kiss, but he maintained control of it the whole time. He knew what Nick wanted; he wanted it too. But it wouldn't be fair. They'd tried uncomplicated, and it blew up in their faces spectacularly.

I love you. The words were there, on the tip of Oliver's tongue. They would drain the tension out of Nick's body, take some of the pain out of his black eyes.

And yet Oliver didn't say them. Couldn't find the strength to give that to Nick. Because he'd loved Cooper, and all that was left was this darkened shop. His love wasn't always enough.

Nick stepped back, clearing his throat. "I have to get to work."

The moment was over, and Oliver nearly grabbed at Nick's shirt to find it again. Instead, he said, "Call me on your break."

Nick smoothed down the front of his pants. "I'll try. Might not be a good night for that."

"Yeah. I understand."

After Nick left, Oliver finished cleaning up. No one showed for the workshop, and honestly, he wasn't surprised. He turned off the lights, locked up the shop, and drove home.

He almost didn't see the man on the front porch as he pulled into the driveway. Oliver only spotted him as the dark shape unfolded itself. His heart rocketed to a million in his chest, and his hand was in his pocket to pull out his cellphone. Then the man took a step down, illuminated by the SUV's headlights, and the air inside the vehicle vanished.

Cooper.

Oliver froze somewhere between dialing the nine and the one.

Cooper waved awkwardly, squinting at the car.

Oliver didn't remember turning off the ignition, but the car went silent, and he climbed out, unable to tear his eyes off the man in front of his house the whole time. He had to support himself on the cool black of the SUV's frame because he would have fallen otherwise.

"What are you doing here?" He didn't recognize his own voice.

"Hey, Ollie," Cooper said. "What happened to the Porsche?"

"What are you doing here?"

Cooper smiled. "Can we talk?"

The SUV's automatic lights clicked off, and the driveway descended into darkness.

20

The smart thing would have been to tell Cooper to go fuck himself. Or call Seb, who would have gladly done it over the phone and then come straight to the house to reinforce the message in person.

But Oliver had always been a fool when it came to Cooper, so here he was, unlocking his front door and letting Cooper follow him into the hall.

"I'm sorry to show up uninvited." Cooper shrugged out of his Hugo Boss jacket and held it awkwardly, like he wasn't sure what to do with it. Manners told Oliver to take it, hang it up some-where. Or possibly drop it on the floor. Cooper bought it for his thirty-third birthday. Even though Oliver's house was pristine, letting it slump to the hardwood would be so satisfying. Instead, he left Cooper to figure it out while Oliver went to the kitchen. He pulled out a glass from the cupboard and filled it at the sink. He very specifically did not get one for Cooper.

Had Cooper always had that swagger to his walk? That confi-dent roll to his hips? His hands were in his pockets as he came through the living room, staring around him, taking in Oliver's house. "I like what you've done with the place. Very minimalist."

Oliver swallowed down all the water in one gulp. "What are

you doing here?" He was going to repeat it until he had an answer.

"Are you just getting back from work?" Cooper ran a hand over the granite top on the breakfast bar.

"Shop doesn't run itself." *And I'm all I have, thanks to you.*

"I drove by, earlier. Pulpability. You know that's a terrible name, right?"

Oliver's grip could have shattered the glass in his hand. He considered squeezing harder. A trip to the emergency room would wrap this up quicker than being polite.

And if he called 911, he might even get to talk to Nick, eventually.

The idea of Nick and Cooper in the same place made his stomach roll.

"What. The fuck. Are you doing. Here?"

"How's the store? Have you conquered the Seacroft wellness market? I like the hipster look. That must be doing wonders for your foot traffic."

Dropping the glass was safer than squeezing it until it cracked. It shattered into a million tiny projectiles. The crash and the sound of shards skittering over the ceramic had the desired effect. Cooper's smooth facade, his easy smile, faltered the tiniest fraction, and he danced back, hands coming out of his pockets defensively.

Oliver took the retreat as an opportunity and stepped forward, glass crunching under his feet. He was going to track it through the house, scratch the floors, grind it into the carpet, and he didn't care. Not if it got Cooper's attention. "Get out."

"I called. I emailed. You wouldn't answer."

"You should have taken that as a hint."

"Ollie, I'm sorry!"

"For what?"

"Everything!"

Oliver was breathing hard, sides heaving. "What are you doing here?"

He had never been so angry in his life. Not when Cooper broke his heart the first time. Not that morning at the market when he thought Anya was Nick's wife.

"You need to leave." He'd break something else, something bigger than a glass, if Cooper didn't go.

"Can I—" Cooper held up his hands. "Please. Can we talk?"

"What the fuck for?"

"I—" Cooper glanced around nervously. "Look. Clearly showing up at the house was a mistake."

"You think? And it's *my* house. Not the house. You have no right to this place."

Cooper stumbled. "I need to talk to you. Things have changed. Please. It's important."

An old fear bubbled up. "Are you sick?"

"No."

"Dying?"

"No more than anyone else." Cooper smiled, then seemed to realize that might not be the best choice, and it vanished. "I'm sorry. All right? I surprised you, and that was my fault. Can we start again? Tomorrow? I can come by the store."

Oliver was irked he could say it so easily, like he had any right to be there either. Never mind they had picked out the location together. That was ancient history.

"Fine." If Cooper got out of his house, Oliver would deal with the repercussions in the morning.

"Nine o'clock?"

Too early. Oliver couldn't face him so soon. "Ten."

"I'll be there." He picked up his jacket from where he'd draped it over one of the couch's arms. Oliver was going to have to burn that couch now, which was a shame because Nick had always looked so perfect, laid out naked and wanting on it.

"Ten o'clock." Saying something like "good night" or "I'll see you soon" was too friendly.

"It's good to see you, Ollie." Cooper tripped as he reached for the front door, and evil satisfaction nested in Oliver's chest next to his anger. He kept his lips clamped shut on all the possible pleasantries as Cooper let himself out.

Once he was alone again, the house spun around him. Headlights flashed through the windows as Cooper's car drove away. Oliver collapsed onto the couch and buried his head between his knees.

Cooper. Fucking Cooper.

What the fuck did he want?

Why now?

Why had Oliver told him he'd meet him at the store tomorrow?

And what the fuck was Oliver going to tell Nick?

———

Oliver didn't answer when Nick called on his break. Disappointing, but since he'd called at two in the morning, also understandable.

The town was silent as Nick drove home, but his house was a different story. Hayden sat in his usual place at the kitchen table, chewing on toast and looking half awake. Anya was running around the place like a tornado.

"Oh, thank God you're here," she said as Nick walked in. Her hair was unbrushed, and she was still in a pink T-shirt and checkered pajama pants. "I slept in. I'm never going to be ready to go to work on time. Can you drive Hayden to school?"

Nick was tired, but what was another half hour? "Sure."

She kissed his cheek and then rushed away to the bathroom.

Hayden glared at him from the table. "Are you sure she knows about you and Beardo?"

"His name is Oliver."

Hayden rolled his eyes. Nick went to the coffeemaker, only to find out that, in her panic, Anya had failed to make a fresh pot.

He could have stayed at work for this kind of disappointment.

While he waited for it to brew, and for Hayden to finish getting ready to go, he checked his phone. Still no sign of Oliver. He went to dial the number, but then hesitated. With Hayden judging him silently from wherever he was in the house, Nick wasn't sure what to say.

I love you.

His cheeks heated. Yeah. He'd say that. He'd never get sick of saying that. Maybe someday Oliver would say it back too.

The drive to school was tense and silent, which was to say a typical drive with Hayden. Except where Nick was usually happy to let the silence stretch, now it seemed like he was wasting an opportunity. "Have you talked to your mom? About . . . you know."

Hayden sighed. "My raging homosexuality?"

Teenagers. One minute they were sobbing in your kitchen and stress-puking in your sink, and the next they were letting loose things like that in your car, strictly for the shock value.

Nick kept his hands steady on the steering wheel. "Yeah."

"No."

"Why not? She'll want to know. You know it won't matter to her."

"You didn't tell her, right?" Hayden's voice rose.

"I promised you I wouldn't."

Hayden stared out through the windshield.

"Did you always know?" he asked. "That you were bi?"

Nick sighed. Hayden was avoiding the question, but pushing it would lead to shouting or sulking. "No. Maybe. But not really. Your mom and I were your age when we met, and then my dad died. There was a lot of growing up and a lot of figuring stuff out happening very fast." But two could play this game. "Did you always know?"

Hayden smirked. "Yup."

Nick winced. All those years. How had they not seen it? And why had Hayden felt he needed to keep it a secret?

"You're not—are you—is there anyone who—" They pulled into the school lot, and Nick could have kicked himself for bringing this up when they had so little time left.

"Am I blowing guys in the locker room?"

Nick winced, and Hayden laughed as he pulled his backpack up from the floor.

"Just be careful, okay? I don't want you doing anything you'll regret."

A mean-eyed boy with too many piercings knocked on the passenger side window, making them both jump.

"That's Carson. I have to go."

"Hayden—"

But Hayden was already getting out of the car without so much as a look back.

————

It turned out the combination of bone-deep anger and gut-twisting nerves led to a kind of nauseated numbness, which was what Oliver was feeling by the time he got to the shop the next morning. Twice he'd gone to his phone to text Cooper and tell him to forget it. Twice, he'd bailed because Cooper didn't deserve the satisfaction of knowing how much he'd rattled Oliver. Cooper had always been an expert in reading people. Handy when they worked together. Not so much when he was appearing unannounced in the middle of the night like something out of a horror movie.

The shop was dead, which would have been frustrating. Today, it was irritating, but also convenient because it gave

Oliver room to pace. The extra-large black coffee he'd picked up didn't help. After so many months off caffeine—with the exception of the other day at the diner—trying to walk his talk with the shop, it hit him like a truck. For a moment, he was worried he was having heart palpitations. Cardiac arrest would solve a lot of problems.

By nine forty-five, he was back to angry, and the twitching was under control. The second part was good; the first was a problem. He hadn't handled things well the night before. It gave Cooper the advantage. In fact, Cooper had the upper hand since the moment he announced he wasn't moving to Seacroft with Oliver. Showing up without warning was a continuation.

The door opened at nine-fifty because Cooper would never be late for anything. His face was like cold water down Oliver's spine, which helped solidify his position at least.

"Hey." Cooper smiled.

Oliver swallowed hard. That smile had been for him once. Ten years of memories with that smile, and Oliver would be lying his ass off if he said it didn't affect him. But the ten months of distance between them now meant the smile couldn't mean anything anymore. "Hi."

Cooper was polished and perfect because he'd never let himself be anything else. The closet in their condo had been half the size of their bedroom, wall-to-wall with designer suits, shoes, and so many ties Oliver had once joked Cooper could go a year without wearing the same one twice. This morning, Cooper was in his weekend chic mode, despite it being Tuesday. Checkered shirt rolled up to his elbows, flat front chinos. The ostrich-skin belt was new. "Thanks for seeing me. You look good."

By comparison, Oliver had gone for his deepest, most committed hipster casual. Worn T-shirt, torn jeans. He'd left his hair down.

This was who they were now. Oliver was where they had

planned to be, and Cooper—clean-shaven, his hair perfectly styled—was where they had once been. For all of Cooper's perfect exterior, Oliver didn't want him anymore.

He wanted Nick.

"What are you doing here?"

Cooper smiled, green eyes scanning the store. Oliver knew what those eyes looked like after sixteen hours at the office. Or right after Cooper had just had the best orgasm of his life.

"I like the layout. I thought you were going to put the fridge by the door."

"Old breaker. It kept blowing. There's a short in the building somewhere." That had taken a month to give up on. By the time Oliver finally admitted the fridge wasn't going to go where he'd planned, even the electrician had stopped charging him to come try to find the source of the problem.

Cooper pulled a bottle from the shelf. He held it in his hand. "Mango Tornado?"

"Mango Ginger Zip didn't fit on the label."

"Because you're using the wrong fonts."

Oliver sighed. He didn't want to rehash this. Didn't want to talk about the money he'd spent to redesign everything so that it would be his and not theirs.

"What are you doing here?"

Cooper pulled one of the tall chairs from the counter, giving Oliver an arched eyebrow as it wobbled while he settled into it. He popped the top on the bottle and took a sip, then grimaced. "Kinda sweet."

Oliver sighed hard. "So you're here to swap recipes?"

"I want to talk." This dance was exhausting, each of them parrying, trying to find a way in. Oliver should have stepped aside and let Cooper be the victor, but his instincts wouldn't let him.

"How's Maurizio?" Oliver asked, at the same time Cooper said, "How's business?"

"Oh my God!" Oliver dug his fingers into his hair. "What the fuck are you doing here?"

He'd lost the contest to crack first, so the only option left was to go on the offensive.

"Ollie. I wanted to—"

"No. No." He pulled himself up to his full height. "You do not get to show up here, in my house, in my store, and act like you were in the neighborhood. You gave up that right. It's a big country. You can have any other part of it you want, but this town is mine."

Cooper gave him a crooked smile. "So things are going well, then? They gave you a key to the city?"

"You have thirty seconds to say whatever it is you came here to say, and then you're leaving."

Cooper leaned against his chair, hooking an elbow over the back. The posture said he had no intention of going anywhere, and Oliver was tempted to rip the seat out from under him. "I want back in."

Oliver laughed. "You're kidding, right? After what you did?"

Cooper shook his head. "I'm not asking you to take me back. I know I can't ask for that."

Fucking right he couldn't.

"So you want, what? The business?"

"Like we planned."

"Silent partner? It's going to be hard to run a juice bar from three time zones away."

"I was thinking of relocating. San Francisco's nice, but it rains a lot."

Oh fuck no. That could not happen. Oliver was finally starting to develop some separation.

"What does Maurizio think about small-town living?" Oliver hadn't seen Cooper's new man after everything had all gone down, but that didn't mean he didn't know who he was. Their circles were small, and if Cooper looked like a GQ model on his day off, then everything about Maurizio screamed Italian runway model.

"Maurizio is . . . " Cooper turned the bottle in his hands. "He took a job in Rome. He's gone."

"Gone? Gone as in—"

Cooper glanced away uncomfortably. Oliver should have been thrilled, but instead, he felt sad for what was about to come. "He got a better offer."

Shit.

"Sucks, doesn't it?"

Cooper reached a hand out over the counter. "Look, Ollie. I fucked up, okay? We had a dream, a big dream, and when it came time to go for it, I panicked. I'm sorry. Maurizio offered me a safe way out, and I took it."

And left Oliver to fail on his own.

"I think you should leave."

"Please! Just listen. I know I don't have any right to ask you to give me another chance. I know that getting back together isn't going to be an option for us, and I'm sorry, because we were good together. You know we were good, right?"

"We were good at the game." Oliver hung his head. "We were good at the lifestyle. The work, the late nights." The suits, the cars, the professionally-decorated condo. "But you weren't there when I needed you."

"Because I was scared!"

"You think I wasn't?" Oliver glared at him. "I quit my job. I told my family I had given it all up. I came here." *Without you.*

"I'm sorry, all right?" Cooper came around the counter. "Let me make it up to you. Let me help. I can't fix our relationship—"

"We don't have a relationship." Not anymore.

"But I could help with the business. It would be like we planned. You can be the ideas guy. I'll do the execution. I'm not asking for anything else."

Heat built on Oliver's skin, over the back of his neck and up his scalp. "Let me get this straight. You bail on me ten months ago, because you got a better offer. And then, when that doesn't work out the way you hoped, you show up in the middle of the night, and then slide in here this morning like you never left? You want your part in my business? The one I have spent the last six months growing *by myself*, and you think I'm going to bring you back into the fold?"

"I can help."

"Fuck you, Cooper!" Spittle flew from his lips.

Cooper barely blinked. "You need me."

"Not anymore."

"Yes, you do."

"I think you should go."

"You need me. I've done my research." He glanced around the store. "You think I came unprepared?"

"What research?" Oliver was ready to punch the words right off his lips.

Cooper continued. "I've asked around. I popped by the market last weekend."

"You're stalking me now?"

"Just research. Nothing more. You think I don't know it's not going according to your perfect plan?"

"It's going fine." He wouldn't give Cooper the satisfaction of admitting otherwise, but this dance was familiar. Cooper wouldn't have come here any less prepared than for a trial. He wouldn't have relied on old feelings and shared history to make his case. He'd rely on facts and pain points.

"It's midmorning on a weekday. How many customers have you had so far today? The fridge was full when I got here."

Oliver clenched his jaw. Cooper knew the numbers, the projections. He'd reviewed the revenue models and the estimates. He knew it all, right down to how much foot traffic they'd need on a Tuesday morning to pay the bills.

"Thank you for coming today." Oliver fished an elastic out of his jeans pocket and tied his hair back. "I'd say it was good to see you, but I'd only be lying."

"Ollie, come on." Cooper tilted his head to the side. "Is this about pride? I don't care about that. It could be great. Even if we're not together, we could still do this. I can help you."

"Yeah, until something better comes along."

"This business won't survive the way you're running it."

Maybe, but it would be Oliver's. Just his. He was done wasting any more energy on Cooper and their past.

He pulled the shop's front door open. "Please don't come back. If you want to open up a competing place across the street to drive me out of business for spite, be my guest, but I would appreciate if you didn't step foot in my store or my home again."

Cooper sighed. "If you change your mind, call me, okay?"

Oliver kept his gaze on the old floorboards beneath his feet. He didn't react when Cooper squeezed his shoulder, and if he let the door go a fraction early, so that it caught the heel of one of Cooper's suede Louboutin sneakers on the way out, he had earned the right to be petty.

His attention was caught by a shout and a hurried apology, and Oliver glanced out the window to see Cooper dodging around Avery's fluttering form in the street.

"Hey!" Avery appeared fully recovered from the previous day's migraine as he blew into the shop.

Oliver ground his teeth. He needed three minutes to decompress before he had to put his smiling face back on. "Can I get something for you?" He hoped it sounded friendly.

"Oh! Um. No. That is . . . " Avery ran a hand over his bright red hair, which he'd combed down today, making him look more respectable and less like he was twelve.

"Or do you have new celebrity updates? Because I don't think the vegan baking thing is going to work out." He was pushing the false cheer too hard, but he couldn't help it. Cooper had been watching, asking around. Fuck him for being a stalker.

A coward. Fuck him for being good at his job and catching Oliver unprepared.

"Um. I wanted to ask about food. For me." Avery coughed.

"Something other than late-night energy drinks?"

"Um, well, I guess. Maybe. Depends on what you think."

"Let me get my notepad, and we'll see what we can put together for you." This would be okay. The upside to Avery coming in so fast was Oliver had no time to brood and second-guess himself.

"No!" Avery moved fast, stepping in front of Oliver, surprising him so that he stopped short. "It's not—it's not a meal plan. I mean. I—I had a question. About a meal. Just one."

Oliver tried to follow. "Okay?"

"And the meal is—I mean—the question is. About the meal. The question about the meal is . . ." Avery was gasping like a dying fish, and his freckles were disappearing as he blushed furiously.

Oliver put a hand on his shoulder to steady him, hunching down so they were eye to eye. "Are you all right? Is it another migraine?"

Avery made a small squeaky noise as he shook his head.

"Are you sure?" Oliver was tempted to put a hand on his forehead, like his mom had done when he was little and home sick from school. Avery's face was flushed, his eyes bright.

And then suddenly his mouth on Oliver's was hot, wet, his tongue pushing hard against Oliver's lips, and Oliver was stumbling back in surprise, because Avery was kissing him.

Avery was kissing him!

He grunted, and Avery hopped back before Oliver could even attempt to untangle himself.

"I'm sorry." Avery was breathing hard. "I did that backward. I wasn't going to kiss you until after I'd asked you."

Oliver nearly wiped at his lips with the back of his hand, but he didn't want to hurt Avery's feelings, and anyway, he was too confused to try. He'd probably punch himself in the mouth instead.

"Asked me what?" His voice was as shaky as the rest of him.

"About the meal. Dinner." Avery was vibrating. Or possibly running on the spot very quickly. "Would you have dinner with me?"

Oh. Shit.

Oh shit, oh shit, oh shit.

"Are you asking me on a date?"

Avery nodded. "Maybe? Yes. I think so. Yes. I am. Would you have dinner with me? On a date. With me. Please. Yes."

Fuck. Shit. The list of curses running through Oliver's head grew, and he very nearly thumped his head on the counter to get it to shut up, but he'd only scare Avery.

Avery, whose brave smile was slipping. "I mean. It doesn't have to be a big thing. Like, dinner isn't a big thing. But I like you. I don't know if you've noticed that. I mean. Maybe you have. I guess. But . . ."

Fuck.

"Avery."

His smile faded more. "Or we could—"

"I'm with someone."

Avery's eyes bugged wider, and his mouth dropped open. And then he shivered and snapped his jaw shut. Watching him pull himself together again hurt more than letting him down easy.

"That's cool." Avery ran a hand over his hair, and the motion made Oliver's throat tighten. Had he done that on purpose? Combed it out? Tried to look like someone Oliver would want to go out on a date with?

"I'm really flattered."

"Is it that guy?"

Oliver frowned. "Which guy?"

"The—" He poked a thumb toward the door. "The

237

fancy . . . Um, the hot guy who just left? He was, like, really good-looking. I'd understand if you were with him."

Oliver put his hands on his face and groaned, all efforts to keep this from getting awkward destroyed. Fuck Cooper—again—more—for showing up in the middle of this mess. "No. No, it wasn't him. It's someone else."

"Oh."

Oliver tried to smile. "I'm really sorry. It's very flattering, but—"

"No!" Avery raised his hands. "No, it's cool. I understand. It was just a thought." He backed away, toward the door, and Oliver let him. Asking him to stay longer would only make it worse for them both.

"I'm sorry," he said again.

"Totally fine!" Avery's smile was heartbreaking. "I shouldn't have asked. It's fine. I won't—I won't bother you." He stumbled when his shoulder hit the door, and he flung it open, making it crash against the wall.

Oliver winced as the glass rattled. "Avery."

"No, it's cool. I won't—" The poor kid fled.

The shop fell silent.

"Fuck."

Oliver went to the door and locked it, turning the sign over in the window. They were closed. He was closed. He'd had more than enough for one day, and it wasn't even lunch time.

He slumped in the chair that Cooper had sat in so recently, growling as he scrubbed at his face with his knuckles.

He pulled out his phone and called Nick.

Hey honey, how's your day been?

You'll never guess what happened to me!

I should have let you take me home and fuck me like you wanted to.

If Oliver had let Nick have his way, every way, the night before, how much of this could have been avoided?

The call went to voicemail.

"Hey, it's me. It's Oliver. Um . . . you're probably asleep after your shift. Call me when you wake up. I want to see you. Okay. Bye."

The shop went silent again.

He couldn't stay here.

Oliver grabbed his keys and let himself out the back.

21

*N*ick was dead asleep when his phone chimed. He fumbled for it and turned the alarm off. He hadn't slept well, even worse than usual. Too many mixed-up dreams with Hayden, Anya, and Oliver. Brian had even appeared in one wearing a chicken suit right before Nick's alarm had gone off.

A shower helped, the hot water pouring over his skin. Oliver's shower, with Oliver in it with him, would have been better.

Maybe he should let Oliver talk to Hayden after all. If nothing else, Hayden was going to have to get used to Oliver being in Nick's life.

Except what would that look like? They were all still in this house—him, Hayden, and Anya—with no sign the situation would change any time soon. So Oliver would be what? Always on the outside? Always somewhere Nick snuck off to for a few hours on his days off or between shifts?

He rested his forehead on the cool tile wall. They would make it work. Oliver had stuck with him so far. If a trashed SUV hadn't sent him packing, a few awkward living arrangements weren't going to stop him, would they?

He toweled off and went back to his room to dress. Two-thirty was so much earlier than he wanted to be awake, but Hayden needed to be picked up from school soon.

On his nightstand, the phone rang.

Disappointment burned when Oliver's name didn't show up on the screen. Maybe Nick would try to stop by the store before work again tonight. "Hey, Anya."

"Nick?" Her voice made him pause.

"Yeah."

"Where have you been? I've been calling."

"I was asleep. Sorry, I just woke up. I have to go get Hayden soon."

A strange sound over the phone made Nick's blood go cold. He gripped the towel at his waist and sat gently on the edge of the bed.

"What's wrong?" he asked. The sound came again, and Anya was definitely crying. "What happened?"

"Hayden." Her voice trembled and died.

Nick's grip on the phone was tight enough to make his knuckles ache, and his toes dug into the carpet. "What about him?"

"They arrested him." She sobbed and then gasped in a breath.

Nick sighed. He'd been waiting for this, even if he hadn't realized it until this moment. Somehow, he'd been expecting this phone call for months. "What for?"

"I don't know. They said something about theft. I have to leave work. They've taken him to the police station."

"I'll meet you there." He was already moving, pulling clothes from the dresser.

"They're going to take him away. I'm so scared."

"I know. Don't do anything until I get there. He's a minor. They can't question him until one of us is there with him."

"I don't think they're questioning. They sounded pretty sure. Nick! We're going to lose him."

Nick bit his lip. She needed him to be strong. She needed him to take care of them. "I have to make a call. Don't say anything until I get there."

———

"So let me get this straight." Seb was in his living room, pacing in hurried circles around his couch.

"Please don't." Oliver was lying on the same couch, one arm flung over his eyes.

"Your douchebag ex-boyfriend shows up today, after his Gucci-model boy toy dumps his ass to hop across the pond. In a carefully rehearsed scheme right out of a rom-com, Douchey McGee asks to help save your business in an effort to win back your heart."

"He's not going to win back my heart."

"I notice you didn't disagree with my characterization."

Oliver let his arm drop to the floor. Seb was leaning over the couch, smiling expectantly at him. "Cooper is a douchebag. Continue."

"Right." Seb resumed his circling. "And then Avery, your cute-as-a-button twink of a best customer, who is a mild-mannered accountant by day, while his superhero identity is a Red Bull-guzzling, beet-juice-addicted, videogame fanatic by night, propositioned you, and you turned him down."

"He asked me out for dinner. There was no propositioning involved."

"He kissed you."

"He kissed me."

"With sexual intentions."

"Jesus." Oliver threw a cushion at him. "Where is your other half? Martin would be so much better at this than you are."

Seb tossed the pillow back at him with a laugh. "He's doing something with Penny."

"What kind of something?"

"They're organizing a spring fling at the elementary school. Don't ask me what they're flinging. Or how Martin got involved in all this. They made him MC of a fundraiser once last fall and now he's the committee chair."

Oliver had a pretty good idea how that happened. When the bookstore burned down, Martin had been quietly determined to help Seb get back on his feet, and he'd won over the whole town in the process. "He's too good for you."

"Ain't that the truth. Speaking of which!" Seb poked a finger in the air and started pacing again, moving clockwise this time which was just as well, because the other way had been making Oliver dizzy. "On top of these two men, one ex-boyfriend, one aspiring, who both came into your store this morning, desperate to win your heart, we have Nick. He is your *actual* boyfriend, despite the fact that I am only finding out about this change in your relationship status today."

"It's not like I—"

"Nick," Seb continued, like Oliver hadn't spoken, "who is not answering his phone but who, we assume, is at home sleeping. Home, where he lives in a platonic relationship with his high school sweetheart ex-wife because their teenage son is a criminal mastermind who needs twenty-four-hour supervision or else he might take over the world. Do I have all of that right?"

That last part had some not insignificant embellishments, and Oliver hadn't told Seb that Hayden came out to Nick because that wasn't his story to tell, but . . .

Then again, Oliver should have been having this conversation with Nick. If he had answered his phone any one of the three times Oliver called him after he'd left the shop, it would have been a nonstarter because he would have gone to Nick to sort out what happened over the morning. Instead, he was stuck reviewing it with his shithead baby brother, so Nick had no grounds to complain.

"Yeah, that's pretty much all of it." He winced.

Seb flopped down onto the couch with a heavy sigh, resting one elbow on Oliver's bent knee. "When you blow up your life, you really go for full hellfire, don't you?"

"I saw none of this coming."

"Not even the twink?"

Oliver groaned. Avery was the worst part of it. Collateral damage. "What was I supposed to see? He was sweet. I thought he was interested."

"He *was* interested."

"In juicing!"

"In your sexy hipster bod! He was hot for teacher, and you didn't even know!" Seb laughed, and Oliver kicked at him until he squirmed off the couch and fell to the floor with a thump.

Oliver buried his face in the cushion and waited for Seb's laughter to die. "What do I do?"

"What do you want to do?"

Drag Nick out of bed, buy two first class tickets to Fiji, and never look back?

Oliver pulled his phone out of his pocket and started dialing. "I should call Avery and make sure he's okay."

Seb made a noise like a buzzer and grabbed the phone out of Oliver's hand. "Wrong answer. The correct answer is let the uber-nerd lick his wounds for a while, then try to win back his business with a bouquet of fresh cilantro and sweet pea shoots."

That was the thing that worried Oliver the most. Avery would be embarrassed, possibly hurt. He'd more or less said he wouldn't be coming into the store again. He really had been Oliver's very best—nearly only—customer, and losing him now would be devastating, on top of Oliver enjoying his company.

"Can I make a suggestion?" Seb said. He was now lying on the floor, his body stretched out parallel to Oliver's on the couch.

"Will you do it even if I say no?"

"Of course."

"Then no."

Seb laughed softly. "What do you love about the juice bar?"

"That's a question, not a suggestion."

"Thank you, counselor, I'm aware of that. Please answer it."

Oliver leaned over the edge of the couch. "Been watching *Law & Order* reruns again?"

Seb smiled. "Martin has a secret crush on early twenty-first century Benjamin Bratt and doesn't want to tell me."

"You'll be watching *Miss Congeniality* next."

Seb grunted and pushed himself up on his elbows. His platinum hair was askew. "Are you being a dick on purpose, or are you avoiding my question because your answer is 'nothing?'"

Oliver's grin spread as Seb scowled at him, but then he actually thought about the question and rolled back onto the couch. "I don't know. It's been so hard lately. So many little hurdles to get over and—"

"My entire life's work was destroyed last fall, and Martin and I were building the new gallery within a month."

"It wasn't your *entire* life's work. Just the stuff you didn't sell."

Seb flipped him off, then settled to the floor again with a grunt. "My point is, there was never a question in my mind that I was going to rebuild. The fire was awful, and I'll never get those pieces back, but I knew what I wanted. If the juice bar burned down tomorrow—"

"Shit, that's exactly what this day needs."

"Shut up. If the juice bar burned down tomorrow, would you turn around and rebuild it all over, or would you do something else?"

Oliver went to laugh at the ridiculousness of the question. What a pointless hypothetical. The building was freshly renovated, with new smoke alarms and everything. Oliver had never been in the bookstore, but from what he understood about the fire, the place had been a tinderbox for decades.

But just as he was about to come back with his usual sarcastic reply, he stopped. "The store was Cooper's idea."

"Not yours?"

Back then, Oliver had been living on coffee and cigarettes, choking down the occasional smoothie when Cooper forced it on him. "He was trying this new thing. Juicing everything in the house. God, the mess. The counters were sticky all the time."

"I always knew he was a kinky bastard."

"Shut up." Oliver laughed, but he quieted quickly. "I gave up a lot to start this business. Everything."

"I'm not denying that."

"And now you're telling me it was a mistake?" He shifted on the sofa, picking at the upholstery.

"Not if you love it."

Oliver stared up at a small crack in the ceiling. He'd have to get Seb's landlord to look at it.

"If you don't love it, though," Seb continued when Oliver didn't say anything, "that would be okay. You don't have to follow through on everything. Sometimes it's okay to walk away."

"But I quit my job. I moved here."

"And I love having you here for these little heart-to-hearts. But, Ollie, you've only ever been one person, your entire life. You followed one path from the time we were kids until the time you got your fancy legal job with your fancy legal boyfriend in your fancy legal condo. I, on the other hand, have spent my entire life with questionable revenue streams and dubious housing. Trust me when I say it's okay to fuck up from time to time. Change is good."

"Dubious housing?"

Seb shuddered. "Let me tell you about the apartment I had when I dropped out of art school. It wasn't really even an apartment. Just a room with a big closet that had a toilet and a shower. It was so dark and damp in there that mushrooms grew on the tile in the summer and—"

"Okay, okay!" Oliver pulled himself up to sitting and ran his fingers through his hair.

"All I'm saying is, your dickhead boyfriend left you high and dry, right after you made a massive life change, and you did what you could to hold the rest of the pieces together. That's admirable. But if it's not the thing you really want to be doing, why are you doing it?"

Oliver groaned and tipped his head over the back of the sofa. Seb was right—or he was making sense at least, which was irritating in its own way. Pulpability was challenging, but not especially satisfying. He wanted to help people, but lately, the residents of Seacroft had made it clear they didn't want his help. Not like this, anyway. If he weren't trying to keep the business afloat, what else would he do?

He hunched forward so he was looking down at his brother, still lying on the floor. "When you're not being an asshole, you're actually pretty smart."

Seb grinned at him. "That's my secret. I'm always—"

Oliver's phone rang, the sound loud in the quiet apartment. Oliver pulled it out of his pocket and warmth swept over him when he saw Nick's name. He stepped over Seb as he answered the call. "Hey, baby. How's your day going?"

"Oliver? Hayden's in jail. I need you."

liver stared at himself in the mirror. The suit fit perfectly, but then, that was the beauty of a bespoke suit.

Going home to change might have been the height of self-indulgence, but he needed the armor, and he'd given Nick explicit instructions to tell the police Hayden wouldn't be talking to anyone without his lawyer present, so he had time.

He ran a hand over his beard and then through his hair. They didn't fit with the tailored black of his jacket, but that was fine. He wasn't the guy who wore suits like this every day anymore.

Oliver drove across town and strode into the police station with the confidence of years of training and practice. He introduced himself to the officer at the desk and was taken down a dim hall without much fanfare.

Hayden was sitting at a table in a cramped room. Anya sat next to him, looking small. She stood when he walked in. Her mascara was smeared under her eyes, but she straightened and came around the table to shake his hand. "Thank you so much for coming."

"Of course."

Beyond them, Hayden sighed heavily. He was spread out in his chair, taking as much space as he could. For all his mother was so obviously shaken, Hayden looked like everything about this turn of events was incredibly inconvenient.

"Have you spoken to the police?" Oliver asked.

Anya shook her head. "No. Nick told us that you said not to."

"That's good." He tried not to sound too invested when he said, "Where's Nick?"

"I'm here."

Oliver turned to find Nick standing in the doorway, a uniformed officer hovering behind him. Nick held two paper coffee cups.

"Hi." His eyes were tired, but his smile was warm.

Something inside Oliver clicked into place. Nick. He would do anything for Nick. "Hi. Everything okay?"

Nick nodded and walked across the room to hand one of the coffees to Anya. They stood there, shoulder to shoulder, and she leaned into him while he wrapped an arm around her. Oliver might have been jealous, except for the twin expressions of worry and fear on their faces. They were every inch the terrified parents, and he was here to help them win this fight.

"I'd like to speak with my client and his family," Oliver said to the officer, who nodded and shut the door. Two sets of eyes were pinned to Oliver, waiting expectantly, while Hayden traced a fingernail over the battered tabletop.

"Let's have a seat." Oliver pulled a chair away from the table. Muscle memory had him taking out a notepad and several pens and setting them down in front of him. The movement was familiar and foreign, something he had done thousands of times in his old life, something he hadn't needed to do in months.

"So how does this work?" Anya asked.

"Ideally, Hayden tells me what happened in his own words." He hoped they got the hint. It wouldn't help to have them filling in the silences with speculation and half-baked hypotheses. Parents did that, instinct pushing them to protect their kids.

"I stole some tablets from the guidance counselor's office." Hayden's voice was flat, and Anya made a soft sad noise that had Nick pulling her close.

Oliver kept his focus on Hayden. "You're not disputing it?" With teenagers, you usually got everything *except* a full confession. Denial, deflection, shifting of blame. For Hayden to come right out and admit what he'd done was notable.

"There was a box of them delivered while I was working in her office. She had to go to the bathroom. I took a few and put them in my backpack. I thought she wouldn't notice right away."

"But you were going to give them back, right?" Anya asked.

Hayden glanced at her out of the corner of his eye. "Then I would have said I borrowed them. You don't give back things you steal."

Anya covered her face with her hands. Nick's eyes were wide and begging as he stared at Oliver.

Oliver folded his hands on the table. "Do I want to know why you stole them?"

Hayden shrugged, but didn't say anything.

"Answer him." Nick's voice was deep, at the edge of angry, but Oliver held up his hand.

"Sometimes it's better not to." He turned his attention back to Hayden. "You know it's bad, right? You were already on home confinement, and while theft of a single tablet could be considered minor in many circumstances, since we're talking about multiple units here, with your record, it's unlikely that anyone is going to be lenient. We're looking at extending your sentence for sure, and probably incarceration in a juvenile facility."

Anya was crying for real now, big tears down her cheeks. The lines on Nick's face got deeper with every second. Hayden continued to stare at the table like he was building up his X-ray vision capabilities.

"So if there is anything you can tell me that will help me explain why you did what you did, or any reason why the rest of your sophomore and most your junior year shouldn't be spent in jail, now would be a good time to share it."

Hayden continued to scratch at the table.

"Hayden." Anya's voice was thin and tear-soaked. "Honey. Please. You have to tell him. We love you, please. We'll help you any way we can, but you have to tell him what happened."

The only indication Hayden heard her was the whitening of the knuckle on his index finger where he traced an invisible line on the chipped wooden finish.

"Hayden." Where Anya's voice was a plea, Nick's was firm. His next words would be a command, and Hayden tensed.

Oliver stood abruptly, his chair scraping over the floor. The move was a distraction, more than any real need to get up. But putting Hayden on the defensive would not help any of them. "Can I talk with you both for a minute?"

Anya and Nick followed him out into the hall. The second the door was closed, Anya went to pieces, sobbing in Nick's arms. Nick smoothed her hair down her back and stared at Oliver over her shoulder, black eyes desperate. "He's been like this since we got here. Won't say anything else. It's like he's given up."

Oliver wanted to touch him so badly, tell him it was all going to be okay, but this wasn't the place, and he couldn't promise that. He didn't know all the particulars of Hayden's case, but his history wasn't good. "What have you guys had to eat today?"

Nick shrugged, and Anya shook her head, like they didn't understand the question.

Oliver glanced down the hall. The station was quiet, which was to be expected in a small-town police department on a Tuesday afternoon. He suspected no one would mind if he dragged this client conference out a bit.

He spoke directly to Nick. "Go get something to eat. I'd like to talk to Hayden alone."

"Can he do that?" Anya asked Nick.

"I'm not the police. Hayden's my client. With your permission, I'd like to talk to him." The request was this side of ethically dodgy, but then, so was representing your lover's son without disclosing the relationship.

Nick stared at Oliver, and he tried to give them his most professional and reassuring smile.

"Come on," Nick said. "We'll go across the street and get a sandwich. We don't have to be gone long."

Oliver relaxed and stayed in the hall as Nick led her away. Nick glanced over his shoulder once, before they turned the corner, and mouthed, *Thank you.* Oliver tipped his chin toward him, but he didn't want thanks yet.

He pulled off his jacket as he went back into the room. Hayden had his cheek pressed to the table, hands over his head.

"Do you know how often they disinfect that tabletop?" Oliver asked as he sat down.

Hayden peeled his face off the table to glare at him. "Are you going to tell me how fucked I am again?"

"I'd prefer not to. Your dad hasn't told me much about your situation."

Hayden laughed. "Too busy sucking your dick?"

If this kid thought he was going to ruffle Oliver's feathers with a couple dick jokes, he was going to be disappointed. "So why don't you tell me what happened?"

"I already told you." Hayden flopped back in his chair, long limbs splayed in all directions.

"That's not what I asked." Oliver kept his voice icy calm.

"You asked what happened."

"I meant last year. There's no point in trying to defend you for this if I don't understand what happened last year. The first time you got arrested."

Hayden sighed. "It's in my file. I'm sure there's a copy around here somewhere."

"I want to hear it from you."

"Well, I don't feel like talking about it." Hayden crossed his arms over his chest. When he glared, he looked so much like Nick, it nearly broke Oliver's heart. So much of the father in the son, and the distance between them was painful.

"Hayden, I'm your lawyer."

"I didn't ask for a lawyer."

Oliver continued, unperturbed. "Anything we say here is protected by confidentiality. I don't have to disclose anything you tell me unless it's as part of your defense or if I'm asked a direct question in court. But aside from that, I'm not allowed to share anything you tell me with the police, your teachers—"

"I know all of this."

"—Or your parents."

The room fell silent. Hayden kept glaring, dark eyes flashing black and brown, angry, frustrated.

Frightened.

"Is there anything I should know about last year? Anything that could help me, even if you don't want your parents to know?"

"No." But the dark eyes blinked and darted away.

Yes, there is.

"Your dad said you were bullying a kid in your class."

Hayden shrugged, but he still wouldn't turn his eyes back to Oliver's. "He was a loser. It wasn't a big deal."

"Your dad said he was gay."

Another shrug.

Oliver made notes on his legal pad. Nothing important, only the recipe for *Mango Tornado*, but Hayden wasn't watching him, and it bought him some time while he planned his next approach.

"Your dad told me you came out to him."

Hayden's eyes shot back to his face, and he met it blandly. The statement was a risk, but Oliver needed to make some headway. "What if I did?"

Oliver leaned back in his chair and loosened his tie. "It's a big deal. I was a bit older than you are when I told my dad. I was so fucking scared, I nearly threw up in our backyard."

Hayden sneered. "Are you trying to bond with me here?"

"I'm saying it's a scary thing. And before? Before I came out? I was a mess. I'd always known I was gay, but I was so scared that my parents were going to be angry. I was so scared about what my friends would say. I told a few of them in my sophomore year of high school. Everyone said it was cool, but after that, not all of them would come over to my house anymore."

Hayden rolled his eyes. "They sound like a bunch of dicks."

"It's really hard. Coming out gets talked about like you make a big announcement and then the world knows. And some people are cool about it, and others are dicks, but at least everyone knows and you can move on with your life."

Hayden laughed bitterly. "Yeah, maybe if you live in a Hallmark movie."

Oliver smiled sadly at him. He wished he could tell him it would be okay, but the old anxieties never quite went away. There would always be that moment when you read a new acquaintance and decided how much to tell them. The moments when you used "partner" instead of "boyfriend" and let the people in the room assume what they want. It got easier, but it was never fully easy.

"You have to decide who you're going to trust. Family. Friends. You have to decide which of them will have your back."

"People are jackasses."

"A lot of them are. And sometimes you'll choose to trust the wrong people. And sometimes people change." Like Cooper. For so long, he had been who Oliver needed. He'd be a mess of ulcers and heart conditions if Cooper hadn't looked after him for as long as he had.

"I bet no one ever screwed you over," Hayden said.

Oliver gave him a half-hearted grin. "I was in love with someone for a long time. And when we were ready to be together, make a change that would mean it would just be us, living our life the way we wanted, he left me." Oliver had spent the last months telling himself he was the one who chose to leave because it meant he'd still been in control. But the truth was it had all been Cooper, and Oliver was too afraid to admit he hadn't seen it coming.

Hayden swallowed, and the room fell into silence. Oliver waited. Hayden had to trust him, but he couldn't let this get too far off course into his own personal life, or the whiplash would be brutal for both of them when he tried to steer it around to Hayden's story.

"That sucks for you."

"It really did. And for him. It was a big step for both of us, and in the end, he wasn't ready to make it."

"Do you hate him now?"

Hate was a strong word. This year had been complicated, buried in waves of anger, sadness, disappointment. But Oliver had never hated Cooper. "I feel sorry for him. He missed out on something that could have been really great, and I think he's only figuring that out now."

A single tear rolled down Hayden's cheek. Oliver pressed his lips together to keep from reacting. If he pounced on whatever Hayden was feeling, the kid was as likely to bottle it back up as he was to let it out.

"Just because I was mad at him doesn't mean I don't understand why he did what he did, or that I don't still care about what happens to him." And that was the truth. Oliver would never be in love with Cooper again, but maybe, after everything, he could forgive him.

Hayden swiped at his tear with the back of his hand. "He wasn't my friend." His voice was wobbly. "Mom and Dad always call him my friend, but he wasn't."

"Who?"

"Chris. Christian. The guy I—the guy I got arrested for—" He coughed, and his cheeks started to redden.

"The kid you were bullying?" Oliver kept his tone steady. This was progress, but he couldn't rush it.

Hayden nodded, teary eyes spilling over. "He wasn't my friend."

"Okay." Classmate. Acquaintance. The semantics were irrelevant. Unless—

"He was my boyfriend."

Unless he was more than a friend.

Oliver should have brought a glass of water. That was his usual ploy to give himself time to steady his heartbeat and shaking hands in situations like this. But he'd been rushed, and the setting was unfamiliar, and so he only had the pen and pad on the table. He went back to writing out the recipe for Mango Tornado. The letters were jagged and uneven, but it gave Hayden space to pull himself together a bit.

"Did you hear what I said?" The kid's voice was high, desperate.

"He was your boyfriend."

"Yeah."

"Were you together for a long time?" Better to ask simple questions than push for the sequence of events that went from young love to cyberbullying.

"Seven months."

"That's a while." For a fourteen-year-old, that would have felt like a lifetime.

"We didn't tell anyone. Nobody knew."

"That's okay. You didn't have to."

"I know that, all right?" Hayden slammed a palm on the

desk, but Oliver kept up his note-taking. A pound of carrots. Remove the pits from the mangoes. "His parents were super strict, and my family . . ." He laughed. "You've met my family."

Oliver bit back the instinct to defend Nick. "Telling families can be hard."

"And none of our friends knew. They would have said we were gross. Disgusting queers. They wouldn't have understood."

"I'm sorry you didn't have anyone you thought you could tell."

Hayden wiped at his nose again, tears starting once more. "Carson found us, after school one day."

The name scratched at the back of Oliver's brain, but he didn't interrupt Hayden.

"He's a loser. He's supposed to be a year ahead of me, but he keeps failing so he was in a lot of my classes. We weren't doing anything wrong, me and Chris. Just kissing and stuff. Boyfriend stuff. Nothing wrong."

A sick feeling spread in Oliver's stomach. He hadn't had his first real boyfriend until he'd gone to college because nothing stayed a secret in the confines of a high school.

"Did Carson hurt you?"

Hayden wiped at his eyes and sniffled loudly. "He called us fags. Said we were dirty. Said he was going to tell everyone. I couldn't—no one was supposed to know. Chris's family. They're super conservative. If they knew Chris was gay, they'd send him away."

Nick had said that Chris was at a private school now, after the bullying. Whatever came next, Hayden had lost his boyfriend either way.

"You tried to protect him?" He shouldn't put words in Hayden's mouth, but the distress in his eyes was real, and he could panic and shut down at any minute, so Oliver needed to keep him talking.

Hayden nodded, using the collar of his T-shirt to scrub away the wet streaks on his face. "I told Carson not to say anything. I told him I'd do anything if he didn't out Chris. His homework. I'd help him study. Anything he wanted."

Carson. The name clicked into place. Hayden had asked to borrow Nick's phone, the night Oliver had been there, to call Carson about homework. "When did all this happen?"

"Last February. When I was still in ninth grade."

More than a year.

"So what did you do?"

Hayden's face crumbled. He needed a tissue, but Oliver didn't have any, and he wasn't leaving to ask for one. Walking out would give Hayden time to build his defenses back up. Instead, he handed the kid the bright red pocket square from his jacket.

Hayden blew his nose loudly into it. "I broke up with him," he rasped. "I told him I had been lying the whole time. That he was gross and I was fooling around to see what it was like, but that I was straight and I didn't want to see him again."

Oliver nodded. He'd figured as much. "And then what happened?"

"He didn't believe me!" Hayden's voice broke. "He said he loved me and that he knew I was protecting him. But Carson wouldn't stop. He kept telling me . . . He said I had to . . . " Hayden was sobbing now, big, body-wracking shudders.

Oliver came around the table and put a hand on his shoulder. That was enough. He could piece together the rest. Carson's threats had escalated, and with it, Hayden's tactics to get Christian to give up on him, until it would look like bullying to the outside observer instead of desperation.

"Did Carson ask you to steal the tablets?"

Hayden shuddered under his hand, but he nodded. "He told me to call him. On Saturday."

When Oliver had been there. His horror mounted.

"He said this was it. That I had to steal them from the guidance counselor's office. If I didn't, he'd met this girl online who goes to the same school as Chris. He said he'd tell her he saw Chris giving me a blow job after gym class. But he also said this would be the last time. His dad got a new job, so they're moving away this summer. I had to do this one thing, and then he'd leave us alone."

That wasn't a guarantee. Even if the kid moved away, the reach of the internet was long. It could be enough, though. Hope was enough.

And yet it made everything more complicated—or more personal at least. Hayden's harasser called him last Saturday while Oliver had been there, sprawled over Nick's lap, distracting him from his son. If Oliver had stayed home, would Nick have known? Overheard, maybe? Would he have been able to stop it?

"Did you ever try to tell anyone—" Oliver very purposefully didn't mention Nick's name, "—about this?"

Hayden shook his head. "Because then Carson would have told everyone about me and Chris. It was my fault. I should have been more careful. Chris was always so worried, but I thought we'd be okay and—I had to fix it. By myself. No one else could help."

Oliver knew that feeling intimately. He'd spent the last year convinced he needed to rebuild his life on his own, but all that led him to was Seb's couch with his arms thrown over his face, wondering how it came to this.

Better, though, than Hayden's situation. The scene at Nick's made so much more sense. The anger, yes, but the desperation too. The fear because someone else was pulling Hayden's strings, and he thought he couldn't tell anyone. Harassment could easily have fuelled the shattered glass of Oliver's SUV window, scattered around Hayden's feet. It had been a cry for help, and neither Oliver nor Nick had known what they were seeing.

"He said this would be the last one," Hayden said softly. "The last time, and then he'd leave me alone."

"And that's why you told your dad that you were gay? Because you thought it was almost over."

Hayden mopped at his face with the pocket square as he nodded. "Because he gets this look on his face when he talks about you. It's not fair. How come he gets to—and I can't—" He picked at the tabletop with a fingernail. "Except I guess my timing sucked because now I'm here, and it doesn't matter."

It would always matter. Regardless of what happened next, Hayden's identity would always matter.

"You've got me. I'm going to make this better."

———

The sun had gone down by the time they left. Nick felt a hundred years older. He and Anya came back from Oliver's mandated lunch hour to find Hayden puffy-eyed and miserable while Oliver talked quietly with two police officers. As the story came out, Nick's body pressed in on itself, his bones aching and his muscles cramping.

At some point, a commotion erupted at the front of the police station, and an officer led in a mean-eyed teenager with a dozen piercings in his lip and nose. He shouted obscenities and called Hayden's name, even though he couldn't possibly know Hayden was in the building too. Carson. Now Nick knew who he was, the sight of him made Nick want to burn the place to the ground for hurting his kid. Only Oliver, with his steady presence and confident movements as he helped Hayden write up a statement and spoke with the police, kept Nick on an even keel.

In the end, they let Hayden go home. The bracelet was still on his ankle, but Nick was confident they were going to come to the end of this soon.

"Thanks," he said to Oliver, as they all stood in the parking lot. "Thank you."

Oliver smiled at him. He was devastating like this: the dark suit, the white shirt, and thin tie. Throughout this whole terrible day, Oliver had been a pillar of calm. Nick would be grateful until the day he died. Regardless of how Oliver felt about him in a day, a week, a month—and honestly, after the mess of today, Nick didn't understand how Oliver still hadn't run for the hills—Nick would love the man in front of him forever.

"We'll need to get him different representation before his next court date. This isn't my field, and it's not a great idea for me to do it with us—" He leaned forward and gently kissed Nick's temple. "Sorry. Lawyer brain. We'll talk about it later."

Too many things Nick wanted to say, but they had an audience, so in the end he squeezed Oliver's hand and turned to go. Anya was still unsteady, and they also had a lot to talk about, but as he moved toward their car, Anya put a hand on his shoulder. "Where are you going?"

"Home with you guys?"

She kissed his cheek. "Why don't you go home with Oliver?"

"But—" They had so much to work through.

"He saved us, probably all of us, today. Don't make him go home alone."

Nick glanced over his shoulder to where Oliver was walking across the lot toward his SUV. "Are you sure?"

She gave him a gentle shove. "Nothing is changing tonight. We'll talk in the morning."

He caught up to Oliver as he was getting into the driver's seat. Oliver's eyes widened as Nick climbed in beside him. "What are you doing?"

"Going home with you. If that's okay."

Oliver's smile gleamed in the dark. "More than okay."

The SUV purred to life, and they sat silently as Anya pulled out ahead of them and turned toward the street. Nick's chest tightened as the old sedan drove away.

"What is it?" Oliver squeezed his hand.

Nick cleared his throat. "They're going to leave again." Soon. With the truth out about Carson and his harassment, Hayden's house arrest would be over. Without the thing on his ankle, he and Anya had no reason to stay at the house.

Oliver sighed. "Nick. Baby."

"It's okay. It's fine." It would be. They wouldn't go far, and Nick wouldn't keep the same distance he had for all those years. He was still learning how to be a father, but Hayden needed him, underqualified or not. "Thank you. For coming. For helping him. I didn't know who else to call."

"You call me. Always."

Nick stared out the window. He couldn't even see Anya's taillights anymore. "It's a mess. And every time I think it's going to get better, there's another layer, another pile of shit. Something else I couldn't see coming. Maybe it will be better now, or maybe this is just another calm before a whole new storm. If you didn't want to be a part of this, I'd understand."

Oliver's fingers on his chin were soft but firm. His mouth was demanding. Nick held his breath, not wanting to absorb the hope from that single kiss, in case it was all he'd ever get.

Oliver sat back in his seat. "You always call me. No matter what."

"But—"

"I love you. You, Nick. I will always want to help you. Take care of you. Nothing you can tell me or show me will change that. Ever."

Nick tried to breathe now, but the air was trapped by the lump in his throat. "Oliver, I—"

"I love you." Oliver's throat worked hard too. "Let me take you home and show you how much."

He pulled them out onto the street. They were silent for a

block or two, until his laughter cracked though the inside of the car. "Want to hear a funny story? It'll help to break the tension."

Nick grinned at him. His insides had been in knots for hours. Anything Oliver had to say would be a welcome relief. "Sure."

"Cooper showed up uninvited at my house last night."

"Caramel." This was not a story Nick needed to hear right now.

Oliver grinned and put a hand on Nick's knee. "Trust me."

It came out, all the details. Oliver's face was blank as he talked about Cooper, which was good, because Nick was still fighting the need to hunt the bastard down and punch him for hurting Oliver in the first place, and then again for showing up like he had any right to be there.

"But what did he want?" Nick asked.

Oliver turned onto his street. "Absolution. Maybe a second chance. I don't know."

"Well, he'll have to find it somewhere else." Nick tucked a strand of Oliver's hair behind one ear, and Oliver shivered.

"There's uh—there's one other thing," he said, lower lip between his teeth.

"What?"

"One of my customers asked me on a date today. I tried to let him down easy, but—"

"Triple caramel sundae with extra sprinkles!"

They let themselves into the quiet house. Oliver's house. Still perfect, polished, like its tenant, but homey now. Comfortable.

Like Oliver.

Nick pulled him close, and Oliver melted against him when their lips met. This, too, was like coming home.

"I love you," Oliver whispered against Nick's lips.

"You too. I don't know what I would have done without you today." He slipped the elastic in Oliver's hair loose.

"It felt good to be able to help."

263

Nick pulled Oliver's perfect shirt out of the waistband of his pants. "I'm going to wrinkle the hell out of this suit."

Oliver laughed and pushed him away. His eyes were hot as he pulled the tie from around his neck. "I'd like to see you try."

———

Nick was deep inside Oliver, holding them as close as he could. They lay on their sides, and Nick thrust lazily, moving enough to keep them both hard, not enough to make them come. He could stay like this all night, listening to the rustle of the sheets on their skin and Oliver's soft grunts and sighs as Nick worked him.

He'd half expected to be too tired for sex, but Oliver's skin under his hands, his tongue in his mouth, was enough to keep him going.

"I love you." Nick might never get tired of saying that.

Oliver writhed, twisting back to wrap one hand around Nick's neck and pull him in for a kiss. His beard brushed against Nick's cheek, rough on his skin, and it made his heart speed up. His. Oliver was his, to touch, to taste, to have. Finally.

His cock pulsed, making Oliver moan, and Nick thrust deep, loving the way Oliver responded under his body.

"More," Oliver panted. "Please, baby. Give me more."

Nick bit at his earlobe. "What did we say about pet names?"

"You love it." Oliver laughed as he pinched Nick's thigh, then growled deep in his chest as Nick palmed his cock to stroke him.

He did love it. With Oliver, the name went straight to Nick's gut, something needy and desperate hidden inside of it.

He thrust in again, hard, and Oliver arched against him.

"Baby. Please. I need you."

"What do you need?" He kissed the spot at the base of Oliver's skull, burying his face in the coil of hair there.

"You. Oh god." Oliver bucked as Nick pushed into him again. "You. I need you. Now. Please."

Nick rolled away, pulling out of Oliver.

"What?" Oliver's head turned toward him.

"Come here." He sat up, bracing himself against the headboard. Oliver, hair tangled, eyes glassy, followed, crawling up his body, dragging his finger's over Nick's bobbing cock. The weight of him, the heat, as he seated himself back down on top of Nick, taking him deep inside, had Nick's eyes rolling back in his head.

"I don't know what I did to deserve you, but I am going to hang on to you with everything I have." He buried his hands in Oliver's hair, holding it tight, tipping Oliver's mouth back to take it with his own. Oliver groaned, body tightening around Nick when he rolled his hips.

"I'm so glad we couldn't do uncomplicated." Oliver whimpered as Nick bit down on the heavy cord at his neck. Nick thrust up, holding Oliver down on him as he rocked, and Oliver went boneless against him.

"You're so good," Nick said. "Mine. You're so mine."

"Yes." Oliver's blunt nails dug into his shoulders while his hips rolled. "Yes. Yours. I'm yours."

Nick rubbed his thumb over the head of Oliver's cock, spreading the bead of pre-come over the tip, loving the way Oliver clenched and shivered. He explored further, knuckles dragging up and down, making him pulse and jump against his hand.

He thrust up again and again. With gravity working against him, he didn't have much range of motion, but each thrust had Oliver crying out as his lips dragged over Nick's skin, and that was all he needed. He stroked Oliver, who surged in his palm while fucking himself down on Nick's cock.

"You're doing all the work," Nick said.

"Shut up and make me come."

Who was Nick to say no to a request like that? He licked a stripe down his palm and jerked Oliver for real, his head moving in and out of Nick's grip in rapid thrusts.

"Yes." Oliver was a storm against him, and the headboard rattled against the wall. Nick mashed their lips together as Oliver shuddered and bucked against him. Nick pulled him tight, his own orgasm building in his gut and his balls.

Oliver came first, a series of long, low gasps as his ass clenched around Nick and come splashed against both their stomachs. Then Nick spiralled after him, locking Oliver's body against him as his cock pumped his release.

They were all limbs and sticky heat when they pulled themselves apart. Nick's hands felt too big, and he tried to kiss Oliver, but his mouth landed between his temple and his eye.

"I don't think I'll be able to walk tomorrow." Oliver lifted his head to smooth his hair down the back of his neck, then buried his face in the crook of his elbow.

"Don't be dramatic." Nick nipped at one of Oliver's flat nipples before he slid off the bed to go deal with the condom.

"I wasn't being dramatic. I was being complimentary." He yelped when Nick came back from the bathroom and tossed a wet cloth that landed on Oliver's stomach with a soft splat.

"Clean up. You'll get gross if you stay like that, and I'm not going to want to let you up once we're in bed."

Oliver grinned evilly at him as he wiped the come off his belly. "I thought we were in bed. You're the one who got out of it."

Nick glared at him as he folded himself back down onto the mattress. Oliver wrapped himself around Nick again, biting gently at his chin.

"You okay?" he asked.

Nick ran a hand over Oliver's hair and down his back, breathing in his scent and grounding himself. He was here. With Oliver. Anya and Hayden were elsewhere. Not far, but the separation between them was already growing.

"Hey." Oliver nuzzled at his throat. "Stay with me."

"I'm trying." He was. He wanted Oliver, wanted to build

something with him. It was hard to picture, but he had faith they'd make it happen.

Oliver's tongue did distracting things in the hollow between Nick's collarbones. "Want to hear another funny story?"

Nick laughed and kissed the top of his head. "Does it involve another ex-boyfriend showing up out of nowhere? Or someone who would like to be your boyfriend but isn't me? Because I just had my dick in your ass, and now is not a good time for that kind of story."

Oliver pinched him, then squirmed until Nick had him trapped under his body, pressing him down. Nick kissed him, trying to print Oliver's taste in his brain. All of it. He wanted all of it.

"Seriously though." Oliver broke away long enough to speak. "I need to tell you something."

Nick rolled onto his back. "Fine. Tell me."

Oliver followed him, resting his chin on Nick's chest, trailing small kisses on his skin that made it harder to hold onto his anxiety. "I think you should know, before you go all in with me, that there is a very good chance that I could be unemployed within the near future."

"Unem—" Nick lifted his head.

Oliver's eyes were serious, but they didn't look worried. He ran a hand over Nick's cheek, before sliding it down his chest, covering his heart. "The store. It's not—today, with Hayden. I'm good at that. I was always good at that. And I think the juice bar was me holding on to a dream that wasn't really mine. Or I was trying to prove that I could make it a success after my relationship with Cooper failed so badly. But the thing is, there isn't anyone left who cares whether the business lives or dies."

"I care." Nick struggled to follow what Oliver was saying.

"About the juice bar?" Oliver's grin tugged at one corner.

"About you."

"Exactly. About me. And I care about us. But I've been

spending a lot of time and energy trying to keep something afloat when, maybe, I don't believe in it all that much to begin with."

Nick stared up at the ceiling, letting the heat of Oliver's body bleed into his. "So what will you do instead?"

Oliver kissed his chest. "That is a completely different question. Something that can wait until tomorrow."

"But—"

"Tomorrow." Oliver leaned up to kiss his mouth. "What's the worst that can happen?"

*O*liver grunted as he tied off the sign on the booth's frame. The sucker weighed more than he'd expected.

"Got it?" Nick asked from where he was doing the same thing on the other side.

"Think so. Why is it so heavy?"

"Wood's like that."

Oliver stood back so he could examine their handiwork. Around him, market vendors were getting their own booths set up. Nick came to stand beside him, their shoulders bumping under their heavy plaid work shirts.

"The name is terrible," Nick said.

Oliver bit his lip to hide his smile. "It's cute."

"It's terrible. I can't believe I let you talk me into it."

Nick's Nacks. Not his best work, but the way the tips of Nick's ears went pink every time Oliver said it out loud was worth the awkwardness. "People like puns."

"Puns are the lowest form of humor," Seb said, as he came up the aisle with Martin. Between them, they carried a bushy Christmas tree.

"I can't believe I said okay to this." Nick glared at the sign.

"You wanted to call it Wooden Winter Creations." Oliver

helped his brother get the tree into the stand, pretending he didn't see the way it wobbled once they had it upright. He'd argued for an artificial one, but Nick said people would like the smell.

"What's wrong with 'Wooden Winter Creations?'"

"It's seasonal, for one thing. What if we wanted to sell some of these in the summer?" He hauled a box out of the back of the truck. Their truck. Silver and domestic and nothing like the old Porsche. It even had windows that went up and down on all sides.

"They're Christmas tree decorations. Why would we want to sell them in the summer?" Nick pulled the second box out while Oliver ground his teeth. They'd been having this argument for weeks, and most of it stemmed from Nick's discomfort about selling anything he'd made in a public venue. The name was an easy straw man for his fear no one would be buying.

"I think the name is sweet," Martin said.

Seb wrapped an arm around his shoulders and puffed his chest out. "Well, there you have it. Dr. Lindsey has spoken, so let's put an end to this."

Martin grinned at him and kissed Seb's cheek. "I have to go check on the volunteers at the concession stand."

Seb kissed him back, mussing up his carefully brushed brown hair. "I'll go with you. Think they'll let me test the mulled wine?"

The Seacroft Christmas Market sparkled around them as Oliver and Nick finished setting up their booth. They had been a late addition. Oliver needed to do some fast talking to get on the waiting list, and in the end, they'd gotten lucky because one of the quilters came down with the flu and couldn't find anyone to run her booth. So, once again, their location wasn't ideal, tucked away in a far corner past the fruitcake and the teddy bears made out of old sweaters, but Oliver was determined to make this a success for Nick.

"Hey, guys!" Brian and Jess stood at the booth.

"Hi!" Oliver glanced up after they hung the last wooden decoration on the tree. Each one had been sanded and stained until it shone. "Nick, come say hi!" Oliver turned to find Nick very obviously and unsuccessfully trying to hide his big frame behind the Christmas tree. He gave Oliver a guilty glare, peeking around the side, but then shuffled over.

"Looks good!" Brian shook Nick's hand, and the familiar face appeared to steady Nick's nerves, because he straightened and gave a tentative smile.

"Come see." He drew them forward to look at his knick-knacks or his wooden winter creations, whichever they preferred. He showed off the various ornaments he'd made over the last few months with quiet pride. Watching him made Oliver's chest warm, glad to see Nick enjoying himself, even a little.

Anya and Hayden left at the end of the summer. They'd rented a two-bedroom apartment close by, but Nick had been gloomy for weeks before and after their move. Oliver tried to help him stay positive, but the truth was, the departure was sad, and no amount of "look on the bright side" and "they're not that far away" would magically make it all better. No one believed the three of them cooped up in Nick's house had been a long-term solution for anything but mass casualties, but seeing them go had still been hard.

Oliver tried his best to help, and Nick spent more and more time at Oliver's place, saying his own house was too empty to be alone in. Finally, in September, Oliver suggested they start moving some of Nick's things over.

It had been a slow invasion, almost like Nick was afraid to let go of the old house. His workshop tools were the last items to come over, even though, in fact, they were the things Oliver was most looking forward to having in his house. Everything else was old and worn, and Nick didn't appear to have many happy memories attached to any of them.

So Oliver decided to help him make some new memories. It started with him asking Nick to show him how to make something simple on the lathe, but after Oliver nearly took off his index finger, they agreed it would probably be better if Nick worked and Oliver supervised.

"Have you seen Martin?" Jess asked as Nick handed her a paper bag with the Nick's Nacks logo stamped on it. Inside were three snowmen that she had selected, each carefully wrapped in their own box.

"He said something about volunteers and mulled wine." Oliver pointed down the aisle in the direction Seb and Martin had gone.

"Right." Jess stood on her toes to kiss Brian's cheek. "I'm going to go find him. You take your time."

"How have you been?" Brian asked Nick, once Jess had disappeared into the crowd.

Nick blew out a breath and glanced at Oliver, who tried to give him a reassuring smile while also not looking like he was eavesdropping, which he totally was. He busied himself rearranging the tree so the gaps left by the newly departed snowmen weren't too obvious.

"Pretty good," Nick said.

"Night shifts are quiet without you."

Oliver's chest hurt as the silence between the two men grew. Nick had left the department at the beginning of November. It had taken a lot of late-night talks before he admitted duty kept him at the dispatch desk and not love. Coaching him through turning in his resignation had been one of the most satisfying things Oliver had ever done, except for watching the gleam in his eye as they signed the lease papers on a storefront, right next door to Seb's gallery.

Brian glanced around the booth. "This looks . . . " His eyes settled on Oliver, who gave up any pretense of not listening, and Brian smiled. "This all looks really good. I'm happy for you."

Nick clapped his friend on the back, following his eyeline. "Yeah, it's pretty good. I think I have you to thank for it."

Nick was selling himself short, but Oliver was feeling the holiday spirit, so he let it slide. "We're having a demo party on New Year's Day," he said instead. "You and Jess should come. We want to get moved in before the spring."

Brian grinned. "I do love a sledgehammer. I'll be there. Not sure about Jess, though. The doctor said she's not supposed to do any heavy lifting until the babies arrive next summer."

Nick's eyes widened. "Babies?"

Brian's grin turned sly. "Twins."

"Babies!" Nick turned to Oliver, clasping his hands tightly. "We're going to be uncles!"

Oliver laughed. "How do you figure that?"

"Well, Brian is Martin's brother. And Seb and Martin are together. And Seb's your brother. So . . ." He frowned, trying to do that math.

Brian laughed. "You two will definitely be uncles."

Nick beamed and blinked rapidly to hide tears Oliver was pretty sure he wasn't meant to see. "That's—that's amazing, Brian. I'm really happy for you."

When Brian left to catch up with Jess, Oliver slid a hand around Nick's waist and kissed him softly at the temple. "Uncle Nick."

Nick blushed and hunched into his jacket.

"And see," Oliver said, "you sold three snowmen already!"

Nick's eyes widened. "Oh shit! They're friends! And they're having a baby . . . er . . . babies. I shouldn't have charged them. That wasn't right! It doesn't count if you sell them to friends."

Convincing Nick to try selling some of his creations, instead of letting them build up in the basement, had been the hardest part of all. He'd resisted, deflected, procrastinated, and every other thing he could think of in order to avoid it. When Oliver hadn't relented, he'd offered selling them online.

"No," Oliver had said. "Part of this is getting you back out in the community. You've spent all this time being a part of it but not."

"I've been busy," Nick grumbled.

"I'm not denying that. But it's different now. I'm here. I'll help you do it. I won't let you fail."

Nick didn't relax until well into the first hour of the Christmas market, even though a number of townspeople stopped to admire his ornaments. Many bought at least one, and a few stuck around to chat about what else Nick could make while Oliver helped the remaining shoppers.

Picture perfect. The night was clear, bright stars competing with the twinkling lights Martin's volunteers hung for the weekend. Carolers roamed the market. Across the crowded aisle, Oliver spotted Avery, his red hair shining under the glow overhead. For a split second, his eyes met Oliver's. He gave him a tentative smile, and Oliver returned it, along with an only slightly more confident wave. Avery's grin widened, but then an older woman with strawberry blond hair said something to him, and he glanced away before they disappeared into the crowd.

"I saw plans online for a Shaker-style dresser," Nick said, drawing Oliver's attention back as well.

"Oh yeah?" He tried not to pounce on the comment. When he'd proposed opening a showroom for Nick's furniture, Nick balked. Hard. But when Oliver took him to see the vacant shop one Sunday morning after brunch with Seb and Martin, and Oliver explained his vision for the hundredth time, Nick started to throw in ideas. Furniture he could make. Small historical details from the town that could be added to the store for authenticity. His eyes were full of an enthusiasm Oliver didn't get to see very often.

And Oliver would be close by once the new store opened. They'd organized the demo party to knock out some walls in the apartment above the shop and convert the two small bedrooms into an office, from which Oliver could run his new law practice.

"Sorry we're late!" Anya hurried up to the booth with Hayden dragging behind her. She stared pointedly over her shoulder at him. "Someone couldn't find his phone."

"Hey, buddy. Thanks for coming." Nick hugged his son awkwardly, but awkward was an improvement for them at least.

"So you've got all your stuff." Anya tugged at the backpack slung over one of Hayden's shoulders. "And I'll pick you up tomorrow morning before lunch."

"Mom!" Hayden shrugged her off. "Stop. I'll be fine."

Oliver glanced at Nick and gave him a sympathetic smile. They were making progress, the three of them, to build a relationship, but the hurdles from Nick and Hayden's difficult history, versus the ones that came up because Hayden was nearly sixteen—and had all the attitude to show for it—were hard to distinguish.

The market and the rest of their plans for tonight were a pretty big deal, though. Although Hayden had been willing to spend time with his dad, warming up to Oliver took longer, and coming over to the house even longer again. Too many residual feelings from that awful night at Nick's. So they'd started small. A few hours in the afternoon for Nick's birthday. Dinner on nights when Anya was working.

Tonight, though, Hayden would be helping out at the market, and staying over in the guest room at Oliver and Nick's house. He'd made a few pointed comments about Nick and Oliver not being gross while he was there, but honestly, the lead up to the market and having Hayden stay with them made Nick so nervous there wouldn't be anything on his mind but sleep by the time they all got home tonight.

Home.

When Oliver packed up his broken heart and moved here, he'd had one goal: succeed in the plan he and Cooper built and prove he could do it on his own. As he watched Nick lead Hayden around the stall and explain the setup and the pricing, he had to admit he hadn't pictured it turning out this way.

And he wouldn't trade it for anything.

"You think they're going to be okay?" Anya asked as she came to stand by him.

Oliver laughed softly as father and son worked through an order form with twin expressions of focus on their faces: their dark brows drawn together at the same angle, mouths pressed together in the same determined line. Hayden put the dimensions of the sample order in the wrong row, and got frustrated when Nick pointed it out, but they settled down quickly, and Hayden started a new form while Nick watched over his shoulder silently.

Imperfect, but getting better every day.

"I think we're all going to be okay."

THANK YOU

Thank you so much for reading Cold Pressed. There are more Seacroft stories coming, so please keep in touch!

In *Hot Potato*, Avery finally learns to spread his colorful wings and fly, with a little help from the newest member of the Seacroft Fire Department.

And if you missed it, check out *Top Shelf*, where Seb's cynicism and snark are won over by Martin, the shy professor who works downstairs.

Follow me on Amazon to be notified of new releases, or come join my Facebook readers group (facebook.com/groups/allisonsalist). Or sign up for The A-List, my monthly newsletter for new releases, giveaways, and recommendations at allisontemplebooks.com/newsletter.

The kindest thing a reader does for an author is read their book. The second kindest is to recommend it. Please take a minute to leave a review on Amazon or Goodreads, so other readers will know if this story is for them!

ABOUT THE AUTHOR

Whether I knew it then or not, I've been a writer since the second grade, when I wrote a short story about a girl and her horse. My grandmother typed it out for me and said she'd never seen so many quotation marks from a seven-year-old before. I took that as a challenge and have tried to break that record in all the stories I've taken on since then. It's good to have goals, right?

I live in Toronto with my very patient husband and the world's neediest cat. I try to split my time between writing, community theater stage management, and traveling anywhere that has good wine. Tragically, this leaves no time to clean the house.

ALSO BY ALLISON TEMPLE

Top Shelf (Seacroft Book 1)

Martin is a ghost. Well, not really, but he might as well be. Job gone, home gone, self-respect gone, and no one even seems to notice. The only person who really sees him is Seb, the artist who lives above the used bookstore.

Seb haunts the edges of Seacroft in search of beauty. He knows how to excavate the hidden value in abandoned things—whether it's in the pages of forgotten books or in Martin's stuttering attempts to rebuild his life—and transform them into works of art.

Two lost souls, Seb and Martin discover the strength they need to face eccentric townies and their dysfunctional families together. But as friendship sparks toward something more, neither man wants to risk what they've only just found. It takes two to fall in love, but it will take the whole community to bring their beauty to life.

Available on Amazon and Kindle Unlimited

(http://mybook.to/TopShelf)

The Pick Up

Kyle's life is going backwards. He wanted to build a bigger life for himself than Red Creek could give him, but a family crisis has forced him to return to his hometown with his six-year-old daughter. Now he's standing in the rain at his old elementary school, and his daughter's teacher, Mr. Hathaway, is lecturing him about punctuality.

Adam Hathaway is not looking for love. He's learned the hard way to keep his personal and professional life separate. But Kyle is struggling and needs a friend, and Adam wants to be that friend. He just needs to ignore his growing attraction to Kyle's goofy charm, because acting on it would mean breaking all the rules that protect his heart.

Putting down roots in this town again is not Kyle's plan. As soon as he can, he's taking his daughter and her princess costumes and moving on. The more time he spends with Adam, though, the more he thinks the quiet teacher might give him a reason to stay. Now he just has to convince Adam to take a chance on a bigger future than either of them could have planned.

Available at all online book retailers

(http://books2read.com/thepickup)